# INTRODUCTION

*Cupcakes for Two* by Birdie L. ███
Cynthia Lyons leaves a broker███████████████ applies
for a new job as a bed-and-br███████████████ be
Taylor—a demanding, negativ███████████████ cé,
Max—hires her. Yet there is ███████████████ sive
eyes. If she stays on at the bed-and-brea███████ vhat
it is?

*Blueberry Surprise* by Wanda E. Brunstetter
Lorna Patterson is a young widow who returns to college, hoping to become a music teacher. The last thing she is looking for is love, but Evan Bailey, a college student, is a persistent man who has recently taken Cynthia Lyons' online cooking class. Can God take two people so different and help them find their heart's desire through a blueberry surprise?

*Bittersweet Memories & Peppermint Dreams* by Pamela Griffin
After nineteen years, Erica Langley is going home again; yet the prospect is bittersweet. Ron Meers becomes more to Erica than a nice guy helping her find her roots and solve the mystery of her troubling past. In the hopes of winning his heart through his sweet tooth, she takes a "sweet treats" cooking course through Cynthia Lyons' school. Her sad attempts at baking should have him running the opposite direction, but he doesn't. Still, if he does care about her, why is he so distant?

*Cream of the Crop* by Tamela Hancock Murray
When photographer Gwendolyn Warner takes an assignment for DairyBaked, she's ecstatic. But the son of the owner, Sebastian Emerson, objects that he never authorized a new photographer. Gwendolyn tries to impress him by promising the best dessert ever. She enrolls in Cynthia's Internet school. When she manages to flub the recipe, she's sure she'll be fired. The Lord has used lesser ingredients to fulfill His servants. How will He turn the heat up now?

# Sweet Treats

A Heapin' Helpin' of Love Is Dished Up
in Four Fun Romances

WANDA E. BRUNSTETTER
BIRDIE L. ETCHISON
PAMELA GRIFFIN
TAMELA HANCOCK MURRAY

BARBOUR
PUBLISHING

ISBN 1-59310-142-2

All Scripture quotations are taken from the HOLY BIBLE, NEW INTERNATIONAL VERSION®. NIV®. Copyright © 1973, 1978, 1984 by International Bible Society. Used by permission of Zondervan Publishing House. All rights reserved.

Cover image © Waha (Photonica)

Illustrations by Mari Goering.

This book is a work of fiction. Names, characters, places, and incidents are either products of the author's imagination or used fictitiously. Any similarity to actual people, organizations, and/or events is purely coincidental.

Published by Barbour Publishing, Inc., P.O. Box 719, Uhrichsville, Ohio 44683, www.barbourbooks.com

*Our mission is to publish and distribute inspirational products offering exceptional value and biblical encouragement to the masses.*

 Member of the
Evangelical Christian
Publishers Association

Printed in the United States of America.
5 4 3 2 1

# Sweet Treats

# Cupcakes
# for Two

by Birdie L. Etchison

# Dedication

To my mother, Naomi Leighton,
one of the best cooks ever!

# *Chapter 1*

C ynthia Lyons grabbed her luggage and wheeled it toward the street where a taxi waited. She slung her carry-on bag over her shoulder, pushed a lock of blond hair out of her eyes, and ran to the curb.

"I need to get downtown in thirty minutes. Here's the address." She thrust a small piece of wadded up paper in front of the driver's nose. "Is that possible?"

"Get in, lady. We'll try, but no guarantees."

He started to get out to help with the luggage, but she waved him away. "I'm used to taking care of things myself. Thanks anyway."

Seconds later, the taxi pulled away from the cars parked three deep and was soon in the throng of Portland, Oregon, commuters.

"You aren't from here, are you?"

"No. Is it that noticeable?" Cynthia took a deep breath, willing herself to relax. A job interview shouldn't ruffle her. She had lots to offer a bed-and-breakfast operation.

He looked at her in the rearview mirror. "If you were, you

wouldn't have asked if I could make it. It's a straight shot once I get on I-84 heading west."

"That's great. I have an appointment," she said, "and one can't be late for a job interview."

"No problem. We'll make it with time to spare. Traffic is light."

"Thanks" was all Cynthia could manage as a sudden feeling of regret—or was it alarm?—went through her. It was ludicrous leaving Martinez, California, as she had. Stealing away, practically in the middle of the night, leaving her business to Jan, her friend and associate. If only Max had just left her alone. She thought that chapter of her life was over, but he'd returned, acting as if things would pick up as before—and wouldn't take no for an answer. Her thoughts turned to that day when they'd argued.

"Max, we have nothing in common. I need to find someone who believes as I do."

"Are you back to that church thing?" He'd laughed as he said it, showing how unimportant her belief was to him. He was ruggedly handsome and, at six feet three inches, towered over her, almost taking her breath away. "Why does that have to get in the way? It sure doesn't need to."

"I'm not going through it again, Max. Please don't come around anymore."

"And I'm not giving up, not by a long shot." He stood in the doorway, his eyes narrowing. "I'll be back." He left, banging the door hard.

"But you're over him," Jan argued. "You said so yourself just last week."

"I am, and yet I'm not." She'd paused over the box she was packing.

"It's dumb and crazy! Taking off when you have this fantastic business going."

"Which you'll keep going just fine." Cynthia had glanced up, pressing a kink out of the lower part of her back. "Where's your confidence, girl?"

Jan taped the top of the box closed. "I just want you around, that's all."

"I'll probably be back. Give me a year to do *something* else, *somewhere* else, and you'll find me here on your doorstep."

Jan impulsively hugged her. "Oh, I hope so."

Cynthia had stored her bed and other items she wanted to keep, packing her clothes and her favorite recipe collection. If the job didn't pan out for the bed-and-breakfast in Astoria, she would just find something else. She'd circled an ad about a full-time position in a cooking school in Portland, and there'd even been one for an online cooking instructor. Not that she'd *ever* consider doing anything online. Did people get paid for online classes? She knew she could work anywhere. It was just that the job in Astoria sounded so great.

Cynthia recalled the ad: "Victorian House. View of Columbia River. Elegant. Full house expected through fall."

It was August now, and she was prepared to be busy for four months, maybe longer, as some might want to get away for the holiday season. She loved decorating for Christmas.

Cynthia stared at her finger where a beautiful two-carat solitaire had been. Her heart should be healing, still. . . . One didn't get over a relationship overnight. If she knew all that, why did it continue to hurt? Cynthia thought of a quote she'd read in the newspaper. A person wrote to an advice columnist, asking: "Why does love hurt so bad when it's gone?"

"It doesn't," was the answer. "It only hurts when it's still there." Cynthia guessed it was still there.

The taxi wove in and out of traffic. Cynthia's thoughts came back to the present. She glanced at her watch. She had twenty minutes, but the way the driver was going they'd be there in time, though perhaps not in one piece.

"We'll soon cross the Broadway Bridge. Be there in five minutes, miss."

Cynthia stared at the skyscrapers looming ahead on the horizon. Portland's skyline was impressive, definitely larger than Martinez, the small, east-bay town where she had lived most of her life. On her own since her mother died six years ago, she still missed Mom more than she'd ever thought possible. Memories of Mom's gentleness, her guidance, and the fact that she was home with her Lord were the only things bringing peace to Cynthia now.

She glanced out over a river as the steel grating on the bridge jiggled the taxi and tickled the soles of her feet. The driver turned and stopped at a traffic light at the end of the bridge.

"That's the Willamette River. You pronounce it Wa-lamm-et, not Will-a-met."

"Oh, I know that," Cynthia said with a chuckle. "I'm from California, after all."

He looked at the slip of paper and double-parked in front of an immense building with interesting cornices and huge pillars.

THE GARFIELD, a sign said. OFFICE SPACE, STUDIO APARTMENTS, and LOFTS FOR LEASE.

"This is it?"

He nodded. "That's the address you gave me."

This time Cynthia let him assist her with the large suitcase, then wondered what to do with a suitcase and the carry-on when she went in for the interview. She should have thought of that before now.

Cynthia gave the driver a good tip and headed up the steps, pulling her bags behind her. Surely there'd be a place to leave her things. A corner of the waiting room, perhaps.

She dug in her purse for the name and phone number. *Gabe Taylor.* Cynthia hoped there would be a register inside. She pushed the door open and struggled with her luggage. A man hurried past, then returned to hold the door open.

"Coming to stay, I see," he said with a jovial look.

"Actually, I'm looking for Gabe Taylor's office. Would you happen to know where it is?"

"Sure. It's the third floor up, office to the left; far end."

Cynthia got into the elevator after a woman came out, wondering if the tall beauty might have applied for the position as manager of the bed-and-breakfast.

The woman smiled, one of those half smiles people do when they catch you looking at them, then hurried by.

Cynthia found the name she was looking for etched in silver on the door and turned the knob.

She had hoped the receptionist would show her a place to stash her luggage, but there was no waiting room. As the door came open, she almost fell into the room as the suitcase slipped from her grip. A young man at a desk with his feet propped on top nearly fell over backward in his surprise.

"Hey! Don't you knock before entering a room?"

Her face felt hot. "I. . .that is, I assumed there was a waiting room and a. . ." She blushed even more. "I'm so sorry."

"You're here about the position?"

"If you mean the manager of the bed-and-breakfast, yes."

"Have a seat."

His eyes were a deep brown, and she felt herself becoming lost in his steady gaze.

Glancing at her luggage, a slight smile turned up at the corners of his mouth. "Planning on staying awhile I see. You must be Cynthia Lyons."

She held out her hand. "And you're Gabe Taylor."

He nodded. "I'll just take your résumé and get back to you tomorrow."

"I can wait," Cynthia said. She wanted to add that she had nowhere to go, but thought better of it.

He sat, looked at the folder, then back at her, then at her résumé again, as if he didn't know what to do.

"I need to know today, if possible. It will determine whether I rent a car and start out, or stay in Portland to begin looking elsewhere."

"I see." He leaned back and seemed to study her more closely. "Do you usually call the shots when you go on an interview?"

Cynthia felt the color rise in her cheeks again. "No. This is an exception, as I think I'm perfect for the job and can't wait to get started. I'm sure there's lots to do."

Gabe couldn't believe he was even considering hiring this woman. She had a lot of nerve, coming in here and exerting her way like that. She stood no bigger than a minute and, diminutive as she was, he sensed she was strong and determined—good qualities when running a business. And he needed someone like that, especially since he planned on leaving for New York soon—permanently.

He started reading again, fingering his chin as he read. "You had your own catering business?"

"Yes. Cynthia's Catering has been quite successful. My specialty is a variety of desserts. I make the most fancy cupcakes you ever saw—decorating the tops with special designs, all edible, of course. A friend is running the business in my absence. I also have letters from satisfied customers, should you care to see them."

He waved his hand. "No, that won't be necessary. What concerns me, however, is that you're not looking for a long-term job." He looked up, meeting her gaze again.

"Oh, no," Cynthia said. "I want it to be permanent. I just meant my business is in good hands."

"You had orders from some big names in the Bay Area?"

"Yes. Like I said, there are letters—"

"No, I don't want to see any letters." Gabe looked at her thoughtfully. "What I need to know is what you might have on the menu for a typical Sunday brunch."

Cynthia leaned back. "Probably my Egg Blossoms with Hollandaise, or French Toast Soufflé. Either one gets rave reviews and is absolutely delicious."

Gabe arched an eyebrow. "And is this going to cost me an arm and a leg?"

Cynthia straightened her shoulders. "Surely you want something to bring people back! I assure you I use only the best ingredients. Butter, cream, the finest of sugar—"

"I'm sure you're right—I mean about bringing them back. And word of mouth works wonders in this business."

He tapped the form with a pencil, then finally pushed his chair back. "Okay. You're hired. Strictly on a trial basis, you understand."

"Of course."

"And I expect a full report each and every Monday morning."

She raised her chin, almost in defiance. "No problem there. I keep close and accurate records."

"So, if you're ready, and I assume you are, we'll take off and head to Astoria."

"We?"

"As a financial advisor, I'm my own boss, and I made no appointments until later this afternoon."

"I see."

Cynthia couldn't help wondering if he had other job applicants to interview, but decided not to ask.

"I suppose you're wondering about other interviewees?"

She glanced away. "The thought did cross my mind."

"The ad you saw was the second one I ran. On a whim I put it in the *San Francisco Chronicle*. Seems nobody wants to take on a B and B this time of year. It's the end of the season.

The rainy season is ahead. Now come spring, customers will be banging the door down."

"I like the rain," Cynthia said. "It's soothing."

"Then you should love Astoria." He paused at the door. "Why would you leave California this time of year, anyway?"

The knot grew in Cynthia's throat. It was her business, and she didn't think she needed to explain anything to him. He needed someone to operate his B and B, and that was all that mattered.

She looked up. "It's a personal matter, but it won't interfere with my work. Not in the least."

"Very well, then. I ask for two-weeks' notice. I have someone who ran the B and B for the past few weekends, but she does it only as a favor."

A favor? Cynthia wondered about that. She guessed there was more to this than he was willing to discuss. Not that she cared. She wasn't here to fill anyone's shoes. It was simply a job.

"Let me get my coat, and we'll be off."

Cynthia closed her eyes for a brief moment, thanking God for getting her here safely, for helping her to land the job, and also for this man who was getting to her more than she wanted him to. There was something about his face, the thick thatch of hair that appealed to her, but she didn't like the thoughts going through her head. She was definitely not ready for romance.

# Chapter 2

The parking lot was two blocks from Gabe's office, and as Cynthia struggled to keep up, Gabe forged ahead, pulling her larger suitcase behind him.

"You'll like the bed-and-breakfast," Gabe said, once they were inside his Mercury and heading west.

"How long have you owned the B and B?"

He grinned. "Forever. I grew up in it."

"Oh." She glanced at his profile and suddenly saw not a bigwig financial advisor, but a man who still had the small town in him though he tried to appear otherwise.

"I was raised in a little town, too," Cynthia said.

He gave her a quick glance, his eyebrow raised. "I didn't think there was such a thing in California."

"Very funny. Actually, Martinez is a wonderful place, and I wouldn't trade the memories of Mom and me walking to the park on Saturdays, listening to concerts every summer, and visiting the farmers' market Thursday afternoons."

"And your mother? Where is she now?"

Cynthia felt her insides tighten. Would she ever get over the loss of her mother? "Mom died the year I started my catering business. I wish she knew how successful I am at a job I love."

"And just maybe she does." He smiled again and she felt a jolt. Gabe must be a Christian, or he wouldn't have made that comment.

Cynthia smiled. "I like to think so. What about your parents?"

"Both gone. I don't remember my father at all. He died when I was five, then Mom a few years ago, and just last year Grams died. She was a strong, determined person, as you might have guessed."

"Yes. And so it was handed down to you."

"Yeah, that's my life story in a nutshell."

They drove silently while a gospel CD played from the car stereo. Her life had changed so much. After losing her mother, she'd dropped out of college and started cooking for one of the restaurants in her neighborhood. She'd met Max, who pushed her into the catering business. "Anyone who cooks with flair, as you do, should cook for a living." Max found her clients, all businesspeople, but Cynthia preferred cooking what she liked, not what they ordered. Still Max prodded her. Then she found herself pulling away, wanting a different lifestyle than he did. *It all seems so long ago now.*

Gabe hummed one of the tunes while Cynthia watched the countryside fly past. Gabe looked in her direction a few times, and she felt good as she hummed along.

"I see you like the CD."

"I enjoy music. Always have."

Gabe put on the blinker and pulled up in front of a small restaurant nestled in a wooded setting. "This is my favorite eating place, speaking of small towns. It's by far one of the best between Portland and Astoria."

The café was located beside a small stream. The sound of the brook soothed Cynthia, and she felt the tension leave her body. There was something so relaxing about the water.

The waitress came, and they ordered coffee and large bowls of clam chowder.

The coffee was hot, the chowder seasoned and full of clams. Cynthia decided it was similar to her recipe. She'd have to commend the chef.

As if reading her thoughts, Gabe asked, "How does this match up to what you make?"

"Excellent," Cynthia said, setting down her soup spoon. "I'm glad we stopped."

Gabe leaned forward. "You have an interesting manner," he said, catching Cynthia off guard with his sudden statement.

"Oh, and why is that?"

"You seem to be easily pleased."

"And most of your friends aren't?" she had to ask. Was he alluding to previous girlfriends? Cynthia wanted to know, though it was none of her business. She found herself more than casually interested in this person sitting next to her. He was nothing like Max. His earlier haughty, all-business mood had given way to a captivating manner, and she discovered she wanted to know him better. That would be impossible since he lived in Portland. Their business transactions would probably be via the phone or computer.

"I'll pay for my meal," Cynthia offered, but Gabe waved her off.

"This was my idea, and I'll handle it, including the tip."

Nearly an hour later, they pulled into Astoria, and Cynthia gasped when she saw the immense Columbia River. Earlier she'd caught glimpses of it as they drove along the highway, but now the river beckoned with its vast miles and miles of blueness. Hills resembling green velvet on the Washington side of the river appeared to touch the sky overhead. Cynthia took a deep breath. "It's beautiful."

Gabe grinned. "If you like this, wait until you see the view from Taylor's Bed and Breakfast."

Gabe turned and drove straight up a hill. Astoria reminded her of San Francisco. Contrary to popular belief, people living in the Bay Area did not go into San Francisco often unless they worked there. With her business, she'd hired a driver part-time to deliver her meals.

"So, what do you think? I know our hills don't compare to San Francisco, but we like them."

"Oh, I love the hills. It's a gorgeous spot, and I can see it's the perfect vacation place for travelers."

"Except when there is snow or ice. That holds us captive, but it happens rarely, so don't worry about it."

Gabe hopped out and took a deep breath. "I tend to forget how clean the air is here. I love this town."

*Then why did you leave?* Cynthia wanted to ask.

Cynthia stared at the huge house that seemed to tower over her. The dead-end street turned into a hill of green brush. The B and B, a turn-of-the-century Victorian, was painted a deep scarlet. The bay windows were outlined in navy blue, while a sky blue shade accented the gingerbread. A turret on the north side added to the charm. A small yard drew shade from a huge maple that dominated an overgrown flower garden. Already Cynthia's mind whirled with ideas for improving the yard.

"What do you think?" Gabe was at her side, his gaze meeting hers, waiting for an answer.

"It's perfect!"

"Wait until you see the inside."

Steps led up to the wraparound porch, and Gabe produced a set of keys; then they were inside.

Cynthia loved older homes. She marveled at the winding stairway, the highly polished wood, a carved banister, and the rose wallpaper leading up to the next floor. The foyer was perfect with a window bench and a rack for wraps and umbrellas. The area rug was starting to fray, but that was a minor problem.

"Do you want the grand tour now or to just discover it on your own?"

"Now, please."

They climbed the stairs to the second floor, which had four bedrooms. Two were spacious with their own private baths, while the other two rooms shared a bath. Old-fashioned light fixtures gave the appearance of gaslights from long ago.

"It's charming," Cynthia said, clasping her hands.

"The four-poster beds have been in the family for three generations. Just before she died, Grams ordered these matching feather comforters, ruffles, and shams."

"I want to stay in each room a night," Cynthia said. "They're so spacious, and the view—people will love that!"

"I didn't tell you an important part," Gabe said, interrupting Cynthia's reverie.

She turned from the window. "And what is that?"

"You're going to need help. I usually hire high school girls, but Rainey found them unreliable. Sometimes they show up for work, sometimes not."

"Rainey?"

"The person I mentioned who helped me out."

He appeared uncomfortable, and she wondered if Rainey could be an old girlfriend.

"Perhaps the wages weren't high enough, so there was no incentive to do a good job," Cynthia said.

Gabe frowned. "If I pay more than the minimum, I won't make a dime."

Cynthia looked out the window at the river. "I wouldn't worry about it. Things will work out."

"So, do you still want the job?"

"I do, Mr. Taylor. I really do."

They finished the tour, and Gabe showed Cynthia where the fuse box, furnace, and water valve were located. "Everything's been updated, but you just never know." He opened a long cupboard in the kitchen. "Here are candles in case the electricity goes off, and hurricane lamps are on the table in the parlor."

"Does the electricity go off often?"

Gabe nodded. "We have some great storms here, so be prepared." He handed Cynthia his business card. "Contact me if anything goes wrong. And there's always e-mail."

Gabe brought in Cynthia's suitcase, toting it to the small room off the kitchen. He paused in the doorway, as if he needed to add something. His expression said he wanted to stay, and she found herself not wanting him to leave. He had an almost lost look as he ran his hand through his thick hair.

"I'll be in touch. Almost forgot. The computer's in the alcove off your bedroom."

Cynthia walked over, offering her hand. "Thanks for the job. I'll take good care of things here."

He left suddenly, and then came back in. "About a car. The Chevy is over at Rainey's. I'll stop by to ask her to drop it off here. I'd just go get it, but," he said, pausing to look at his watch, "I have a four o'clock appointment."

Cynthia walked out on the porch and said good-bye. A light mist was falling, and it looked like fog rolling in across the river. It made her suddenly feel bereft.

She leaned against the door and closed her eyes. A lot had happened since she'd caught the flight from Oakland. She had much to be thankful for. She lifted her face. "Thank You, Lord, for bringing me this job in such a lovely spot. I ask for Your guidance, and may I do a good job for Mr. Taylor— Gabe. Amen."

Cynthia opened her eyes. "Oh, and Lord, please take away this feeling that is surfacing. Gabe cannot possibly have any interest in me. Let me just do the job and not think about him. Thank You. Again, amen."

After unpacking and slipping into her favorite navy blue sweater, Cynthia explored the food cupboard. Supplies were low, and already she had a list going in her mind. *Guest book needed. Flowers for the foyer, new rugs, new drapes for the living room, and the floors need work.* Was Gabe going to agree to her suggestions? At the thought of his lopsided grin, she felt a sudden surge of energy. Tomorrow she'd go to town to explore.

Gabe drove the four blocks over and asked Rainey to drop off the car.

Rainey pushed her hair behind her ear. "Don't you want to come in for a spot of tea?"

Gabe shook his head. "Thanks, but no. Need to get back for an appointment."

Rainey looked away, and Gabe felt the old familiar thread of guilt. He'd hurt her, he realized, but he did not love her and knew that wouldn't change. What they once had was the remnants of a first love. After high school graduation Gabe left Astoria. He had big plans. Rainey went to the local college, got her teaching degree, and was content to stay here. They'd grown in different directions. There was nothing wrong with that. They'd talked about it and agreed to stay friends. So why did he feel guilty when she looked at him?

She gave him an impulsive hug, promising to drop the car off the next day. "And, Gabe, take care of yourself."

"You, too." He looked back briefly and waved.

Gabe drove down the hill toward Highway 30. As Cynthia Lyons' face came to mind, he felt good, almost lighthearted. She was a gem—something told him so—and he knew the B and B was in good hands. She'd been so enthusiastic—like a child on Christmas morning. He could move to New York now and fulfill his dream to make it in the big city.

As he drove over the miles, he kept thinking about Cynthia. There was something that drew him to her, and he wasn't sure what it was. How different she was from Natalie Wiegant. Elegant, efficient Natalie. They'd been dating two years now, and the relationship seemed to be going nowhere. He thought of her in her expensive designer suit, high heels. . . and those beautiful violet eyes. She could have been a model but had chosen finance for a career. Natalie attracted attention wherever she went, and it had been fun attending a host of parties and being part of the in scene.

They'd had a disagreement last week, and her words still stung.

"You're just a mama's boy, Gabe. You need to start moving."

"Moving?"

"Yes. Remember your New York dream."

"Of course."

Natalie had sauntered across the room—she never just walked—and pointed. "I think you can take the boy out of the small town, but you can never take the small town out of the boy."

Gabe tried to shake the words as he drove on, his thoughts scattered. He had to prove Natalie wrong. And now that the B and B was taken care of, he could and *would* move on.

Gabe hadn't prayed much lately—he wasn't sure why. Busyness. Worry. Trying to get everything together for the New York move. As he approached the industrial area of Portland, he prayed aloud: "Lord, is this new path the right one? How am I to know? Does anyone ever know?"

Cynthia Lyons came to mind again. She intrigued him, but her boldness bothered him. Yet it was that boldness that made her perfect for the job. If she liked the B and B, and every indication pointed to that, she might be there for years. He could live his dream, keep in touch, and come home for a few weeks each summer.

His apartment seemed emptier than usual, and Gabe thought about being back in Astoria, watching while a certain person walked through the house, exclaiming over every feature. He'd felt joy being around her, and for the first time in a long while, he realized how much his life had lacked the very essence of joy. Was Cynthia Lyons bringing joy into his world again?

His head was saying, "New York, New York," but his heart was saying, "Cynthia, Cynthia." It was not a good sign.

# Chapter 3

The next morning Cynthia called her friend Jan, back in Martinez, to tell her the news. "I got hired, Jan. I'm now the manager of the most wonderful B and B ever, with a magnificent view. You've got to come see it."

"Hey, good for you!"

"You busy?"

There was an audible sigh.

"Is something wrong?" Cynthia asked.

Her good friend chuckled. "No, it's just that I have lots of orders for this coming weekend. Oh, and I got a call from an online cooking school. They are looking for an instructor to handle a column on sweet treats. Just once a week. You post recipes and go in a chat room to answer questions."

"Sweet treats?"

"You know, desserts."

"Why not just call them desserts?"

"Guess they wanted something different. How do I know? You can call or not; it's up to you."

"Are you feeling overwhelmed? Do you want me to move back?"

"Before you even start your new job? Don't be silly. The little gal you hired will work out just fine. Oh, and Max called, demanding to know where you were. I said I hadn't heard from you—which was true. Finally got rid of him."

A funny ache went over Cynthia. Max had been a part of her life for so long. She found herself thinking of only the good times, not the difficult ones, and wondered if that was what other women did, following a breakup.

"How's he doing?"

"I didn't ask. Look, call me tomorrow," Jan said. "I have to go shopping."

"Yeah, me, too," Cynthia said. "I'm looking forward to it. You wouldn't believe this quaint town. I hope I can find Portobello's."

"Think you'll stay for a while?"

Cynthia felt a sudden lurch. "You know I think I might."

"And everything's okay?"

"Yeah, except—"

"*Except?*"

"Mr. Taylor is brusque, but cute."

"Whoa, girl. You know you can't go from the frying pan to the fire."

"Don't worry. The feeling isn't mutual."

"So, you going to follow up on the cooking class?"

"Yeah. Sounds interesting. Guess I should at least check it out."

Cynthia jotted down the Web site and e-mail address.

"Thanks, Jan. I'll let you know what happens."

A short time later, Cynthia sat at the computer and keyed in the Web site.

*Online instructor needed. We need someone who makes scrumptious desserts. There is a cry from several would-be bakers wanting to learn how to make fantastic Sweet Treats. E-mail for more information.*

The instructions were clear:

*We want simple, easy-to-do recipes.*
*Post a cooking lesson once a week.*
*Offer at least three recipes. Nothing exotic, but down-to-earth home cooking.*
*Give specific instructions.*
*Measurements must be exact.*
*Close with a request for questions.*
*Go online once a day; say every evening at six. If there are questions from online cooking students, answer the questions.*

The idea intrigued her. There was not the slightest doubt in her mind that she could do it. It wouldn't interfere with her work here at the B and B. Her evenings would be free; she would post her recipes, field questions, and still have energy to handle guests and bake her specialty cupcakes and bread. Yes, God certainly knew how to answer prayer—by giving her not one, but two jobs.

There was more. The sponsor wanted six sample recipes, plus a few tips. Cynthia pored over her recipe books that evening and finally selected six:

Apple Crisp—Crisp because it's far easier than trying to make piecrust.

Bread Pudding—an old standard, uses something everybody has on hand.

Chocolate Chunk Cookies—an old standard, but better than the traditional ones.

Berry Cobbler—to make when berries are in season, but can also be made with berries found in the frozen section of any supermarket.

Pudding Cake—an elegant dessert for company in a variety of flavors.

Pound Cake—something Grams made.

They wanted simple. Cynthia knew simple. She had learned simple at her grandmother's knee. Grams loved to cook, and Cynthia had watched, standing on tiptoes, as Grams showed her how to make piecrust, cookie crust, crisps, buckles, and flans. She'd made an apple crisp when she was six. That would be her first recipe to put online. She began jotting down a few hints.

*Buy Granny Smith apples for cooking, as they are tart and crisp. They make for great cooking. The biggest job for this recipe is peeling the apples, quartering to get the core out, and the slicing. Try to make uniform slices. And for those* who are going to ask, No, you cannot, you MUST NOT use canned apples.

Cynthia jotted the recipe from memory:

*Slice up 6 apples into a baking dish. I prefer a round glass bowl, but anything works. Apples brown quickly, so you might want to make the topping before peeling apples.*

   *Topping: Use 1½ sticks butter that has softened. This means taking it out of refrigerator two hours before. And it must be butter. Real butter. No margarine and no whipped butter. 1½ cups white sugar, 1 tsp. cinnamon, and ½ tsp. nutmeg. Mix these together until crumbly. Pat that over the top of the apples. Bake at 375 degrees for approximately an hour. It depends. If you like your apples not to be cooked up, take crisp out after 45 minutes.*

   *Serve with whipped cream or ice cream. Best served while warm. So, plan on taking crisp out of oven an hour before you serve dinner.*

Cynthia posted a few cooking tips and a hint of what would come the following week.

By the time she had finished, it was almost noon. She was behind on the schedule she'd set up the night before. Schedules were a must if she were to accomplish several tasks.

The next thing was the grocery list. She'd buy two pounds of Granny Smith apples to test her recipe, and while in the apple section, she'd select five or six Braeburns for the table. She'd found the perfect cut glass fruit bowl in the pantry.

Cynthia always had a bowl of fruit on the counter of her kitchen. It cheered her. Thinking of how juicy the apples tasted brought a smile to her face.

But now she jotted things down on a task list. Fresh flowers were another must. She needed a bouquet for the foyer as guests arrived, for the middle of the large table, and one for each bedroom—carnations, preferably, as she could easily find them in colors to match the décor of the room.

Cynthia wanted to replace the drapes but knew there might be resistance there. Gabe would not see the need. Still, she put it on her list. She'd cover one thing at a time.

Cynthia went to the office. Crammed behind the kitchen, the office had undoubtedly been a storage room in the earlier days. She'd like to return it to a storage room and put the office in the alcove off her bedroom. The computer was already there, and there was room. It was the perfect place, besides being airy and sunny. She needed sun. According to the weather forecaster, there'd be showers today, and this was *August*. Rain in August! Unheard of in California. She supposed she'd get used to it. But why would people want to vacation if the weather was lousy? Yet there were two bookings for this weekend; one Friday night, the other on Saturday. Both would stay two nights.

Dressing in corduroy pants with a red sweatshirt, Cynthia was finally ready for shopping. The phone rang, just as she grabbed her backpack.

"Cynthia? Gabe here. How's it going?"

Cynthia took a deep breath. "Yes, everything is fine, but it's raining. The sun comes out, and then it disappears."

He laughed. "Tell me something I don't know."

"Does it always rain here in the summer?"

"Without fail."

"Nobody will come."

"They will. Did you notice the games in the closet? And the assortment of videos?"

"Yes, but—"

"They're for people to play when they can't go outside. There's also a new movie house with six theaters downtown. It's just like Portland."

"I haven't been out to explore yet, but intend to go now."

"Any questions?"

Cynthia cleared her throat. "I'd like some new everyday china, as what you have is a hodgepodge of things."

"Didn't seem to bother Rainey."

*I'm not Rainey,* she wanted to say, but held her tongue.

"The drapes also need replacing. I think they've been there for a long time—"

"That's what gives the house its charm," Gabe interrupted.

"I don't mean to buy something modern, but replace these with new ones. We can use the same fabric and color. I'm sure we could find a seamstress who'd take on the job."

"Try vacuuming them. I'm sure there's lots more wear in them."

"Okay, I'll try it." She wanted to mention flowers and the guest book, and possibly a new throw rug, but thought she'd better wait. They'd definitely lock horns.

The items Gabe addressed were unimportant. He suggested she keep a running itinerary of her days; e-mail him any charges she made; and to call immediately if there were problems.

Problems? What sort of problems was he referring to? She supposed she would find out soon enough.

Cynthia felt as if she was putting brakes on her feet as she started down the hill. She glanced at the clouds scudding across the sky that had been blue moments earlier, but now looked dark and threatening. She hoped Rainey brought the car over soon. She guessed if it rained too hard, she'd just call a taxi, if they had one in such a small town.

Her list was in her backpack, and she thrust her hands into her pockets and hurried on. The air was brisk, but definitely not cold. At home she'd be in shorts and a tank top by now. One thing was certain: She'd have to buy some jeans and sweaters as she hadn't brought but two warm outfits with her.

The first stop was the florist. Large bunches of roses in every color imaginable filled huge baskets on the sidewalk leading into the store. Inside was a flurry of action with one young girl talking to a customer while an older lady brought out a bouquet of salmon gladioli. Her dark hair was pulled back into a ponytail and tied with a red scarf.

The woman stopped and smiled. "Good morning, can I help you?"

Cynthia nodded. She could stay in this place forever. It was almost as good as her kitchen when it smelled of baking bread and cakes.

"How early must I order flowers?"

"If you put in an order today, I can have them tomorrow. All our shipments come from Portland, just two hours away."

"Yes, two hours away. I came from there yesterday."

"Oh!" Her cheeks flushed as a smile crossed her round face. "You're new to Astoria. Welcome!" She held out a hand. "I'm Mary, and this is my flower shop. Just opened up last March."

"It's wonderful."

Cynthia explained she was the new manager of Taylor's Bed and Breakfast, pointing up the hill.

"Yes," Mary said. "I've lived here all my life and know the Taylor family well. I just went into this business as it's been a longtime dream of mine."

Cynthia smiled. "I think fulfilling dreams is important in life. I wish you every success."

"How is Rainey doing, anyway?"

Cynthia tried not to look surprised. Was something wrong with Rainey? And who was this woman who had helped Gabe out?

"I don't know," she mumbled. "We haven't met yet." *Is there something I should know?*

"She's been ill, I understand. She'll come around when she's on her feet again."

"I hope so. She's bringing me a car, Mr. Taylor said."

"Gabe," Mary said. "We all go on first-name basis around here. And Gabe is one of us, whether he likes to think so or not."

Cynthia wondered about the remark as she moved on into the store, admiring the various displays of fresh flowers and a few plants. She wanted to buy everything she saw.

"I'd like to order fresh flowers to be delivered on Friday." Cynthia hesitated and looked at Mary's face.

"I'll go with the lilies in that pink tone. They're so fragrant."

"That they are."

"Okay, and yes, we deliver, but I'm wondering, is this order for the B and B?"

"Yes. Is that a problem?"

"Gabe's never ordered flowers before."

"It's a must. He'll agree."

"Okay. I'll write it up."

Since Cynthia was walking, she bought only a few things on her grocery list. She'd come again tomorrow. And maybe she'd bring some of her bread or a plate of cupcakes for Mary. She'd make the ones with flowers on top.

Just as Cynthia started to climb the hill toward the B and B, the sky opened and rain soaked her before she got there. Thankfully she'd had her items in a plastic bag and not a paper one. This wasn't the usual "mist." It *was* going to take some getting used to.

# Chapter 4

Rainey dropped the car off the following day. If she rang the bell, Cynthia had not heard it. She was busy responding to the online instant message from the cooking guru.

"We're going to call your class The Lion Cooks. A little play on words. What do you think?"

"Sounds fine to me," Cynthia answered. "I'm looking forward to it."

"We'll start on Tuesday. Is tomorrow too soon?"

"I look forward to it!"

Cynthia shut the computer down and went outside to look at the side yard again. She needed to prepare the ground for the bedding plants she wanted. A little color would help immensely. A dusty blue Chevy sat in the driveway, and then she noticed the envelope under the doormat. The keys. But why hadn't Rainey come in? She looked up the street in the hopes of seeing someone walking, but there was no one. For once the sky was a cloudless blue, and the air felt warm. She went back inside to check on the bread rising in the pans.

Soon the kitchen would be filled with the fragrance of rosemary and dill. She'd just turned the oven on when the phone rang.

"Did you get my e-mail?"

"Well, and good morning to you, too."

"Good morning."

"I did."

"And?"

"I'll mail the amount by the end of the day. Oh, and Rainey dropped off the car."

"Good. Did she come in?"

"No, which I thought strange."

"You'll meet her one of these days. She's kind of a loner."

"I gathered that."

"I'm coming down this weekend," he said then.

"You are?"

"Thought you might need someone there."

"I know I can handle it." Her pulse raced, though she told it not to.

"I'm sure you can, too."

That night Cynthia went to the message board, looking for responses from online students. She found several. She didn't realize how little some of the readers knew.

"Does it matter what kind of apples I use?" was the first question. "I have these red ones; I don't know what they are."

"I have a can of applesauce, can I use that?" was another.

And yet another: "Do I need to peel the apples?"

Then: "My husband prefers peaches. Can I make a crisp with peaches?"

Cynthia replied:

*You can use any apples; it's just that Granny Smiths are the best for cooking. Applesauce is not going to work. You need fresh apples. And, yes, please peel them.*

*You can make peach crisp. Ripe peaches would be the best, but canned can also be used. Use half the sugar, though.*

*Quick breads are next. I hope you have loaf pans. If not, buy one or two now. Buy the regular size, not the small ones.*

*Bon appétit!*
*Cynthia Lyons*

On Wednesday Gabe phoned again. "What is this huge floral expense?"

Cynthia braced herself. "A bed-and-breakfast should have fresh flowers to greet the guests, and a bouquet in their room. It sets forth the right ambience."

"And I say the view is what brings them there—and will bring them back."

"I know. That, too."

"Maybe you'd better run things by me before you buy."

"Okay. Sure."

Rainey came over the next day. She knocked first and then opened the door. "Hello, anyone here?"

Cynthia dried her hands—she'd been peeling veggies to add to a stew that she'd be eating the rest of the week. "Yes, I'm here. In the kitchen." She held out her hand to a young woman who was tall and had broad shoulders, but looked about the same age as Cynthia. She knew immediately who it was.

"Hi, I'm Rainey."

"You should have just come in—you must know this place better than I do! I'm Cynthia and so glad to meet you."

"Mary said you were hoping I'd stop by. Been sick, but feeling better now." Her eyes swept over the room, and Cynthia knew Rainey was noticing she'd moved some things around.

"It's different," Cynthia said. "I hope you like it."

"Yes, it's just that Gabe doesn't like change. Has he seen it yet?"

"No, but I guess he will on Friday. He said he's coming down." Cynthia gestured toward the kitchen. "Come on in, and I'll put the kettle on for tea, or whatever you'd like. There's cola in the refrigerator."

"You are a dynamo," Rainey said, "and I'll have tea."

Cynthia pulled out a kitchen chair and put the heat on under the kettle. "I like to keep busy, that's true."

"Gabe was lucky to find you."

"I am lucky the B and B needed a manager, and I couldn't have found a more beautiful spot."

"Astoria is wonderful. We who live here tend to take it for granted."

"Can't get used to the rain, though. I mean it's summer! Look at the clouds—and they just hang over, making it cool and damp."

"It's always been that way. You just get used to it."

"Maybe you do, but I must admit I miss the sunshine in California."

"And the busy freeways, the fires, and floods?"

"You're right. Tell me, did I hear that you and Gabe went to school together?"

Rainey's long, slender fingers wrapped around her cup of tea. She lifted it to take a drink then lowered it onto the saucer. "I have known Gabe since kindergarten. Our mothers were best of friends."

Cynthia wanted to ask if they had been boyfriend and girlfriend, but didn't.

"Yes, I loved him. Might as well tell you now, as you'll hear it from the grapevine. I know he loved me once, but his dream was to move on to Portland and begin his business there. Astoria is too small."

"Maybe he will change his mind." Cynthia squeezed a spot of lemon into her tea.

"No, there's Natalie now. She has him wrapped around her finger, as the saying goes. She's not right for him, but he can't see it. She smells of success, and that's what he's looking for now."

"And what do you do?"

"Teach. At the grade school. Music and art."

"That certainly sounds successful to me."

"Small time, though. Small school. No challenge. But I like it here. Don't imagine I'll ever move. At least I don't have the inclination now."

Later, over a bowl of beef stew, Cynthia thought of the wistful look on Rainey's face. She loved Gabe. When she spoke of him, her eyes lit up, but she'd accepted the fact that what they once had was a thing of the past. Just as Cynthia realized her first boyfriend had left her behind. First love was intense and could be so crushing.

Cynthia went over her notes for the second online class. Quick breads. She had posted a request for favorite comfort foods. She knew she'd get things like mashed potatoes and macaroni and cheese, but when she asked specifically for desserts, chocolate in any shape or form topped the list, but pudding was second. And there were so many kinds of puddings.

*Puddings. They were a favorite with the pioneers. Simple; not too many ingredients, usually something they had in the pantry. If you have four ingredients, you can make several puddings.*

The phone rang. A reservation for a month away. After marking the calendar, Cynthia mixed up batter for cupcakes. She'd purchased a large mixer with a stand the second day after taking the job. She couldn't live without a mixer that whipped up things in one minute instead of taking ten. She didn't put that on the charge; she'd take it with her wherever she went. The way things were going, Gabe might look for someone who didn't care what the B and B looked like and had no designs to improve it.

Cynthia wasn't into clothes and jewelry, but she insisted on having comfortable, beautiful surroundings—like the bedroom she was supposed to sleep in. It had drab beige walls, white curtains, and a white bedspread with a pink fringe. She hated the whole room. She ordered a new throw rug for beside the bed; a colorful patchwork quilt, pillows with shams, and a dust ruffle;

curtains in a cozy, warm lilac; and found a picture for the wall over the bed. It was a small child on his knees beside his bed, reciting: "Now I lay me down to sleep. . ." A Monet with irises was on the opposite wall. Now she could sleep here. She put down her expenses, not charging for the two paintings.

Gabe called the next morning. "What's this quilt, ruffled sham, and curtains expense? I thought all the rooms were fine the way they were."

"That's for my room."

"*Your* room! Who is going to see your room?"

"I am," Cynthia said, trying to keep her cool.

"Surely your walk-through with guests does not include your room," he said, as if not hearing her.

"Of course my room is off limits, but I cannot sleep in an all white room! Makes me think of a hospital."

"Seemed to be okay for Rainey—"

"Perhaps you should hire her back."

"She can't work now. She's a teacher."

"Well, I'm sorry, but I had to make a few changes, and I thought you'd understand."

"Within reason, yes."

"Tell me what amount that might be."

There was a long silence, and she could hear him leaning forward in his chair and then the sound of shuffling papers. "I have no set amount, Miss Lyons, but just within reason."

"So the Persian rug I ordered for the front hallway is not within reason?"

"Persian rug? In the hallway? Isn't that where the forest green rug is now?"

"Yes, but it's stained and half of the fringe is missing."

"Miss Lyons, I think I better go over the place with you so I can see for myself how many changes you want to make." He cleared his throat. "And it just might be possible that I can get a better deal on prices. Did that thought ever occur to you?"

"Oh, I'm a bargain hunter, Mr. Taylor. A dear lady in Mary's church made the quilt. We bartered."

"Bartered?"

"Yes, I'm baking bread for her son's restaurant. You know that cute, cozy one down on Marine Drive?"

There was another long silence. "How about the curtains?"

"Made by another friend. I had to supply the material, so that's the expense you see."

Cynthia heard Gabe's chair scrape again, a deep sigh, and then a voice that sounded clipped. "I *will* be down this Friday."

"I can handle it. Really I can. Don't you trust me?"

Another pause. "It isn't that. I just need to know what else you want done. It needs my approval. It *is* my house, after all."

"Will you be here in time for dinner?"

"Dinner?"

"Yes. I can cook for two as easily as one."

"Well, I hadn't thought about it. What time would dinner be?"

"After the hors d'oeuvres."

"Okay. Sounds good. What will you cook?"

"I don't know yet. Is there anything you *cannot* eat?"

"Just liver."

"It won't be that as I don't care for liver, either."

Cynthia pored over her recipes that night and decided on

the salmon chowder. She'd also make her parsley bread sticks and apple crisp for dessert. It'd make a well-rounded meal.

Should she invite Rainey? That would be a pleasant surprise for Gabe, and it might be nice to have an ally—that is, if Rainey agreed with Cynthia's plans.

Two more guests registered for Saturday, Sunday, and Monday nights. This would make Gabe happy. He might forgive her the expense of the Persian rug. She found it at a secondhand store, but hadn't told him that. He'd find out soon enough. Anything was an improvement over the green thing that had been there forever. Of course it matched the heavy green velvet drapes at the bay windows. No amount of cleaning, shaking, or pounding had helped. They had to be replaced.

Cynthia hummed as she made a list of ingredients she needed. The salmon chowder had been a favorite when she'd catered. Not that it was the main dish, but many people preferred a chowder or soup instead of salad. It worked especially well when she offered a tray of cut-up veggies and some nice dip or spread. She decided to include hummus, as well.

Rainey declined the invitation when Cynthia called.

"I have a faculty meeting—yeah, I know. Weird time to have it on Friday evening, but nobody on this board is normal."

"If you can get away, come for the snacks and dessert."

Gabe had told her from the first that there'd be no wine served. "I prefer nonalcoholic drinks," he'd said. "If guests have to have that glass of wine, they can go elsewhere to have it." Cynthia agreed with this reasoning.

At three, Cynthia was ready for her guests. The guest book

lay open and waiting for people to sign. She'd found a wonderful fancy pen with a long feather. The rooms were clean; the house smelled of fresh bread. Soon it might smell like salmon, but that was okay. There was no better smell than that of onions cooking with a wonderful fish or beef.

Cynthia sat on the front porch in the chair looking out over the view. A barge went down the river, and she wondered what it would be like to have the job of navigating a barge up and down the river. She thought it would be boring, but supposed the people who ran it loved the river and could not imagine working on land.

Gabe arrived before the guests from Missouri. She waved and then stopped. Someone was in the car with him. Had he mentioned he was bringing anyone? No, she was sure not. It was probably the girlfriend Rainey mentioned. That was fine. Cynthia would see what her ideas were on what was needed in the house. She might want Gabe to spend even more money.

They got out of the car, and Cynthia went down the steps to greet them.

# Chapter 5

C ynthia watched while Gabe went around and opened the car door. A long-legged woman emerged and stood with her long golden hair gleaming in the sun.

"This is Natalie," Gabe said. "Natalie, this is Cynthia Lyons, the new manager of the B and B."

Cynthia offered a hand to the graceful woman who towered over her. Natalie wore a stylish suit with a diamond pin in the lapel.

"I've heard a lot about you, and you've been here less than a week?"

"Yes, that's right." Cynthia looked back at Gabe, who appeared suddenly uncomfortable.

"Cynthia is a caterer, also," Gabe offered.

"Yes, darling," Natalie trilled, "you told me that on the way here." She turned and looked at the old Victorian house. "So this is the place I've heard so much about." She smiled dryly again. "Gabe's been raving about the B and B for so long. I finally had to see the new diva who is changing everything and giving him a headache."

Cynthia felt her composure slip. *Does this woman have a knack at making one feel bad, or what?*

"Yes, well, I've done what I can." Cynthia walked around to the side of the house. "I put in a new flower garden—petunias, pansies. . . What do you think?"

"I prefer roses," Natalie said, "not that I've ever planted any. I'm far too busy with my consulting firm." She studied one long fingernail. "I hear roses are a lot of work."

Gabe looked at the riot of color and nodded. "Petunias are what Grams always planted. How did you know?"

Cynthia smiled, glad that Gabe had taken time to look at the bright spot. "I didn't, but I was told by the local nursery person that petunias thrive here."

"When do we see the house?" Natalie asked, walking up, linking her arm with Gabe's. She gazed at him with a look Cynthia couldn't quite decipher. It definitely was not adoration.

"Yes, let's go inside," Cynthia said, leading the way as if it were her own house. "I'll put on the kettle for tea or make coffee. We can have a snack now or wait for the guests."

"I say let's have a tour first and then decide," Gabe said.

"You know, darling, I really don't want to stick around to wait for guests. After the tour, I'd like to go to that place on the waterfront. It's highly recommended in the cooking magazine I subscribe to."

"Yes, well—"

"I have salmon chowder for dinner," Cynthia said. "It's a new recipe, and it's just out of this world for taste—"

"My dear, I think you've played the Suzie Homemaker role nicely, but don't overdo it—at least not on my account. I can't even boil water and don't need someone to make me remember how awful I am."

Cynthia felt as if she'd been slapped. She wasn't trying to impress the woman at all. It hadn't been her intention. She liked to cook, and better yet, liked to share the food she prepared.

"Whatever you have planned is fine," Cynthia said. "Perhaps the guests coming in today will want a bowl of chowder."

"Perhaps they will."

Gabe had not said a word, but Cynthia heard his sharp intake of breath. He might have spoken, but Natalie was far too busy chatting.

Gabe said he thought the floors were wonderful, but she need not have gone to that much trouble. He also liked the way she'd changed the living room around. That surprised her, as he was the sort "who didn't like changes."

"I've seen it," Natalie said, "so that should keep you happy." She glanced at Cynthia. "You're doing a good job, I see, which is good as Gabe won't be around to come checking on you every week, or twice a week—whatever it's been. He's going to New York to live come November."

"You are?" Cynthia blurted out, then realized it was none of her business what Gabe did with his life. He was her boss; she had a job, and that's all that mattered. Why did she care what he did? A small lump formed in the bottom of her stomach when she realized that he was going away and probably looking forward to it. Yet she thought she could detect a "small boy" part about him that maybe he didn't know was even there.

"Natalie, I don't think you need to go around telling my plans—"

"I didn't know you were going to New York," Cynthia said. "Not that you shouldn't, but isn't it tough getting a job there?"

"I have connections," Natalie said, purring like a kitten, taking his arm again in that possessive way she had. "Gabe will do well. He has a friend who will show him the ropes, and he'll be on Wall Street in no time."

Gabe's face went blank, and Cynthia wondered what he was thinking about. She didn't know him well enough to interpret all of his expressions, but she'd guess that he might not be completely sold on the idea.

"I know," Gabe said then. "Since Natalie wants to try out this restaurant with its four stars, we'll do that, and then come back to meet the guests."

"Oh, darling," Natalie interrupted, "I do get bored so quickly in small towns. You know that."

Cynthia looked away. How could the woman be bored in a spot this beautiful? Had she even noticed the view? The beautiful home she was in? She hadn't mentioned the touches Cynthia had worked so hard on—the napkin rings on the already set table, the bloom of flowers in the hall, the gorgeous Persian rug in the foyer. She had not noticed a thing, not even the cooling apple crisp on the counter.

But Gabe had noticed the crisp and insisted on having "just a tiny taste."

One taste led to another until Cynthia had dished up at least a third of the apple dessert.

"This is just like my Norwegian grandmother used to make," Gabe said, polishing off the last spoonful.

"And I just so happened to get that from Nonie, who was my

Norwegian grandmother," Cynthia said. "I'm glad you like it."

"No, dear," Natalie said when Cynthia again offered her just a small portion. "It's my figure, you know. I don't eat sweets these days."

"I'm sorry to hear that," Cynthia said. "I find eating one of my true pleasures of life."

Gabe grinned, and Cynthia smiled back. She knew he liked eating, but she also surmised he wouldn't say so, not wanting to invoke another barbed comment.

"I'll be here waiting for the Hendersons," Cynthia said, walking the two to the door. "They are from Missouri and wanted to see what it was like in our wonderful Pacific Northwest, or at least that is what they said online."

"Well, you take care of your guests," Natalie said, patting Cynthia's hand as if she were a small child. Cynthia moved back, saying nothing.

Glad they were gone, she put Gabe's bowl and spoon in the dishwasher. She would invite the guests to share the chowder with her. Why not? If they wanted to go out, that was fine, too, but she had an idea that they might just want to relax tonight and enjoy the conversation. She had put together a scrapbook showing sights to see in Astoria. They could look around on Saturday since they were staying two nights before heading down the coast toward Lincoln City and another B and B called Ocean Lake.

Cynthia let her thoughts return to Gabe and Natalie. Natalie was the right person for some man, but was Gabe the one? She couldn't quite put her finger on how she felt about it, but she didn't think Gabe and Natalie were a good match. Not that it was any of her business.

"Mind your own business, Cynthy," her mama used to say. "It doesn't matter what the neighbors are doing or how they talk to one another. It's their life, not yours."

"I'm just curious," was Cynthia's pat answer. It was true. She loved people and wanted to know what made them tick.

She thought back to the time she'd taken a dish of freshly baked brownies to a new neighbor. The door slammed in her face, the voice behind it telling her to just leave, not to bother them again. Crushed, she'd hurried home and bawled her eyes out.

Her mother had comforted her, explaining that not all people were friendly, no matter how hard one tried to be a good neighbor. Cynthia kept to herself for a few months, but soon she was noticing people and things and was "meddling," as her mother often called it.

Was she meddling now? Why should she care what Gabe did? If he wanted to marry this beautiful, outspoken woman, what was it to her? It was absolutely none of her concern. She had a job, and she would do the job the best she knew how. If it didn't work out, she'd return to San Francisco, and perhaps Max would have a new love interest by then. She would make it, no matter what happened. She was a winner. She knew it, and she was going to keep telling herself that very thing. How could she be anything else with God on her side?

Gabe was never quite sure when it first hit him that Natalie bugged him. Was it her bossiness? She liked to think she had all the answers and her way was the best. When she'd first mentioned moving to New York and finding a job on Wall Street, he realized it had been a dream in the back of his mind. He'd often thought he'd like to live in New York, the financial capital of the world. Somewhere along the way, he had started changing. It didn't seem as important to him. Then Natalie came along and started the fire going again. "Of course you can be a success there," she had said. "I'll be going soon, and I want you to come with me."

He had fallen for the woman completely. So different from Rainey—his old sweetheart from school days—they had broken off their relationship long before he moved to Portland. She had stepped in, helping him out until he found someone to take over the B and B permanently. Rainey was wonderful, and he would always love her like a sister, but he knew they could never be husband and wife.

Could he be a husband to Natalie? He wasn't even sure Natalie wanted that. She seemed content to see him twice a week, to have someone accompany her out for an evening on the town, whether it was a dinner in a fancy, upscale restaurant, or one of the Broadway shows or concerts. She had never mentioned marriage, nor had he. And now that he thought about it, as he sat across from her at the Pelican, he knew he would not be with her forever.

She complained often, like now.

"How this place got four stars is beyond me," Natalie said while they drank coffee. "I have certainly had better coffee in a two-star corner café in downtown Portland."

"Shh," Gabe said, leaning forward. He tried to take her

hand, but she pulled away.

"And why shouldn't they know?"

"Let's just enjoy the evening," Gabe said.

It went from bad to worse. Natalie insisted the salad dressing was "store-bought."

"I've never had such tasteless blue cheese," she whined. "Why, there aren't even any chunks of cheese!"

"We can always go back to have salmon chowder," Gabe suggested.

"Oh, you'd like that, wouldn't you!"

Gabe soon gave up. There was no appeasing her. He would stop trying. He had learned when to talk and when to keep silent. Was that the kind of relationship he wanted? Somehow he didn't think it would be that way with Cynthia. And then he smiled to himself. But Natalie caught it.

"What's funny? You're smiling."

"Oh, am I?"

"Thinking about that country bumpkin back there," she said, pushing her salad aside. "I think she's just right for that job, but don't get any ideas, Mr. Taylor. She sure can't help your career as I can."

"I wasn't thinking about my career."

"And perhaps you should." Natalie leaned forward.

But Gabe didn't want to think about it. For some reason he longed to go back to the B and B, and wanted to meet the Hendersons, picturing them as a down-to-earth couple from the heartland. Perhaps they even had a farm. They would love Cynthia and especially her cooking.

The sautéed prawns came before Natalie could say anything.

"This is all we get?" she asked the waiter.

"It says six to eight on the menu, I believe, ma'am."

Natalie took a bite and shoved her plate aside. "This has certainly not been a pleasant experience," she snapped. "I think whoever wrote that article in my cooking magazine must be the owner. I'd like a chance to write a piece—"

"Natalie, please," Gabe was saying. This was still his hometown, though he hadn't lived here for the past seven years. He still knew most of the people, and if he remembered correctly, the waiter was someone he had known in high school.

"Gabe, if you won't say something, then I must."

Gabe pulled out some money, put it on the table, and told the astounded waiter—George, or whatever his name was—to keep the change.

"You can go on complaining, but you're going to be alone." He turned away. "I'll be in the car waiting."

Natalie followed, brushing past the waiter on her way out the door.

"You humiliated me," she screamed once they were on the sidewalk. "You should have backed me up!"

"What was there to back up? I thought everything was fine."

"Maybe you won't make it in New York then."

"And maybe I won't!"

He held the door open and almost slammed it before she got her high-heeled foot completely in. He so wished he'd never talked her into coming. He'd been trying for months to get her to come to Astoria, but she was always too busy or wanted to try yet another new restaurant in Portland. Well, this was a first and a last. He sure wouldn't make this mistake again.

"I suppose you're going to pout all the way back to Portland," Natalie snapped, staring straight ahead.

"No, I'm not. We're stopping back at the B and B, and I'm having a bowl of salmon chowder."

"Oh no you're not!" Natalie's eyes blazed.

"I'm driving and I say I am."

"I couldn't possibly stand to be in the same room with Miss Perfect anymore."

"Okay. Sit in the car then. I'll try to be quick."

That is what she did as he went inside. A navy blue car with Missouri plates was in one of the parking spots, and he heard Cynthia's voice carrying from one of the upper bedrooms. His heart did a funny lurch as she came down the stairs, asking the guests to wait until she returned. He figured she probably thought it was another guest.

"Gabe!" Her eyes widened as their gazes met. "But, I thought—"

"I know. Natalie didn't like the food, and I'm back here, wanting to meet the guests and hoping there's enough chowder for me."

"Of course. Come on up while I finish their tour. They can select their favorite room, and then I'll put the chowder on. Surely Natalie will come in?"

"No, I don't think so."

The next hour was pleasant, and the chowder was better than Gabe could have imagined. He had a winner in Cynthia Lyons. He had thought so before, but after tonight, he knew so. You didn't have to hit him over the head to make a point.

Cynthia knew the couple would take the Garden Room. As they brought in their suitcases and hauled them up the narrow staircase, she went down to put the chowder on. They had agreed they would like to have a bowl of salmon chowder, and then join Cynthia and the owner. She'd hastily explained that he was in town briefly and would like to try her new recipe.

"I've only had salmon once," Mr. Henderson said. "Wasn't too happy with it. Guess I'm a beef and potatoes type guy. Most of us farmers are, you know."

"But we would love to try it again, now wouldn't we, Chester?" Mrs. Henderson said.

The four sat around the smaller of the two tables and had thick wedges of Cynthia's bread with bowls of steamy salmon chowder.

"So what do you think?" Cynthia asked after everyone had had at least two spoonfuls.

"This is wonderful," Mrs. Henderson said.

"I agree. It's sure got a good flavor."

"I've never tasted anything like it," Gabe said.

"And?" Cynthia asked. "That's good or not?"

Gabe grinned. "Good, of course."

They were just polishing off the chowder when a horn honked. Gabe's eyebrows lifted. "Oh, I think that's my friend in the car."

"Well, why didn't she come in?" Mr. Henderson asked. "Does she have the plague or something?"

"No. We just had a spat, and she insisted on staying in the car."

Gabe felt for his keys just as they heard a car start, and when he looked up, he realized he'd left them in the ignition.

"She didn't drive off and leave you, did she?" Mrs. Henderson asked.

Gabe shrugged. "Nah. She'll be back. She's gone down to the corner store, probably."

But Natalie did not return, and after they had the cheese and fruit platter Cynthia had prepared, Gabe said he'd have to rent a car.

"If we were going that way, we could take you," Mr. Henderson offered.

"I could take you, I suppose," Cynthia offered and then remembered she had two more guests coming in.

"No, the rental car will work fine."

Long after the Hendersons had settled down for the night— at nine they said it seemed like eleven because of the time change—Cynthia went online to see if there was anyone in the chat room or if there were any questions.

"Dear Lion, I made the apple crisp tonight, and my husband ate half of it! I want some more apple recipes. Thank you, Laurie."

Cynthia quickly replied, then shut off the computer. This was going to be fun. And she loved the people who were staying the weekend. But what she couldn't get out of her mind was Natalie and the way she had behaved. And even more, she thought about Gabe, wondering if he was truly happy with the situation. Somehow she felt he belonged here in

Astoria, where his heart seemed to be.

Gabe had two hours to think as he drove east toward Portland. Going through the familiar towns gave him small comfort. He had felt embarrassed tonight with Natalie making a spectacle over the dinner. Why was she so negative about things? He thought again of Grams and the lessons he'd learned at her knee. Her voice seemed to come to him now in the darkness and stillness of the car as he sped over the miles to his Portland apartment.

"Don't ever hurt anyone intentionally," Grams had said. "And if someone hurts you, give them the benefit of the doubt. But if they are taking advantage of you, stand up for your rights. God will give you the strength to do that, if you but ask."

*Is this what Natalie is doing to me now? Am I letting her do it because I need her help with my goals to become a top financier?*

A full moon shone overhead, and Gabe remembered his childhood, walking along the riverbank, looking at the stars overhead, wondering if he would be someone someday.

"But you are someone," Grams said. "God doesn't make junk. Just be true to your inner self. Be the best you can be."

Gabe breathed a prayer, the first he'd said in a long while.

*Lord, I need Your guidance. I need insight. Is Natalie the right person for me? If so, why does Cynthia's face keep popping into my mind? Could I be blinded by the need to succeed instead of leaning on You?*

It was late when Gabe arrived at his apartment. He saw the Mercury parked on the street, and Natalie stood on the sidewalk, her arms crossed.

"Give me the keys," he said.

"I suppose you're angry."

He didn't look at her. "Not angry, but my eyes were opened tonight."

"Meaning?"

"Meaning that you and I don't have a real relationship. Meaning that I won't be seeing you again."

"And all because of one incident where I lost my temper?"

Gabe sighed. "No, Nat, it's more, much more than that. I don't have enough time to explain it, not that you'd listen if I did—"

"So, that's it? You're breaking off with me just like that?"

Gabe didn't have to look to know that her eyes were blazing.

"You'll feel differently tomorrow."

"I wouldn't count on it." He moved toward the porch.

"Well, if that's how you feel—" She removed the ruby ring he had given her on her birthday and flung it at him. "I hope you have a wonderful life with Miss Goody Baker!"

Gabe said nothing but strolled up the steps and put the key in the lock, sudden relief filling his being.

# Chapter 6

August turned into September and then October. Cynthia kept busy with the online cooking classes and the B and B, which was full during the week, not just on weekends. She had hired a young woman whose husband was out of work to help clean and make up the beds after the guests left. Cynthia had not taken an order for cupcakes in over a month, but she still delivered her special bread once a week to the restaurant in town. Mary delivered fresh flowers twice a week, including small bouquets for each bedroom.

Cynthia was happy with the way things were going, but there was an unexpected ache that went through her. It had to do with Gabe. Soon he'd be gone to New York, and the thought unnerved her, though she wasn't sure why.

New drapes hung at the bay windows, though they were pulled back and held with a matching bow. Gabe had agreed to replace two more rugs and let her take out the wall-to-wall carpeting in the bedrooms. She hated the carpeting. It didn't add to the feel of the Victorian home. But the biggest and most wonderful surprise was when Gabe brought the small fountain to put in the parlor. It added charm, and its trickling sound mesmerized everyone. She remembered the afternoon with fondness.

"This is to appease you as I said no to the outdoor fountain."

"Oh, it's wonderful! I can't wait to set it up."

"Has the raccoon been back?"

That was the reason he'd said no to a fishpond or a waterfall. Both attracted wild animals, and there were certainly some in the hills behind the Victorian.

"I saw footprints yesterday."

Cynthia had mixed feelings about chasing the animal away. The first time she'd caught a glimpse, the raccoon limped off. Later she saw where his right foot was mangled. "Probably from a trap," Gabe said.

The guests had left by noon, and no one was expected that evening. One free night. Cynthia felt heady.

"When do you go back?" she asked. She liked the way his shoulders hunched over the fountain project, the sunshine from a nearby window gleaming on his hair. She had the sudden urge to touch him but stepped back.

He stood, rubbing his back. "I can't lean over for long. It's an old football injury."

"I can do this," Cynthia said.

"I know." Gabe's face suddenly looked flat. "I don't think there's anything you *cannot* do."

"I didn't mean it to sound that way."

"I know," he repeated.

He took her arm suddenly. "Let's go outside; soak up some sun."

Cynthia followed him out the door and down the steps. A riot of color from the impatiens and petunias nearly took her breath away. "I love this spot."

"I know. It's beautiful now, and I appreciate how you've brought it to life. Come sit for a minute."

Cynthia had talked him into the concrete deacon's bench. It was ideal for inclement weather and the dampness Astoria experienced year-round.

She put pads on the bench each day, bringing them in at night or at the first sight of rain. Funny how the small misty showers bothered her no longer. She found she liked how the rain made everything greener and cleared the air.

"I suppose you'll be moving on one of these days," Gabe said.

Cynthia met his steady gaze and looked away again. "I don't know why you think that."

"Someone with your obvious flair for decorating needs to find a better-paying job."

"I'm happy with what you pay me. After all, I don't have rent to pay, and the food is covered. I think it's a good deal."

"How's the online cooking class going?"

"Great." Cynthia thought of her last posting. Peach Treats. "I keep getting new students. The latest is a guy who wants to impress his girlfriend."

"A guy, huh?"

"Men do like to cook, you know. Why do you suppose all the classy restaurants have men chefs? When they cook, they do it with flourish. They're never afraid to try new things."

"You try new things."

"Yes, I do."

"What treat do you have today?"

Cynthia laughed. "Oh, so is that a hint?"

Gabe stood. "I really need to get back to Portland," he said abruptly.

"Without a slice of peach pie?"

"Peach pie?"

"Made first thing this morning. I had to try this new piecrust."

Gabe stayed another hour, having two pieces and taking a slice with him when he left. Cynthia cleaned off the table. Something was bothering Gabe; it was so evident. She'd tried to get him to talk, but he wouldn't. He'd broken off with Natalie; that had happened right after that visit when she'd driven off in the car. No, it was something else. Had he met another woman?

With the rest of the afternoon free, Cynthia checked the phone, making sure it would pick up messages, and headed out, her sweater over her shoulders. She took the last piece of peach pie to Mary. Mary always appreciated her cooking, about as much as Gabe. She'd found a true friend in Mary.

As Cynthia got to the bottom of the hill and onto Main Street, a familiar car went by. Gabe. And beside him sat Rainey. *Rainey.* Was he seeing her again? Friends, he'd said more than once, but was it really only that? Rainey was laughing, and it looked as if they were driving back to Portland together.

"Hey, haven't seen you in a few," Mary said. "How did you like the last flowers I sent? I thought the dahlias were especially colorful."

"Gorgeous. I've never seen such a variety of colors and blooms." Cynthia set the sack on the counter. "Peach pie. Tell me if you like the crust. It has just a smidgen of cornmeal."

"Cornmeal?"

"Yeah. Saw the recipe in *Sunset* magazine."

"Can't wait to try it, but I'll wait until I get home and put my feet up and have a cup of java with it."

Cynthia turned to leave.

"Hey, what's up? Don't you feel like talking, or are guests coming in this afternoon?"

"No, I have a few hours. I just wanted to walk down by the river."

"Is something wrong?"

Cynthia opened her mouth to speak but closed it again. How could she tell Mary what was in her heart—how she had fallen in love with her boss, a man who clearly got agitated with her for things, and who thought of her only as the woman who ran his bed-and-breakfast with precision and dignity?

"You don't have to tell me if you don't want. That's okay. I think I know anyway."

Cynthia spun around. "You *know*? But you couldn't know."

"Could so."

Cynthia looked at her friend, the only real friend she had here. "I will muddle through it, as I do all my problems."

"It may not be as bad as you think."

"Meaning?"

"It concerns Gabe. And I think he's equally smitten but won't admit it. Not yet, anyway."

"He's going with Rainey again."

"They're friends."

"Yeah, you said that before."

"It's true."

"Well. . ." Cynthia paused in the open doorway. "I just don't think you know what I'm thinking about."

"It's a business deal," Mary said then.

"A business deal?"

"Yes. And that's all I'm going to say about it."

A business deal? What would that be about? Did it have something to do with Gabe's going to New York?

The walk along the river was tranquil. A large ship was anchored, and a barge moved slowly toward Portland. One day she wanted to go on the excursion boat that traveled back and forth from Portland. Across the Columbia River, to the Washington side, hills all green and woodsy seemed to meet the sky. Cynthia had driven over once just to see the hills up close. It was beautiful. But what wasn't beautiful in the Northwest?

Cynthia strolled past the old railroad depot. It sat empty and neglected, as if waiting for someone to come along and refurbish it. She could see a restaurant going in. Many cities across the United States had turned their old train stations into works of art. She'd seen one in Bennington, Vermont, when traveling there with her mother just a year before she died. Her one dream was to travel back to the place of her birth, and so they had. Dreams should be fulfilled, if possible.

Cynthia touched the red brick. It would be standing long after she was gone. The old building had possibilities. She had ideas, but nothing with which to do anything.

Cynthia knew she was a dreamer. She'd always been a dreamer. Her mother told her she was like her father. She wished she'd known him better. She wished they could have shared their dreams. Did he see old, dilapidated buildings and imagine them as magnificent structures again? Did he drive through a town and imagine what it would be like to live there? Did he enjoy the sunrises and sunsets as much as she did?

Max had laughed at her dreams. He never understood. He wanted to please her, but in the end he had stopped trying. The fact that he denied there was a God was something Cynthia couldn't tolerate. Why, God was everywhere she looked. He guided and directed her. How could anyone deny His existence?

A breeze blew in from the west. The Pacific Ocean was not far away; its tides ruled the mouth of the Columbia. The waves picked up as she turned and headed back up the hill.

The phone was ringing when Cynthia returned to the B and B.

"Hello, Taylor's Bed-and-Breakfast. May I help you?"

"Cynthia?"

Her heart lurched. "Gabe? I thought you were on the road."

"I am."

"And?"

"I felt I left with things unsaid."

"I saw you go by with Rainey. She's going to Portland with you?"

"No, I dropped her off at the edge of town at a friend's."

"Oh." Now Cynthia felt dumb.

"What's playing in the background?"

"Willie Nelson," Cynthia said.

"Willie Nelson? You like his music?"

"It's a tape Mom gave me one Christmas. There are a few songs that make me think and put things into the right perspective."

"I see. Cynthia, I—"

"Yes? What?"

"Oh, never mind. I wanted to run something by you, but I think it can wait. Take care."

The phone went dead before she could say good-bye.

"We never learn until it's too late," Willie sang, his words filling the now vacant sitting room. Why did that song haunt her so?

Two reservations came in, and soon Cynthia was busy in the kitchen. She wanted to try something new with cupcakes. She'd have cupcakes in the next online class. There was so much one could do with cake.

The doorbell rang. Cynthia dried her hands and hurried to answer. Mary's husband stood there, a smile on his face. "I know this isn't the regular delivery day, but these are special."

"Special?"

"The order just came in on the phone."

"Well, aren't you the speedy one to deliver so fast?"

"Wait until you see the card."

"The card can't be as special as these peonies. They are beautiful!"

Cynthia recognized Mary's spidery handwriting on the small enclosure. It was addressed to her, not the B and B.

*I don't think you realize how much your help means to me. Have a wonderful week. Gabe Taylor.*

Cynthia smiled. Only Gabe would add his last name as if Cynthia didn't know who he was. She found the lovely milk glass vase in the pantry and filled it with water, adding a teaspoon of sugar. Peonies didn't have a long life, but she wanted these to last as long as possible.

Gabe called Mary's Bouquets after leaving Astoria. He should have stopped at the store, but the idea hadn't occurred to him until he dropped Rainey off.

"You're in love, Gabe," Rainey had said, looking up at him with a sudden smile.

"Don't be ridiculous," he snapped.

"Yeah, I'm right."

The Mercury stopped, and she opened the door. "You don't want to admit it, but your fast reaction in denying it is all the more reason I believe it."

"Rainey, I'm just getting over Natalie—you know that."

"So?"

"I can't possibly consider even looking at another woman, let alone have a relationship."

"What? You didn't have a relationship with Natalie. She talked and you jumped. Is that what you call a relationship?"

"I thought it was at the time."

"Still going to New York?"

"Of course. Bought the airline ticket last week."

Rainey smiled again. "Anything can happen, Gabe. *Anything.* Trust me on this."

Gabe drove off in a huff. He hated it when she insisted she could read his mind. She was almost as bad as Natalie.

*Cynthia.* Was it true? He found himself thinking of her endlessly. When he tried to push the thought aside, her smiling face came back to haunt him. How could he be so foolish to fall for someone now? Someone like her?

*Someone like her?* The thought suddenly hit him. What did he mean by that? Any man could consider himself lucky to have a woman like Cynthia. She was smart, an innovative cook, fixed things, had a good mind... She wasn't a beauty, but she had a good, homespun quality about her, someone his grandmother would have loved on the spot. And Grams was picky about whom she liked and didn't.

He picked up his cell phone and dialed Mary at the florist shop.

After passing through the small town of Clatskanie, Gabe considered all the reasons why this was not the time to fall in love. It had not been long enough since his relationship with Natalie. Was he over her? And Cynthia had been with a man in California—Max, he thought she'd called him. It could be that she was still in love with him. Besides, he remembered reading that one should wait four years before another relationship. *Lord, is that true? Do I want to get involved with this woman?*

*And why not?* a voice seemed to say.

Yes, why not?

Gabe didn't take rejection well. For that reason, he had to take things slow. Then he thought about New York. He had always dreamed of living there, of getting a slice of the fast lane. How could he not go now? His friend Jeff expected him. Natalie had closed the door on any help, but he wondered if she could have helped him much anyway. No, he must go. It was a done deal.

The traffic was worse than usual as Gabe drove through the streets of downtown Portland. He loved the town, but the traffic was one huge headache. He longed for Astoria and the quiet nature—the lack of cars, trucks, and noise. Noise always had bothered him. He missed the bellow of a ship's horn, the *clackety-clack* of a train on the tracks below. These sounds put him to sleep at night, made him long to travel, to leave the town of his childhood, and go to the city.

Here he was about to leave and go to one of the largest cities in the world. How would he fare? Would he like it as much as he once thought he would? He guessed he would never know until he tried it.

The last cooking class had been a success.

"Noodle pudding? I would never have thought of noodles as being dessert. Thanks for the interesting and delicious recipe."

Cynthia smiled, remembering the visit to a neighbor when she was five. Gloria lived alone and had a wooden leg. The wooden leg intrigued Cynthia. It was the only reason she went with her mother. She hoped to see what a wooden leg looked like. She recalled going into a house that was dark and musty smelling. They entered the kitchen, where the woman sat. "She never gets up to answer the door," her mother explained beforehand. "It takes too long to walk with crutches, you know."

"But if she has a wooden leg, can't she walk on it?"

"Yes, of course, but it's much easier not to."

When they entered the cluttered kitchen, the smell of vanilla emanated from the oven.

"You're just in time to take my noodle pudding out of the oven," Gloria said. "And then you can share it with me."

"I brought cookies," Cynthia's mother said, holding up a small white bag. "They came from the bakery over on Tenth."

"Oh, how delightful. Please set them up on that counter." Gloria pointed.

Cynthia watched while her mother opened the oven door, pot holder in hand.

She wondered what a noodle pudding could be. It didn't sound like anything she'd like.

"We'd be delighted to have a small dish with you," her mother said.

"No," Cynthia started to say, but her mother elbowed her, and Cynthia changed her no to a "yes, thank you."

"Noodle pudding comes from my grandmother, who loved cooking."

Cynthia kept trying to see the wooden leg, but both legs were covered with denim. Cynthia brought two bowls to the table while her mother brought the third bowl and cream she'd found in the refrigerator.

"This is just wonderful that you want to share with us."

Cynthia nodded. "Yes, thank you very much."

Cynthia knew she'd have to hold her nose to get the pudding down. But on the third bite, when she breathed suddenly, a sweet taste filled her mouth, and she ate the rest with gusto.

"I do need this recipe," Cynthia's mother said, and Cynthia nodded in agreement.

Gabe's face came to mind again, but she pushed it aside. He had sent her flowers. Why, she didn't know, but it wouldn't be for the right reason, not the reason she hoped for. She'd enjoy them, anyway.

Cynthia decided to make another noodle pudding and take some to Mary and her family. She was just removing it from the oven when the doorbell rang. No guests were coming, and Mary was still at work.

Rainey stood with jacket in hand. "It does make one sweat coming up that hill," she puffed.

"Come on in. I heard you went to visit a friend."

"Oh, so Gabe called you."

"He did."

"And sent you flowers?"

"Yes, but how did you know?"

Rainey slipped out of her loafers and placed the jacket in a small heap on top of her shoes. "Gabe said I should stop to see the new changes. He seems quite happy about everything."

"Not that he wanted to spend any money—"

Rainey laughed. "That's Gabe all right. He's tight, but that's good in a way. Means he has a good business head on him. He should do fine in New York."

*New York.* How Cynthia wished she had never heard about

it. It made an empty hollow feeling inside her, one that wouldn't go away.

"After a tour, you can have some noodle pudding with me."

"Noodle pudding!" Rainey exclaimed. "Is that a dessert?"

"Yes. I believe it's Armenian. A neighbor in my old neighborhood used to bake it a lot."

"I'll try anything once," Rainey said, following Cynthia up the stairs.

"It *is* beautiful," Rainey said. "Gabe said you had the magic touch, and I can see he is right."

"I'm glad you think so."

After standing and enjoying the view from the north bedroom window, the two went back downstairs to the kitchen. Rainey accepted the bowl and claimed it was delicious. "So this goes on your Web site?"

"Oh, not mine," Cynthia said, removing the bowls. "I just send in my column once a week, and then each night I see if anyone has posted a question or comment. Sometimes they send recipes for me to try."

"And you're not too busy with the work here?"

"Usually not."

Rainey left, and Cynthia's thoughts included Gabe again. She hoped Gabe had arrived home all right. She wished Portland wasn't a two-hour drive away. Yet the distance hadn't stopped him before. But New York, that was another matter. It was time to shift gears and go online to see if there were more messages. She turned on the computer and relaxed when she heard the steady hum.

# Chapter 7

In the past few months, Cynthia had covered quick breads, puddings, cookies, crisps and flans, and cakes. Her next lesson was to hone in on decorative cupcakes. She had never made any for Gabe, and she now regretted it. Gabe had left for New York two weeks before, and she had not heard a word. Funny how quickly she'd become used to hearing from him, having him drop in, feeding him some of her cooking, and sending him home with a goodie to enjoy the next day. He always called, thanking her. If only they didn't spar so much. Cynthia was a strong person; she'd always known that. She liked having control. A lot of changes had been made to the B and B since she came. The latest was the remodel of one bedroom, which was now pet-friendly.

At first Gabe said no to every suggestion. And so she'd worked and finished one thing at a time. When he saw it, he liked it. He just didn't like it when the bills came in.

"I'm not made of money, you know."

Cynthia laughed. "No, but think of all the money you saved on labor."

Every Friday morning she mowed the lawn and edged it. Some places would expect to pay a gardener, and she'd tactfully pointed out that fact.

The ongoing bill was for the flowers that Cynthia insisted on ordering. The house must look inviting. Word of mouth brought others to the B and B.

Cynthia looked out at the view of the river she'd grown to love. She couldn't think of living anywhere else. It was serene except when the winds came and blew up a storm. When the water was choppy and frothy, she imagined what it must be like to be out in a boat then.

Cynthia dropped Gabe a snail mail note at the end of his first week in New York.

*Just wanted to tell you that we had a full house last week-end. More people coming for midweek. Then it should start slowing down, though I don't know why. The weather is glorious. But I really am writing to see how you're doing. Do you love New York? I've always wanted to go, but maybe it's one of those dreams I'll never fulfill.*

She wanted to say she missed hearing from him, missed seeing his face, but the words stayed inside her, along with the hollow emptiness.

Why didn't he write? Even if it were just a sentence or two, she'd at least know he was doing okay.

Cynthia made a potpie and invited Rainey over.

"I just wanted to visit. . .see if you had heard from Gabe," she said before Rainey slipped out of her sweater.

"I have not. And I assume you haven't, either."

"Did he always want to go to New York?"

Rainey nodded, taking a piece of the Mexican fudge Cynthia offered her. "Yes, he did. Talked about it as far back as I can remember."

"Then it's good he's doing it. I think life is too short not to do what you've always wanted to do."

"And you?" Rainey asked. "What's your heart's desire?"

Cynthia poured tea and motioned for Rainey to sit at the small table in one corner of the kitchen.

"I think I'm pretty much doing it. I've always liked to cook. I started the catering business, as you've undoubtedly heard about, and now I'm managing one of the loveliest B and Bs in the Northwest. I bake what I want when I want, and I am now teaching others a love of cooking—or hope that I am."

Cynthia grabbed a plate off the sideboard and showed Rainey her latest creations. "These are cupcakes I've made for a party."

Rainey's eyes widened. "I like the butterfly design on this one. They're all too beautiful to eat."

"No, they're to be eaten."

"How did you learn this?"

"By trial and error."

The two women talked, and Cynthia found out a lot about Gabe that she had only guessed at before.

"His grandmother doted on him; he could do no wrong."

"I surmised that."

"His father died when he was too young to remember, but my father remembered him as being loud and lusty."

"Gabe certainly isn't loud," Cynthia interjected.

"I know. He never has been." Rainey sighed audibly. "I have loved him for so many years, first as a boyfriend, and now as a brother. He'd do anything for me."

Cynthia wondered if it was really a brother/sister relationship. Some of the best relationships were ones where the two were good, solid friends. You then built more on that foundation. She hoped someday she'd find someone like that. She knew it would never be Gabe. They disagreed on a lot of things, and though she found him attractive and felt she was falling in love with him at one point, she realized they couldn't make a go of it.

Long after Rainey left, Cynthia thought about her life and what she would now do differently. And she couldn't think of a thing except having a male companion. She missed that very much. There was a show in Astoria she longed to see, but it was no fun going alone. She went out to eat once in a while, but not often, as it was usually a disappointment. She supposed she was like a writer who no longer read a book for enjoyment, but edited every line. Still, a night out could be fun, and someone to help carry the groceries in could be nice. Someday she might realize that dream. There was always hope.

Cynthia cleaned the few dishes up, checked the computer for e-mail—just in case Gabe had written—then started her next column. She liked to keep ahead two weeks in the event she got too busy to do one sometime.

Cynthia turned the last light out and went to her small bedroom at the rear of the house. Sometimes she wanted to be on the tip-top floor as the view was magnificent. But, the innkeeper always had the smallest bedroom.

A sky full of stars was just outside her window, and she marveled in this most wonderful creation. She never tired of looking at the sky and the stars. The moon was but a sliver, making her think of a piece of pie.

Cynthia couldn't sleep, not even after reading a couple chapters in Hebrews. Usually she felt comforted from the faith verse, but not tonight. Her mind kept going back to Gabe and how she felt when he was around. The times they didn't get along were when they argued over the telephone. When he was here, she could ply him with one of her entrees or a fancy dessert, and he was happy. Sometimes they walked down the street to stroll along the river. There they talked about a lot of things, but never business. They left the B and B behind. She liked thinking about those times, knowing they wouldn't happen again. Gabe had carved out his niche; he would stay in New York and forget his simple life in Astoria, and Cynthia had to accept that fact and get on with her life.

# Chapter 8

Cynthia had boxes of cake mix lined up in a row: chocolate and vanilla, two favorite flavors. She also had butter, powdered sugar, food coloring, vanilla extract, and lemon. There were also cupcake papers, which she usually didn't use, but she knew they would be easier for the girls to handle while icing and decorating their cupcakes.

"How do I get myself into these things?" she said to Jan, who had called wanting to know how things were going.

"Because you're a glutton for punishment," Jan retorted. "At least that's what my mom used to say."

"It seemed like a good idea at the time."

Cynthia had met the local Junior Girl Scout leader at the florist shop.

"We're having a celebration coming up in honor of Juliette Lowe, our leader. We have a skit, a program showing what we do, but we need to make some money. I keep trying to come up with an idea. Do you have any?"

"No, afraid not," Mary said, as she wrapped a silver ribbon around a bouquet of scarlet mums.

Cynthia walked on into the shop and, as always, had to put her two cents' worth in. "I think it would be fun to have a cupcake raffle. It's not as expensive, the girls could make fancy cupcakes, and people would bid on them."

The leader's face lit up, and she said it was a good idea, but who would help the girls?

"I could. Since cupcakes are my specialty, I have lots of photos and ideas."

"Trust me," Mary said with a nod. "Cynthia Lyons is a wonder when it comes to food. I say go for it!"

Here they were now, ten girls with frosting on the counter, floor, on everyone's apron, and even on a few noses. But the cupcakes were coming along nicely. Each brought a cake mix, to go along with what Cynthia already had, and a box of powdered sugar. Cynthia provided the flavorings and decorations. She had a plate of cupcakes for an example, and the girls each chose which one they liked best. The ladybug always won, hands down.

They baked the cupcakes—each girl would do a dozen, and Cynthia would finish up with the rest and donate those to the raffle. The girls would have one hundred and twenty, and Cynthia would add another hundred or so. That should help toward the expenses of summer camp.

Cupcakes adorned the counters, the top of the stove now cooled off, and trays on the dining room table. Cynthia had bought pink boxes from the bakery, so the girls could take their cupcakes to the sale in a pink box. She hoped people paid more than they were worth.

Cynthia finished frosting the first dozen—it didn't take

her long. The girls crowded around, marveling at how fast she worked.

"I've frosted cupcakes for years; I better be fast."

The door opened and she turned, startled. Nobody ever just came in, not even Mary or Rainey.

It was Gabe. Her heart flip-flopped as she wiped her hands on her apron, now smudged with greens, yellows, and reds.

"Why, Mr. Taylor, what a surprise!" She wondered if her face was red as a flush heated it. "I thought you were in New York."

He came into the room and as their eyes met, there was a sudden longing in his gaze—if she was reading it right. Of course she could be wrong. She had been wrong many times in the past where men were concerned.

"This is Troop 44, and I'll let each girl introduce herself, and, girls, Mr. Taylor owns this house. We have him to thank for letting us use the kitchen."

Gabe smiled and nodded as each girl said her name.

"Are there any samples?" he asked, a grin spreading across his face.

Cynthia looked at her masterpieces. "Actually, these cupcakes were made for a raffle tomorrow night. The proceeds go into the girls' camp fund. Now if you'd like to buy one, you can do that."

"Just give him one," Martha said. "He looks extra hungry."

Cynthia nodded. "I suppose I could do that. Let him pick out his favorite?"

"No, I'll buy since it's for a good cause."

Cynthia had not finished all of her cupcakes yet. The frosting was hardening, but that was no problem. She'd just add a teaspoon of hot water and finish the job.

Gabe bought six cupcakes and set a ten-dollar bill on the table. "I hope this is enough."

"That's more than adequate," Cynthia said. "I'll have coffee ready in a jiff, that is if you want to eat one now."

"Does a bear live in the woods?" He grinned.

One of the Scouts wrinkled her nose. "What does that mean?"

"Of course a bear lives in the woods," another girl answered, "so of course he wants a cupcake. That's what he means."

Gabe pulled out a chair. "You never cease to amaze me," he said to Cynthia. "What's it going to be next? You'll invite all the politicians over for dinner?"

"Ha-ha!"

The girls put their cupcakes in their boxes, and soon parents came and picked them up. Gabe had started on his third cupcake. "These are not only works of art; they're tasty, too."

Cynthia wondered why Gabe was here. One didn't usually fly to New York, work a few weeks, and fly home. Had something come up too important not to attend to? Was he selling the B and B because he wanted to buy a place in New York? Wouldn't Rainey have mentioned it when she saw her yesterday?

"You're wondering what brought me back."

"As a matter of fact, yes."

"So am I."

Cynthia raised an eyebrow. "Is this supposed to be Twenty Questions?"

Gabe got up then, wiping the frosting off his chin, and it hit her again how much he was like a little boy. She wanted to run her hand through his hair, wanted him to lift her face to his, but she must stifle the feelings. He'd found someone in New York and had come home to pack up the rest of his things in Portland and would probably sell the B and B by the end of the season, which was soon. She felt a lump come to her throat.

"So, are you going to say why you're here, even if I think I know why?"

"Oh, you think you know, do you?"

"Gabe, just come out with it. You're buying a place in New York and selling the B and B. Never mind the fact that it's been in your family for three generations. Never mind the fact that you have an efficient manager who would give her eye-teeth to live here forever. . . ." She stopped in midsentence, realizing what she'd said.

He stood staring at her, as she tried to recover as quickly as possible. "I shouldn't have said that last part. I'm sorry—"

"Sorry?" Suddenly he was there, taking both hands, removing the frosting-encrusted apron, and pulling her to him. "You'd like to live here the rest of your life? Is this true?"

"Well, I. . ." She looked up into his dark eyes and forgot everything that was on her mind. Only the things in her heart mattered now.

"You are wanting me to kiss you."

Before she could respond, his mouth covered hers, and she felt herself lean into him as if she belonged there, as if she had always belonged there.

"So, that's settled."

"What's settled?" Cynthia stepped back, her hands gripping the sides of her skirt. Usually she wore jeans, but this morning, feeling she wanted to look like an old-fashioned girl, she had donned a skirt with white ruffled blouse. The apron also had ruffles. It lay discarded on the back of a chair where Gabe had tossed it.

"I have something to show you."

"In Portland? I can't leave. Guests are coming today."

"Not in Portland. It's five blocks away, close enough to walk."

Cynthia wondered what Gabe was talking about. She looked at the frosting dried and congealed in the bowl now. She had to finish the cupcakes first. Would he understand? "Give me fifteen minutes, okay? So I can finish? You can put those that are done in one of the pink boxes—"

"Are you always going to be this bossy?"

*Always? Did he say always?* Always conjured up good thoughts in her mind. Happy thoughts. Forever belonged to always. She glanced back at him and found herself in his arms again, being kissed not just once, but twice. Finally he released her.

"I missed you so much when I was in New York."

"I missed you, too. Your calls complaining about the latest expense, you suddenly turning up without calling first. . ."

"You do like being bossy, making the decisions, having your own way."

"Now, just a minute. Everything I did for this B and B made it better, and you know it."

"I like it when you get angry. Do you know your mouth gets all small and your eyes actually flash? I noticed it the first time we met in my office. I said to myself that day, 'Here is trouble.'"

"You did not."

"Did so."

"You never acted like that. I thought you couldn't stand me."

"I was fighting the feeling. You were getting in the way of my dream, my passion to go to New York and become somebody."

"You already are somebody."

"I know. I discovered that while I was gone. It doesn't matter where you are; you're still the same person. And I also knew that God brought you into my life for a reason, and if I didn't get back here, someone else might come along and snatch you up."

Cynthia's head whirled with the suddenness of it. It was happening too fast.

She looked at the frosting and back at Gabe. "This can wait. I've had interruptions before."

"This interruption will be worth it."

"I'm sure it will."

She changed from flats to tennis shoes and grabbed a sweater from the foyer coat rack.

"Where are we really going?"

"To see a house."

"To see a house," Cynthia repeated. She had trouble keeping up with his long stride, until he realized and slowed down. "Here, let me take your hand. That will keep me in pace with you."

Soon they stood in front of an old Victorian, and Cynthia gasped. It looked to be the same vintage as Taylor's B and B. But the paint crumbled, shutters were hanging askew, and the roof was in dire need of repair.

"Whose house is this?"

"Mine."

"Yours? But you never told me you had another house."

"I know, because it wasn't mine. I bought it yesterday; I put down the money after taking out a second mortgage on the bed-and-breakfast, which qualified for a nice loan, thanks to you."

"You really own this house?" Cynthia's mind was reeling.

"Yes. I've loved this house all my life; it's the twin to the bed-and-breakfast. The owners wouldn't sell, though I asked every year. And then Rainey saw that the son who inherited it died of sudden cancer, and she checked around and discovered that his heirs wanted to sell, the sooner the better."

Cynthia looked at the old Victorian, then back at him. "And you're opening another bed-and-breakfast?"

"Yes. That's my plan. But it will take major work, and I need someone who is good with interior design, but I guess she's too busy cooking with everyone in Astoria."

"Gabe! It was a one-time thing. The Girl Scouts, you know?"

"I know. And it's what I've come to admire about you in these past four months. You are so giving and generous and loving to everyone."

His eyes told Cynthia he was once again teasing her, and she playfully pushed him.

"I like all those traits, even the bossiness, as a bossy person gets things done. But the most important one is the loving, and anyone who would help the Girl Scouts make money for their camp is all heart."

A car pulled up and Rainey got out. "I thought you'd be here when nobody answered the door at the B and B. Hello, Cynthia."

"You knew about this?"

Rainey smiled. "Friends know everything, don't they?"

*But you still love him,* Cynthia wanted to say. Sometimes you can't have what you want most, but life goes on, and soon another window opens; she hoped that was true for Rainey. Rainey was a good, thoughtful person. She needed to find someone, too.

"I'll hear if the deal went through tomorrow," Gabe said then. "And I'm setting up an office right here in Astoria, believe it or not. Didn't think they'd ever need a financial advisor, but the time is right; our town is growing, and I think I'll do just fine here."

He turned toward Cynthia and took her hand again. "Rainey, you know my heart. I fought my feelings toward this woman, but you said to just let it go and see what happened. Go to New York. Pursue your dream. Well, the dream changed. And here I am."

Cynthia looked back at the house. Already she had an idea about the color for the outside paint. Light pink, scarlet, and aqua. She'd seen the colors in a magazine once, and they would make this house stand out like the beauty she once was. There would be lots of scraping and peeling, and it would take time, but the end result would be worth it. The flower garden would be in the front of this house, not on the side. There was more room between the house and sidewalk for a huge plot of flowers and a picket fence.

"I think we should go inside," Cynthia said then. "You lead the way, Gabe. I'll take notes about colors and wallpaper and flooring."

Gabe shrugged. "See what I mean about being bossy, Rainey? She gets to call all the shots, and somehow I think I'm going to like that part." He grinned as he paused on the first step. "Maybe I should carry you over the threshold now, but it wouldn't be appropriate since you don't have a ring yet."

Cynthia shook her head. "This is going too fast. I still can't believe any of it. Maybe I better pinch myself."

"You do that," Gabe said, leaning over and kissing the end of her nose. "Hey, tastes like frosting."

They laughed and then went inside the house. Cynthia thought of the frosting and cupcakes she'd just left. Already she knew what she'd do. She'd cut off the side of two cupcakes, frost them together, and put two hearts on top. Her and Gabe's hearts.

Cynthia liked the comfort of his hand holding hers and glanced up and smiled again. It was time for the dream to begin. God had such perfect timing, as always.

# NOODLE PUDDING
## (sometimes called Kugel Pudding)

8 ounces wide egg noodles
1 cup crushed pineapple, drained
2 tablespoons sugar
1 cup cottage cheese, small curd
¼ cup butter, melted
½ cup brown sugar
3 eggs, beaten
1 tsp. vanilla
⅓ cup raisins

Topping:
1 tablespoon butter
¼ cup graham cracker crumbs
1 tablespoon sugar

Cook noodles (slightly overcook them). Combine remaining ingredients, except topping, with cooked noodles in a large bowl. Place mixture in a buttered 9x13-inch buttered baking dish. Add topping. Bake at 350 degrees for 1 hour. A dollop of whipped cream is optional.

## BIRDIE L. ETCHISON

Birdie L. Etchison has enjoyed writing romances for the past ten years. She has also written numerous articles for various publications and been included in several anthologies, the latest being *Prayers and Promises—Armed Forces*. She speaks at writing seminars and co-directs Writer's Weekend at the Beach, a gathering of writers from all over. Walking the beach two blocks from her home on the Long Beach peninsula in Washington State, Birdie finds stories in people she meets and in everyday happenings. "God gave me a passion for writing," she says, "and I'm the happiest when putting characters into a scene that will soon unfold into a story." Birdie enjoys deep friendships with several writer friends. "We all get a boost and encourage and help each other with the writing process." Cooking is a favorite hobby, so it was easy to move inside the head and heart of her heroine, Cynthia Lyons, in *Cupcakes for Two*.

# Blueberry Surprise

by Wanda E. Brunstetter

# Dedication

To my friend Jan Otte,
whose sweet treats have brought joy to so many people.
And to my daughter, Lorine Van Corbach,
a talented musician, who has fulfilled
her heart's desire of teaching music.

# Chapter 1

Rain splattered against the windshield in drops the size of quarters. The darkening sky seemed to swallow Lorna Patterson's compact car as it headed west on the freeway toward the heart of Seattle, Washington.

"I'm sick of this soggy weather," Lorna muttered, gripping the steering wheel with determination and squinting her eyes to see out the filmy window. "I'm drained from working two jobs, and I am not happy with my life."

The burden of weariness crept through Lorna's body, like a poisonous snake about to overtake an unsuspecting victim. Each day as she pulled herself from bed at five in the morning, willing her tired body to move on its own, Lorna asked herself how much longer she could keep going the way she was.

She felt moisture on her cheeks and sniffed deeply. "Will I ever be happy again, Lord? It's been over a year since Ron's death. My heart aches to find joy and meaning in life."

Lorna flicked the blinker switch and turned onto the exit ramp. Soon she was pulling into the parking lot of Farmen's Restaurant, already full of cars.

The place buzzed with activity when she entered through the back door, used only by the restaurant employees and for deliveries. Lorna hung her umbrella and jacket on a wall peg in the coatroom. "I hope I'm not too late," she whispered to her friend and coworker, Chris Williams.

Chris glanced at the clock on the opposite wall. "Your shift was supposed to start half an hour ago, but I've been covering for you."

"Thanks. I appreciate that."

"Is everything all right? You didn't have car troubles, I hope."

Lorna shook her head. "Traffic on the freeway was awful, and the rain didn't make things any easier."

Chris offered Lorna a wide grin, revealing two crescent-shaped dimples set in the middle of her pudgy cheeks. Her light brown hair was pulled up in a ponytail, which made her look less like a woman of thirty-three and more like a teenager. Lorna was glad her own hair was short and naturally curly. She didn't have to do much, other than keep her blond locks clean, trimmed, and combed.

"You know Seattle," Chris said with a snicker. "Weather-wise, it wasn't much of a summer, was it? And now fall is just around the corner."

*It wasn't much of a year, either,* Lorna thought ruefully. She drew in a deep breath and released it with a moan. "I am so tired—of everything."

"I'm not surprised." Chris shook her finger. "Work, work, work. That's all you ever do. Clerking at Moore's Mini-mart during the day and working as a waitress here at night. There's no reason for you to be holding down two jobs now that. . ."

She broke off her sentence. "Sorry. It's none of my business how you spend your time. I hate to see you looking so sad and tired, that's all."

Lorna forced a smile. "I know you care, Chris, and I appreciate your concern. You probably don't understand this, but I need to keep busy. It's the only way I can cope with my loss. If I stay active, I don't have time to think or even feel."

"There are other ways to keep busy, you know," Chris reminded her.

"I hope you're not suggesting I start dating again. You know I'm not ready for that." Lorna pursed her lips as she slowly shook her head. "I'm not sure I'll ever be ready to date, much less commit to another man."

"I'm not talking about dating. There are other things in life besides love and romance. Just ask me—the Old Maid of the West." Chris blinked her eyelids dramatically and wrinkled her nose.

Lorna chuckled, in spite of her dour mood, and donned her red and blue monogrammed Farmen's apron. "What would you suggest I do with my time?"

"How about what you've always wanted to do?"

"And that would be?"

"Follow your heart. Go back to school and get your degree."

Lorna frowned. "Oh, that. I've put my own life on hold so long, I'm not sure I even want college anymore."

"Oh, please!" Chris groaned. "How many times have I heard you complain about having to give up your dream of teaching music to elementary school kids?"

Lorna shrugged. "I don't know. Dozens, maybe."

Chris patted her on the back. "Now's your chance for some real adventure."

Lorna swallowed hard. She knew her friend was probably right, but she also knew going back to school would be expensive, not to mention the fact that she was much older now and would probably feel self-conscious among those college kids. It would be an adventure all right. Most likely a frightening one.

"Think about it," Chris whispered as she headed for the dining room.

"I'll give it some thought," Lorna said to her friend's retreating form.

Evan Bailey leaned forward in his chair and studied the recipe that had recently been posted online. "Peanut butter and chocolate chip cookies. Sounds good to me." He figured Cynthia Lyons, his online cooking instructor, must like desserts. Yesterday she'd listed a recipe for peach cobbler, the day before that it was cherries jubilee, and today's sweet treat was his all-time favorite cookie.

Evan was glad he'd stumbled onto the Web site, especially since learning to cook might fit into his plans for the future.

He hit the PRINT button and smiled. For the past few years he'd been spinning his wheels, not sure whether to make a career of the air force or get out at the end of his tour and go back to college. He was entitled to some money under the GI bill, so he had finally decided to take advantage of it. Military life had its benefits, but now that Evan was no longer enlisted, he looked forward to becoming a school guidance counselor, or maybe a child psychologist. In a few weeks he would enroll at Bay View Christian College and be on his way to meeting the first of his two goals.

Evan's other goal involved a woman. He had recently celebrated his twenty-eighth birthday and felt ready to settle down. He thought Bay View would not only offer him a good education, but hopefully a sweet, Christian wife, as well. He closed his eyes, and visions of a pretty soul mate and a couple of cute kids danced through his head.

Caught up in his musings, Evan hadn't noticed that the paper had jammed in his printer until he opened his eyes again. He reached for the document and gritted his teeth when he saw the blinking light, then snapped open the lid. "I think I might need a new one of these to go along with that wife I'm looking for." He pulled the paper free and chuckled. "Of course, she'd better not be full of wrinkles, like this pitiful piece of paper."

Drawing his gaze back to the computer, Evan noticed on the Web site that not only was Cynthia Lyons listing one recipe per day, but beginning tomorrow, she would be opening her chat room to anyone interested in discussing the dos and don'ts of making sweet treats. Her note mentioned that the participants would be meeting once a week, at six o'clock, Pacific standard time.

"Good. It's the same time zone as Seattle. Wonder where she lives?" Evan positioned his cursor over the sign-up list and hit ENTER. Between the recipes Cynthia posted regularly and the online chat, he was sure he'd be cooking up a storm in no time at all.

When Lorna arrived home from work a few minutes before midnight, she found her mother-in-law in the living room, reading a book.

"You're up awfully late," Lorna remarked, taking a seat on the couch beside Ann.

"I was waiting for you," the older woman answered with a smile. "I wanted to talk to you about something."

"Is anything wrong?"

"Everything here is fine. It's you I'm worried about," Ann said, squinting her pale green eyes.

"What do you mean?"

"My son has been dead for over a year, and you're still grieving." A look of concern clouded Ann's face. "You're working two jobs, but there's no reason for it anymore. You have a home here for as long as you like, and Ed and I ask nothing in return." She reached over and gave Lorna's hand a gentle squeeze. "You shouldn't be wearing yourself out for nothing. If you keep going this way, you'll get sick."

Lorna sank her top teeth into her bottom lip so hard she tasted blood. This was the second lecture she'd had in one evening, and she wasn't in the mood to hear it. She loved Ron's parents as if they were her own. She'd chosen to live in their home after his death because she thought it would bring comfort to all three of them. Lorna didn't want hard feelings to come between them, and she certainly didn't want to say or do anything that might offend this lovely, gracious woman.

"Ann, I appreciate your concern," Lorna began, searching for words she hoped wouldn't sound harsh. "I am dealing with

Ron's death the best way I can, but I'm not like you. I can't be content to stay home and knit sweaters or crochet lacy table-cloths. I have to keep busy outside the house. It keeps me from getting bored or dwelling on what can't be changed."

"Busy is fine, but you've become a workaholic, and it's not healthy—mentally or physically." Ann adjusted her metal-framed reading glasses, so they were sitting correctly on the bridge of her nose. "Ed and I love you, Lorna. We think of you as the daughter we never had. We only want what's best for you." Her short, coffee-colored hair was peppered with gray, and she pushed a stray curl behind her ear.

"I love you both, and I know you have my welfare in mind, but I'm a big girl now, so you needn't worry." Lorna knew her own parents would probably be just as concerned for her well-being if she were living with them. She was almost thankful Mom and Dad lived in Minnesota, because she didn't need two sets of doting parents right now.

"Ed and I don't expect you to give up your whole life for us," Ann continued, as though Lorna hadn't spoken on her own behalf. "You moved from your home state to attend college here, then shortly after you and Ron married, you dropped out of school so you could work and pay his way. Then you kept on working after he entered med school, in order to help pay all the bills for his schooling."

Lorna didn't need to be reminded of the sacrifices she'd made. She was well aware of what she'd given up for the man she loved. "I'm not giving up my life for anyone now," she said as she sighed deeply and pushed against the sofa cushion. Ann didn't understand the way she felt. No one did.

"Have you considered what you might like to do with the rest of your life?" her mother-in-law persisted. "Surely you don't want to spend it working two jobs and holding your middle-aged in-laws' hands."

Lorna blinked back sudden tears that threatened to spill over. She used to think she and Ron would grow old together and have a happy marriage like his parents and hers did. She'd imagined their having children and turning into a real family after he became a physician, but that would never happen now. Lorna had spent the last year worried about helping Ron's parents deal with their loss, and she'd continued to put her own life on hold.

She swallowed against the lump in her throat. It didn't matter. Her hopes and dreams died the day Ron's body was lowered into that cold, dark grave.

She wrapped her arms around her middle and squeezed her eyes shut. Was it time to stop grieving and follow her heart? Could she do it? Did she even want to anymore?

"I've been thinking," Ann said, breaking into Lorna's troubling thoughts.

"What?"

"When you quit school to help pay our son's way, you were cheated out of the education you deserved. I think you should go back to college and get that music degree you were working toward."

Lorna stirred uneasily. First Chris, and now Ann? What was going on? Was she the victim of some kind of conspiracy? She extended her legs and stretched like a cat. "I'm tired. I think I'll go up to bed."

Before she stood up, Lorna touched her mother-in-law's hand. "I appreciate your suggestion, and I promise to sleep on the idea."

" 'Delight yourself in the Lord and he will give you the desires of your heart,' " Ann quoted from the book of Psalms. "God is always full of surprises."

Lorna nodded and headed for the stairs. A short time later, she entered her room and flopped onto the canopy bed with a sigh. She lay there a moment, then turned her head to the right so she could study the picture sitting on the dresser across the room. It was taken on her wedding day, and she and Ron were smiling and looking at each other as though they had their whole lives ahead of them. How happy they'd been back then—full of hope and dreams for their future.

A familiar pang of regret clutched Lorna's heart as she thought about the plans she'd made for her own life. She'd given up her heart's desire in order to help Ron's vision come true. Now they were both gone—Ron, as well as Lorna's plans and dreams.

With the back of her hand, she swiped at an errant tear running down her cheek. *Help me know what to do, Lord. Could You possibly want me to go back to school? Can I really have the desires of my heart? Do You have any pleasant surprises ahead for me?*

# Chapter 2

"What did the ground say to the rain?" Lorna asked an elderly man as she waited on his table.

He glanced out the window at the pouring rain and shrugged. "You got me."

"If you keep this up, my name will be mud!" Lorna's laugh sounded forced, but it was the best she could do, considering how hard she'd had to work at telling the dumb joke.

"That was really lame," Chris moaned as she passed by her table and jabbed Lorna in the ribs.

The customer, however, laughed at Lorna's corny quip. She smiled. *Could mean another nice tip.*

She moved to the next table, preparing to take an order from a young couple.

"I'll have one of the greasiest burgers you've got, with a side order of artery-clogging french fries." The man looked up at Lorna and winked.

Offering him what she hoped was a pleasant smile, Lorna wrote down his order. Then she turned to the woman and asked, "What would you like?"

"I'm trying to watch my weight," the slender young female said. "What have you got that tastes good and isn't full of fat or too many calories?"

"You don't look like you need to worry about your weight at all." Lorna grinned. "Why, did you know that diets are for people who are thick and tired of it all?"

The woman giggled. "I think I'll settle for a dinner salad and a glass of unsweetened iced tea."

When Lorna turned in her order, she bumped into Chris, who was doing the same.

"What's with you tonight?" her friend asked.

"What do you mean?"

"I've never seen you so friendly to the customers before. And those jokes, Lorna. Where did you dig them up?"

Lorna shrugged. "You're not the only one who can make people laugh, you know. I'll bet my tips will be better than ever tonight."

"Tips? Is that what you're trying to do—get more tips?"

"Not necessarily more. Just bigger ones." As she spoke the words, Lorna felt a pang of guilt. She knew it wasn't right to try to wangle better tips. The motto at Farmen's was to be friendly and courteous to all customers. Besides, it was the Christian way, and Lorna knew better than to do anything other than that. She'd gotten carried away with the need to make more money in less time. *Forgive me, Father*, she prayed.

Chris moved closer to Lorna. "Let me see if I understand this right. You're single, living rent free with your in-laws, working two jobs, and you need more money? What gives?"

"I've given my notice at the Mini-mart," Lorna answered.

"Next Friday will be my last day."

Chris's mouth dropped open, and she sucked in her breath. "You're kidding!"

"I'm totally serious. I'll only be working at this job from now on."

"You don't even like waiting tables," Chris reminded. "Why would you give up your day job to come here every evening and put up with a cranky boss and complaining customers? If you want to quit a job, why not this one?"

"I decided to take your advice," Lorna replied.

"My advice? Now that's a first. What, might I ask, are you taking my advice on?"

"One week from Monday I'll be registering for the fall semester at Bay View Christian College."

Chris's eyes grew large, and Lorna gave her friend's red and blue apron a little tug. "Please don't stand there gaping at me—say something."

Chris blinked as though she were coming out of a trance. "I'm in shock. I can't believe you're actually going back to college, much less doing it at my suggestion."

Lorna wrinkled her nose. "It wasn't solely because of your prompting."

"Oh?"

"Ann suggested it the other night, too, and I've been praying about it ever since. I feel it's something I should do."

Chris grabbed Lorna in a bear hug. "I'm so happy for you."

"Thanks." Lorna nodded toward their boss, Gary Farmen, who had just walked by. "Guess we should get back to work."

"Right." Chris giggled. "We wouldn't want to be accused

of having any fun on the job, now would we?"

Lorna started toward the dining room.

"One more thing," Chris called after her.

"What's that?" Lorna asked over her shoulder.

"I'd find some better jokes if I were you."

The distinctive, crisp scent of autumn was in the air. Lorna inhaled deeply as she shuffled through a pile of freshly fallen leaves scattered around the campus of Bay View Christian College.

Today she would register for the fall semester, bringing her one step closer to realizing her dream of teaching music. The decision to return to school had been a difficult one. Certainly she was mature enough to handle the pressures that would come with being a full-time student, but she worried about being too mature to study with a bunch of kids who probably didn't have a clue what life was all about.

By the time Lorna reached the front door of the admissions office, her heart was pounding so hard she was sure everyone within earshot could hear it. Her knees felt weak and shaky, and she wondered if she would be able to hold up long enough to get through this process.

She'd already filled out the necessary paperwork for pre-admission and had even met with her advisor  the previous week. Today was just a formality. Still, the long line forming behind the desk where she was to pick up her course package made her feel ill at ease.

Lorna fidgeted with the strap of her purse and felt relief

wash over her when it was finally her turn.

"Name?" asked the dark-haired, middle-aged woman who was handing out the packets.

"Lorna Patterson. My major is music education."

The woman thumbed through the alphabetized bundles. A few seconds later, she handed one to Lorna. "This is yours."

"Thanks," Lorna mumbled. She turned and began looking through the packet, relieved when she saw that the contents confirmed her schedule for this semester.

Intent on reading the program for her anatomy class, Lorna wasn't watching where she was going. With a sudden jolt, she bumped into someone's arm, and the entire bundle flew out of her hands. Feeling a rush of heat creep up the back of her neck, Lorna dropped to her knees to retrieve the scattered papers.

"Sorry. Guess my big bony elbow must have gotten in your way. Here, let me help you with those."

Lorna looked up. A pair of clear blue eyes seemed to be smiling at her. The man those mesmerizing eyes belonged to must be the owner of the deep voice offering help. She fumbled with the uncooperative papers, willing her fingers to stop shaking. *What is wrong with me? I'm acting like a clumsy fool this morning.* "Thanks, but I can manage," she squeaked.

The young man nodded as he got to his feet, and her cheeks burned hot under his scrutiny.

Lorna quickly gathered up the remaining papers and stood. *He probably thinks I'm a real klutz. So much for starting out the day on the right foot.*

The man opened his mouth as if to say something, but Lorna hurried away. She still had to go to the business office and take care of some financial matters. Then she needed to find the bookstore and locate whatever she'd be needing, and finally the student identification desk to get her ID card. There would probably be long lines everywhere.

Lorna made her way down the crowded hall, wondering how many more stupid blunders she might make before the day was over. She'd been away from college so long; it was obvious she no longer knew how to function. Especially in the presence of a good-looking man.

Evan hung his bicycle on the rack outside his lake view apartment building and bounded up the steps, feeling rather pleased with himself. He'd enrolled at Bay View Christian College today, taken a leisurely bike ride around Woodland Park, and now he was anxious to get home and grab a bite to eat. After supper he'd be going online to check out Cynthia Lyons' cooking class again. Maybe he'd have better luck with today's recipe than he had last week. Evan's peanut butter chocolate chip cookies turned out hard as rocks, and he still hadn't figured out what he'd done wrong. He thought he'd followed Cynthia's directions to the letter, but apparently he'd left out some important ingredient. He probably should try making them again.

As soon as Evan entered his apartment, he went straight to the kitchen and pulled a dinner from the freezer, then popped it into the oven.

"If I learn how to cook halfway decent, it might help find me a wife," he murmured. "Not only that, but it would mean I'd be eating better meals while I wait for that special someone."

While the frozen dinner heated, Evan went to the living room, where his computer sat on a desk in the corner. He booted it up, then went back to the kitchen to fix a salad. At least that was something he could do fairly well.

"I should have insisted Mom teach me how to cook," he muttered.

As Evan prepared the green salad, his thoughts turned toward home. He'd grown up in Moscow, Idaho, and that's where his parents and two older sisters still lived with their families. Since Evan was the youngest child and the only boy in the family, he'd never really needed to cook. His sisters, Margaret and Ellen, had always helped Mom in the kitchen, and they used to say Evan was just in the way if he tried to help out. So when Evan went off to college, he lived on fast foods and meals that were served in the school's cafeteria. When he dropped out of college to join the air force, all of his meals were provided, so again he had no reason to cook.

Now Evan was living in Seattle, attending the Christian college a friend had recommended. He probably could have lived on campus and eaten whatever was available, but he'd chosen to live alone and learn to cook. He'd also decided it was time to settle down and look for a Christian woman.

Evan sliced a tomato and dropped the pieces into the salad bowl. "First order of business—learn to cook. Second order—find a wife!"

Over the last few days, Lorna's tips from the restaurant had increased, and she figured it might have something to do with the fact that she'd given up telling jokes and was being pleasant and friendly, without any ulterior motives.

"I see it's raining again," Chris said, as she stepped up beside Lorna.

Lorna grabbed her work apron and shrugged. "What else is new? We're living in Washington—the Evergreen State, remember?"

Chris lifted her elbow, let it bounce a few times, then connected it gently to Lorna's rib cage. "You're not planning to tell that silly joke about the ground talking to the rain again, I hope."

Lorna shook her head. "I've decided to stick to business and leave the humorous stuff to real people like you."

Chris raised her dark eyebrows, giving Lorna a quizzical look. "*Real* people? What's that supposed to mean?"

"It means you're fun-loving and genuinely witty." Lorna frowned. "You don't have to tell stale jokes in order to make people smile. Everyone seems drawn to your pleasant personality."

"Thanks for the compliment," Chris said with a nod. "I think you sell yourself short. You're talented, have gorgeous, curly blond hair, and you're blessed with a genuine, sweet spirit." She leaned closer and whispered, "Trouble is, you keep it hidden, like a dark secret you don't want anyone to discover."

Lorna moved away, hoping to avoid any more of her friend's psychoanalyzing, but Chris stepped in front of her, planting both hands on her wide hips. "I'm not done yet."

Lorna squinted her eyes. "It's obvious that you're not going to let me go to work until I hear you out."

Chris's smile was a victorious one. "If you would learn to

relax and quit taking life so seriously, people would be drawn to you."

Lorna groaned. "I want to, Chris, but since Ron's death, life has so little meaning for me."

"You're still young and have lots to offer the world. Don't let your heart stay locked up in a self-made prison."

"Maybe going back to school will help. Being around kids who are brimming over with enthusiasm and still believe life holds nothing but joy might rub off on me."

"I think most college kids are smart enough to know life isn't always fun and games," Chris said in a serious tone. "I do believe you're right about one thing, though."

"What's that?"

"Going back to school will be good for you."

# Chapter 3

Lorna settled herself into one of the hard-backed auditorium seats and pulled a notebook and pen from her backpack. Anatomy was her first class of the day. She wanted to be ready for action, since this course had been suggested by one of the advisors. It would help her gain a better understanding of proper breathing and the body positions involved in singing.

She glanced around, noticing about fifty other students in the room. Most of them were also preparing to take notes.

A tall, middle-aged man, who introduced himself as Professor Talcot, announced the topic of the day—"Age-related Changes."

Lorna was about to place her backpack on the empty seat next to her when someone sat down. She glanced over and was greeted with a friendly smile.

*Oh, no! It's that guy I bumped into the other day during registration.*

She forced a return smile, then quickly averted her attention back to the professor.

"I'm late. Did I miss much?" the man whispered as he leaned toward Lorna.

"He just started." She kept her gaze straight ahead.

"Okay, thanks."

Lorna was grateful he didn't say anything more. She was here to learn, not to be distracted by some big kid who should have been on time for his first class of the day.

"Everyone, take a good look at the seat you're in," Professor Talcot stated. "That's where you will sit for the remainder of the semester. My assistant will be around shortly to get your names and fill out the seating chart."

Lorna groaned inwardly. If she'd known she would have to stay in this particular seat all semester, she might have been a bit more selective. Of course, she had no way of knowing an attractive guy with gorgeous blue eyes and a winning smile was going to flop into the seat beside her.

*I can handle this. After all, it's only one hour a day. I don't even have to talk to him if I don't want to.*

"Name, please?"

Lorna was jolted from her thoughts when a studious-looking man wearing metal-framed glasses tapped her on the shoulder.

She turned her head and realized he was standing in the row behind, leaning slightly over the back of her seat, holding a clipboard in one hand.

"Lorna Patterson," she whispered.

"What was that? I couldn't hear you."

The man sitting next to Lorna turned around. "She said her name is Lorna Patterson. Mine's Evan Bailey."

"Gotcha!" the aide replied.

Lorna felt the heat of embarrassment rush to her cheeks. *Great! He not only saw how clumsy I was the other day; now he thinks I can't even speak for myself. I must appear to be pretty stupid.*

As she turned her attention back to the class, Lorna caught the tail end of something the professor had said. Something about a group of five. *That's what I get for thinking when I should be listening. Maybe I wasn't ready to come back to college after all.* She turned to Evan and reluctantly asked, "What did the professor say?"

"He said he's about to give us our first assignment, and we're supposed to form into groups of five." A smile tugged at the corners of his mouth. "Would you like to be in my group?"

Lorna shrugged. She didn't know anyone else in the class. Not that she knew Evan. She'd only met him once, and that wasn't under the best of circumstances.

Evan Bailey was obviously more outgoing than she, for he was already rounding up three other people to join their group—two young men and one woman, all sitting in the row ahead of them.

"The first part of this assignment will be to get to know each other," Professor Talcot told the class. "Tell everyone in your group your name, age, and major."

Lorna felt a sense of dread roll over her, like turbulent breakers lapping against the shore.

*It's bad enough that I'm older than most of these college kids. Is it really necessary for me to reveal my age?*

Introductions were quickly made, and Lorna soon learned the others in the group were Jared, Tim, and Vanessa. All but

Evan and Lorna had given some information about themselves.

"You want to go first?" Evan asked, looking at Lorna.

"I—uh—am in my junior year, and I'm majoring in music ed. I hope to become an elementary school music teacher when I graduate."

"Sounds good. How about you, Evan?" Tim, the studious-looking one, asked.

Evan wiggled his eyebrows and gave Lorna a silly grin. "I'm lookin' for a mother for my children."

"You have kids?" The question came from Vanessa, who had long red hair and dark brown eyes, which she'd kept focused on Evan ever since they'd formed their group.

He shook his head. "Nope, not yet. I'm still searching for the right woman to be my wife. I need someone who loves the Lord as much as I do." Evan's eyebrows drew together. "Oh, yeah—it might be good if she knows how to cook. I'm in the process of learning, but so far all my recipes have flopped."

Vanessa leaned forward and studied Evan more intently. "Are you majoring in home economics?"

Evan chuckled. "Not even close. My major is psychology, but I've recently signed up for an online cooking class." He smiled and nodded at Lorna instead of Vanessa. "You married?"

Lorna shook her head. "I'm not married now." She hesitated then looked away. "My husband died."

"Sorry to hear that," Evan said in a sincere tone.

"Yeah, it's a shame about your husband and all," Jared agreed.

There were a few moments of uncomfortable silence, then Evan said, "I thought I might bring some sweet treats to class one of these days and share them with anyone willing to be my guinea pig."

Vanessa smacked her lips and touched the edge of Evan's shirtsleeve. "I'll be looking forward to that."

"It's time to tell our ages. I'm twenty-one," Tim said.

Vanessa smiled and said she was also twenty-one.

Jared informed the group that he was twenty-four.

"Guess that makes me the old man of our little assemblage. I'm heading downhill at the ripe old age of twenty-eight," Evan said with a wink in Lorna's direction.

*With the exception of Evan, they're all just kids,* she thought ruefully. *And even he's four years younger than me.*

Vanessa nudged Lorna's arm with the eraser end of her pencil. "Now it's your turn."

Lorna stared at the floor and mumbled, "I'm thirty-two."

Jared let out a low whistle. "Wow, you're a lot older than the rest of us."

Lorna slid a little lower in her chair. *As if I needed to be reminded.*

Evan held up the paper he was holding. It had been handed out by the professor's assistant only moments ago. "It says here that one of the most significant age-related signs is increased hair growth in the nose." He leaned over, until his face was a few inches from Lorna's. As he studied her, she felt like a bug under a microscope. "Yep," he announced. "I can see it's happening to you already!"

Jared, Tim, and Vanessa howled, and Lorna covered her face with her hands. If the aisle hadn't been blocked she might have dashed for the door. Instead, she drew in a deep breath, lifted her head, and looked Evan in the eye. "You're right about my nose hair. In fact, I'm so old I get winded just playing a game of checkers." She couldn't believe she'd said that. Maybe those stupid jokes she had used on her customers at the restaurant were still lodged in her brain.

Everyone in the group laughed this time, including Lorna, who was finally beginning to relax. "The other day, I sank my teeth into a big, juicy steak, and you know what?" she quipped.

Evan leaned a bit closer. "What?"

"They just stayed there!"

Vanessa giggled and poked Evan on the arm. "She really got you good on that one."

Evan grimaced. "Guess I deserved it. Sorry about the nose hair crack."

He looked genuinely sorry, making Lorna feel foolish for trying to set him up with her lame joke. She was about to offer an apology of her own when he added, "It's nice to know I'm not the oldest one in class."

Lorna didn't know how she had survived the morning. By the time she entered her last class of the day, she wondered all the more if she was going to make it as a college student. *This is no time to wimp out,* she chided herself as she took a seat in the front row. *Choir is my favorite subject.*

The woman who stood in front of the class introduced herself as Professor Lynne Burrows.

*She's young,* Lorna noted. *Probably not much past thirty. I would be a music teacher by now if I'd finished my studies ten years ago.*

"Do we have any pianists in this class?" Professor Burrows asked.

Lorna glanced around the room. When she saw no hands raised, she lifted hers.

"Have you ever accompanied a choir?"

She nodded. "I play for my church choir, and I also accompanied college choir during my freshman and sophomore years." She chose not to mention the fact that it had been several years ago.

The professor smiled. "Would you mind playing for us today? If it works out well, perhaps you'd consider doing it for all the numbers that require piano accompaniment."

"I'd like that." Lorna headed straight for the piano, a place where she knew she'd be the most comfortable.

"If you need someone to turn the pages, I'd be happy to oblige."

Lorna glanced to her right. Evan Bailey was leaning on the lid of the piano, grinning at her like a monkey who'd been handed a tasty banana. She couldn't believe he was in her music class, too.

"Thanks anyway, but I think I can manage," Lorna murmured.

Evan dropped to the bench beside her. "I've done this before, and I'm actually pretty good at it." He reached across Lorna and thumbed a few pages of the music.

She eyed him suspiciously. "You don't know when to quit, do you?"

He laughed and wagged a finger in front of her nose. "Just call me Pushy Bailey."

"Let's see what Professor Burrows has to say when she realizes you're sitting on the piano bench instead of standing on the risers with the rest of the choir. You *are* enrolled in this class, I presume?"

Evan smiled at her. "I am, and I signed up for it just so I could perfect my talent of page turning."

Lorna moaned softly. "You're impossible."

Evan dragged his fingers along the piano keys. "How about you and me going out for a burger after class? Then I can tell you about the rest of my faults."

"Sorry, but I don't date."

He snapped the key of middle C up and down a few times. "Who said anything about a date? I'm hungry for a burger and thought maybe you'd like to join me. It would be a good chance for us to get better acquainted."

Lorna sucked in her breath. "Why would we need to get better acquainted?"

He gave her a wide smile. "I'm in choir—you're in choir. You're the pianist—I'm the page turner. I'm in anatomy—you're in anatomy. I'm in your group—you're in my—"

She held up one hand. "Okay, Mr. Bailey. I get the point."

"Call me Evan. Mr. Bailey makes me sound like an old man."

"Evan, then."

"So will you have a burger with me?"

Lorna opened her mouth, but Professor Burrows leaned on the top of the piano and spoke first. "I see you've already found a page turner."

Lorna shook her head. "Not really. I've always been able to turn my own pages, and I'm sure you need Mr. Bailey's voice in the tenor section far more than I need his thumb and index finger at the piano."

Evan grinned up at the teacher. "What can I say? The woman likes me."

Lorna's mouth dropped open. Didn't the guy ever quit?

"You're pretty self-confident, aren't you?" The professor pointed at Evan, then motioned toward the risers. "Let's see how well you can sing. Third row, second place on the left."

Evan shrugged and gave Lorna a quick wink. "See you later."

"Don't mind him," Professor Burrows whispered to Lorna. "I think he's just testing the waters."

"Mine, or yours?"

"Probably both. I've handled characters like him before, so we won't let it get out of hand." The professor gave Lorna's shoulder a gentle squeeze and moved to the front of the class.

Lorna closed her eyes and drew in a deep breath, lifting a prayer of thanks that the day was almost over. She couldn't believe how stressful it had been. Maybe she should give up her dream of becoming a music teacher while she still had some shred of sanity left.

As Evan stood on the risers with the rest of the class, he couldn't keep focused on Professor Burrows or the song they were supposed to be singing. His gaze kept going back to the cute little blond who sat at the piano.

He knew Lorna was four years older than he, and she'd made it clear that she had no interest in dating. Still, the woman fascinated him, and he was determined they should get better acquainted. The few years' age difference meant nothing as far as he was concerned, but it might matter to Lorna. Maybe that's why she seemed so indifferent.

*I'd sure like to get to know her better and find out if we're compatible.* Evan smiled to himself. He would figure out a way—maybe bribe her with one of his online sweet treats. Of course, he'd first have to learn how to bake something that didn't flop.

# Chapter 4

When Lorna arrived home from school, she found her father-in-law in the front yard, raking a pile of maple leaves into a mountain in the middle of the lawn.

Ed stopped and wiped the perspiration from the top of his bald head with a hanky he had pulled from the pocket of his jeans. "How was your first day?"

Lorna plodded up the steps, dropped her backpack to the porch, and sank wearily into one of the wicker chairs. "Let's put it this way, I'm still alive to tell about it."

Ed leaned the rake against the outside porch railing and took the chair beside her. "That bad, huh?"

She only nodded in reply.

"Is your schedule too heavy this semester?" he asked, obvious concern revealed in his dark eyes.

Lorna forced a smile. "It's nothing to be worried about."

"Anything that concerns you concerns me and Ann. You were married to our son, and that makes us family."

"I know, but I do have to learn how to handle some problems on my own."

"Problems? Did I hear someone say they're having problems?"

Lorna glanced up at Ann, who had stepped onto the porch. "It's nothing. I'm just having a hard time fitting in at school. I am quite a bit older than most of my classmates, you know."

Ann laughed, causing the lines around her eyes to become more pronounced. "Is that all that's troubling you? I'd think being older would have some advantages."

"Such as?"

"For one thing, your maturity should help you grasp things. Your study habits will probably be better than those of most kids fresh out of high school, too. These days, many young people don't have a lot of self-discipline."

"Yeah, no silly schoolgirl crushes or other such distractions," Ed put in with a deep chuckle.

Lorna swallowed hard. There had already been plenty of distractions today, and they'd come in the form of a young man with laughing blue eyes, goofy jokes, and a highly contagious smile.

"My maturity might help me be more studious, but it sure sets me apart from the rest of the college crowd," she said. "Today I felt like a sore thumb sticking out on an otherwise healthy hand."

"You're so pretty, I'm sure no one even guessed you were a few years older." Ann gently touched Lorna's shoulder.

"Thanks for the compliment," Lorna said, making no mention of the fact that she had already revealed her age during the first class of the day. She cringed, thinking about the nose hair incident. "I'd better go inside. I want to read a few verses of scripture, and I have some homework that needs to be done before it's time to head for work."

Lorna stood in front of the customer who sat at a table in her assigned section with a menu in front of his face. "Have you decided yet, sir?" she asked.

"I'll have a cheeseburger with the works."

He dropped the menu to the table, and Lorna's gaze darted to the man's face. "Wh—what are you doing here?" she rasped.

Evan smiled up at her. "I'm ordering a hamburger, and seeing you again makes me remember that you stood me up this afternoon."

"How could I have stood you up when I never agreed to go out with you in the first place?" Lorna's hands began to tremble, and she knew her cheeks must be pink, because she could feel the heat quickly spreading.

Evan's grin widened. "You never really said no."

Lorna clenched her pencil in one hand and the order pad in the other. "Did you follow me here from my home?"

"I don't even know where you live, so how could I have followed you?" Evan studied his menu again. "I think I'll have an order of fries to go with that burger. Care to join me?"

"In case you hadn't noticed, I'm working."

"Hmm. . . Maybe I'll have a chocolate shake, too."

Lorna tapped her foot impatiently. "How did you know I worked here?"

He handed her the menu. "I didn't. I've heard this restaurant serves really great burgers, and I thought I'd give it a try. The fact that you work here is just an added bonus."

"I'll be back when your order is up." Lorna turned on her heels and headed for the kitchen, but she'd only made it

125

halfway when she collided with Chris. Apple pie, vanilla ice cream, and two chocolate-covered donuts went sailing through the air as her friend's tray flew out of her hands.

Lorna gasped. "Oh, Chris, I'm so sorry! I didn't see you coming."

"It was just an accident. It's okay, I know you didn't do it on purpose," Chris said as she dropped to her knees.

Lorna did the same and quickly began to help clean up the mess. "I'll probably be docked half my pay for this little blunder," she grumbled. "I ought to send Evan Bailey a bill."

Chris's eyebrows shot up. "Who's Evan Bailey?"

"Some guy I met at school. I have him in two of my classes. He's here tonight. I just took his order."

Chris gave her a quizzical look. "And?"

"He had me so riled I wasn't paying attention to where I was going." Lorna scooped up the last piece of pie and handed the tray back to Chris. "I really am sorry about this."

Chris laughed. "It's a good thing it went on the floor and not in someone's lap." She got to her feet. "So what's this guy done that has you so upset?"

Lorna picked a hunk of chocolate off her apron and stood, too. "First of all, he kept teasing me in anatomy class this morning. Then he plunked himself down at the piano with me during choir, offering to be my page turner." She paused and drew in a deep breath. "Next, he asked me to go out for a burger after school."

"What'd you say?"

"I didn't answer him." Lorna frowned. "Now he's here, pestering me to eat dinner with him."

Chris moved toward the kitchen, with Lorna following on her heels. "Sounds to me like the guy is interested in you."

Lorna shook her head. "He hardly even knows me. Besides, I'm four years older."

"Who's hung up on age differences nowadays?"

"Okay, it's not the four years between us that really bothers me."

"What then?"

"He acts like a big kid!" Lorna shrugged. "Besides, even if I was planning to date, which I'm not, our personalities don't mesh."

Evan leaned his elbows on the table and studied the checkered place mat in front of him. He had always been the kind of person who knew what he wanted and then went after it. How come his determination wasn't working this time? *Lorna doesn't believe me. She thinks I've been spying on her and came here to harass her. I've got to make her believe my coming to Farmen's was purely coincidental.* He took a sip of water. *Although it could have been an answer to prayer. Somehow I've got to get Lorna to agree to go out with me. How else am I going to know if she's the one?*

A short time later, Lorna returned with Evan's order, and he felt ready to try again. He looked up at her and smiled. "You look cute in that uniform." When she made no comment, he added, "Been working here long?"

"Sometimes it feels like forever," she said with a deep sigh.

"Want to talk about it?"

She shook her head. "Will there be anything else?"

He rapped the edge of the plate with his knife handle. "Actually, there is."

"What can I get for you?"

"How about a few minutes of your time?"

"I'm working."

"When do you get off work? I can stick around for a while."

"Late. I'll be working late tonight."

Evan cringed. He wasn't getting anywhere with this woman and knew he should probably quit while he was ahead. Of course, he wasn't really ahead, so he decided he might as well stick his neck out a little farther. "I'm not trying to come on to you. I just want to get to know you better."

"Why?"

Evan reached for his glass of water and took a sip. How could he explain his attraction to Lorna without scaring her off? "I think we have a lot in common," he said with a nod.

She raised one pale eyebrow. "How did you reach that conclusion?"

"It's simple. I'm in choir—you're in choir. You're the pianist—I'm the page turner."

"I'm not interested in dating you or anyone else."

Evan grabbed his burger off the plate. "Okay, I get the message. I'll try not to bother you again."

She touched his shoulder unexpectedly, sending a shock wave through his arm. "I–I'm sorry if I came across harshly. I just needed you to know where I stand."

He swallowed the bite of burger he'd put in his mouth. "Are you seeing someone else? You mentioned in class that you're a widow, so I kinda figured—"

Lorna shook her head, interrupting his sentence. "I'm a widow who doesn't date."

Evan thought she looked sad, or maybe she was lonely. He grabbed the bottle of ketchup in the center of the table and smiled at her. "Can we at least be friends?"

She nodded and held out her hand. "Friends."

# Chapter 5

L orna awoke with a headache. She had been back in college a week, and things weren't getting any easier. It was hard to attend school all day, work every evening at Farmen's, and find time to get her assignments finished. She was tired and irritable but knew she would have to put on a happy face when she was at work, no matter how aggravating some of the customers could be. One patron in particular was especially unnerving. Evan Bailey had returned to the restaurant two more times. She wasn't sure if he came because he liked the food, or if it was merely to get under her skin.

Lorna uttered a quick prayer and forced her unwilling body to get out of bed. She couldn't miss any classes today. There was a test to take in English lit and auditions for lead parts in the choir's first performance.

She entered the bathroom and turned on the faucet at the sink. Splashing a handful of water against her upturned face, she cringed as the icy liquid stung her cheeks. Apparently, Ann was washing clothes this morning, for there was no hot water.

"Ed needs to get that old tank replaced," Lorna grumbled

as she reached for a towel. "Maybe I should stay home today after all."

The verse she'd read the night before in Psalm 125 popped into her mind. *"Those who trust in the Lord are like Mount Zion, which cannot be shaken but endures forever."*

"Thanks for that reminder, Lord. I need to trust You to help me through this day."

———

"I don't see how we're ever gonna get better acquainted if you keep avoiding me."

Lorna sat in her anatomy class, watching a video presentation on the muscular system and trying to ignore Evan, who sat on her left. She kept her eyes focused on the video screen. *Maybe if I pretend I didn't hear him, he'll quit pestering me.*

"Here, I brought you something." He leaned closer and held out two cookies encased in plastic wrap.

She could feel his warm breath on her ear, and she shivered.

"You cold?"

When she made no reply and didn't reach for the cookies, he tapped her lightly on the arm. "I made these last night. Please try one."

Lorna didn't want to appear rude, but she wasn't hungry. "I just ate breakfast not long ago."

"That's okay. You can save them for later."

"All right. Thanks." Lorna took the cookies and placed them inside her backpack.

"I'm going biking on Saturday. Do you ride?" he asked.

"Huh?"

"I'd like you to go out with me this Saturday. We can rent some bikes at the park and pedal our way around the lake."

"I told you. . .I don't date."

"I know, but the other night you said we could be friends, so we won't call this a date. It'll just be two lonely people out having a good time."

Lorna's face heated up. "What makes you think I'm lonely?"

"I see it in your eyes," he whispered. "They're sad and lonely looking." When she made no reply, he added, "Look, if you'd rather not go, then—"

Lorna blew out her breath as she threw caution to the wind. "All right, I'll go, but you're taking an awfully big chance."

"Yeah, I know." He snickered. "A few hours spent in your company, and I might never be the same."

Lorna held back the laughter threatening to bubble over, but she couldn't hide her smile. "I was thinking more along the lines of our fall weather. It can be pretty unpredictable this time of the year."

Evan chuckled. "Yeah, like some blond-haired, blue-eyed woman I'd like to get to know a whole lot better."

Evan studied the computer screen intently. Brownie Delight was the sweet treat Cynthia Lyons had posted on Tuesday, but he hadn't had time to check it out until today. The ingredients were basic—unsweetened chocolate, butter, sour cream, sugar, eggs, flour, baking powder, salt, and chopped nuts. Chocolate chips would be sprinkled on the top, making it doubly delicious. If the brownies turned out halfway decent, he would take some on his date with Lorna. Maybe she'd be impressed with his ability to cook. He hoped so, because so far nothing he'd said or done had seemed to make an impact on her. She hadn't even said whether she'd liked the chocolate peanut butter cookies he'd given her the other day. Lorna was probably too polite to mention that they'd been a bit overdone. This was Evan's second time with these cookies, and he was beginning to wonder if he'd ever get it right.

Evan still hadn't made it to any of the online chats Cynthia Lyons hosted. Now that he was in school all day, his evenings were usually spent doing homework.

Oh, well. The chats were probably just a bunch of chitchat about how well the recipes had turned out for others who had made them. He didn't need any further reminders that his hadn't been so successful.

Evan hit the PRINT button to make a copy of the recipe and leaned back in his chair while he waited for the procedure to complete itself.

A vision of Lorna's petite face flashed into his mind. He was attracted to her; there was no question about that. But did they really have anything in common? Was she someone who wanted to serve the Lord with her whole heart, the way Evan did?

The college they attended was a Christian one, but he knew not everyone who went there was a believer in Christ. Some merely signed up at Bay View because of its excellent academic program. Evan hoped Lorna wasn't one of those.

And what about children? Did she like kids as much as he did? Other than becoming an elementary school music teacher, what were her goals and dreams for the future? He needed to know all these things if he planned to pursue a relationship with her.

The printer had stopped, and Evan grabbed hold of the recipe for Brownie Delight. "Tomorrow Lorna and I will get better acquainted as we pedal around the lake and munch on these sweet treats. Tonight I'll pray about it."

The week had seemed to fly by, and when Lorna awoke Saturday morning, she was in a state of panic. She couldn't believe she'd agreed to go biking with Evan today. What had she been thinking? Up until now, she'd kept him at arm's length, but going on what he probably saw as a date could be a huge mistake.

"Then again," she mumbled, "it might be just the thing to prove to Evan how wrong we are for each other."

Lorna crawled out of bed, wondering what she should wear and what to tell her in-laws at breakfast. Not wanting to raise any questions from Ann or Ed, she decided to only tell them that she'd be going out sometime after lunch, but she would make no mention of where. Her plans were to meet Evan at the park near the college, but she didn't want them to know about it. They might think it was a real date and that she was being untrue to their son's memory. She only hoped by the end of the day she wouldn't regret her decision to spend time alone with Evan Bailey.

At two o'clock that afternoon, Lorna drove into the park. The weather was overcast and a bit chilly, but at least it wasn't raining. She found Evan waiting on a wooden bench, with two bikes parked nearby.

"Hey! I'm glad you came!"

"I said I would."

"I know, but I was afraid you might back out."

Lorna flopped down beside him, and he grinned at her. "You look great today."

She glanced down at her blue jeans and white T-shirt, mostly hidden by a jean jacket, and shrugged. "Nothing fancy, but at least I'm comfortable."

Evan slapped the knees of his faded jeans and tweaked the collar on his black leather jacket. "Yeah, me, too."

A young couple pushing a baby in a stroller walked past, and Lorna stared at them longingly.

"You like kids?"

"What?" She jerked her head.

"I asked if you like kids."

"Sure, they're great."

"When I get married, I'd like to have a whole house full of children," Evan said. "With kids around, it would be a lot harder to grow old and crotchety."

"Like me, you mean?"

Evan reached out to touch her hand. "I didn't mean that at all."

She blinked in rapid succession. "I am a lot older than most of the other students at Bay View."

"You're not much older than me. When I was born, you were only four."

She grunted. "When you were six, I was ten."

"When you were twenty-six, I was twenty-two." Evan nudged her arm with his elbow. "I'm gaining on you, huh?"

Lorna jumped up and grabbed the women's ten-speed by the handlebars. "I thought we came here to ride bikes, not talk about age-related things."

Evan stood, too. "You're right, so you lead, I'll follow."

They rode in pleasant silence, Lorna leading and Evan bringing up the rear. They were nearly halfway around the park when he pedaled alongside her. "You hungry? I brought along a few apples and some brownies I made last night."

She pulled her bicycle to a stop. "That does sound good. I haven't ridden a bike in years, and I'm really out of shape. A little rest and some nourishment might help get me going again."

Evan led them to a picnic table, set his kickstand, and motioned her to take a seat. When they were both seated, he reached into his backpack and withdrew two Red Delicious apples, then handed one to Lorna. "Let's eat these first and save the brownies for dessert."

"Thanks." Lorna bit into hers, and a trickle of sweet, sticky juice dribbled down her chin. "Umm. . .this does hit the spot." She looked over at him and smiled. "Sorry about being such a grump earlier. Guess I'm a little touchy about my age."

"Apology accepted. Uh. . .would you like to go to dinner when we're done riding?" Evan asked hesitantly.

Warning bells went off in Lorna's head, and she felt her whole body tremble. "I'm not dressed for going out."

"I was thinking about pizza. We don't have to be dressed up for that." Evan bit into his apple and grinned.

That dopey little smile and the gentleness in his eyes made Lorna's heartbeat quicken. She gulped. "I–I—"

"You can think about it while we finish our ride," Evan said, coming to her rescue.

She shrugged her shoulders. "Okay."

"So, tell me about Lorna Patterson."

"What do you want to know?"

"I know you're enrolled in a Christian college. Does that mean you're a believer in Christ?"

She nodded. "I accepted the Lord as my personal Savior when I was ten years old. At that time I thought I knew exactly what He wanted me to do with my life."

"Which was?"

"To teach music. I started playing piano right around the time I became a Christian, and I soon discovered that I loved it."

"You're definitely a gifted pianist," he said with a broad smile. "You do great accompanying our choir, and you have a beautiful singing voice."

"Thanks." She nodded at him. "Is that all you wanted to know about me?"

"Actually, there is something else I've been wondering about."

"What?"

"You mentioned that you're a widow. How did your husband die?"

Lorna stared off into the distance, focusing on a cluster of pigeons eating dry bread crumbs someone had dumped on the grass. She didn't want to talk about Ron, her loss, or how he'd been killed so tragically.

"If you'd rather not discuss it, that's okay." Evan touched her arm gently. "I probably shouldn't have asked, but I want to know you better, so—"

137

Lorna turned her head so she was looking directly at him. "It's okay. It'll probably do me more good to talk about it than it will to keep it bottled up." She drew in a deep breath and plunged ahead. "Ron was killed in a motorcycle accident a little over a year ago. A semitruck hit him."

"I'm so sorry. It must have been hard for you."

"It was. Still is, in fact."

"Have you been on your own ever since?"

She shook her head. "Not exactly. I've been living with Ron's parents, hoping it would help the three of us deal with our grief."

"And has it?"

"Some."

Compassion showed in Evan's eyes, and he took hold of her hand. It felt warm and comforting, and even though Lorna's head told her to pull away, her heart said something entirely different. So she sat there, staring down at their intertwined fingers and basking in the moment of comfort and pleasure.

"I'm surprised a woman your age, who's blessed with lots of talent and good looks, hasn't found another man by now."

Lorna felt her face flame. She focused on the apple core in her other hand, already turning brown. When she spotted a garbage can a few feet away, Lorna stood up. Before she could take a step, she felt Evan's hand on her arm.

"I'm sorry, Lorna. I can tell I've upset you. Was it my question about your husband's death, or was it the fact that I said I was surprised you hadn't found another man?"

She blinked away unwanted tears. "A little of both I suppose."

She stiffened as Evan's arm went around her shoulders. "Still friends?"

"Sure," she mumbled.

"Does that mean you'll have pizza with me?"

"I thought I had until the bike ride was over to decide."

He twitched his eyebrows. "What can I say? I'm not the patient type."

"No, but you're certainly persistent."

He handed her a napkin and two brownies. "How do you think I've gotten this far in life?"

She sucked in her breath. How far had he gotten? Other than the fact that he was majoring in psychology, wasn't married, and was four years younger than she, Lorna knew practically nothing about Evan Bailey. Maybe she should learn more—in case she needed another friend.

She tossed the apple core into the garbage and bit into one of the brownies. "Where'd you say you got these?"

"Made them myself. I think I already told you that I'm taking an online cooking class. Right now the instructor is teaching us how to make some tasty sweet treats." He winked at her. "I thought it might make me a better catch if I could cook."

Lorna wasn't sure what to say. She didn't want to hurt Evan's feelings by telling him the brownie was too dry. She thought about the cookies he'd given her the other day. She'd tried one at lunch, and they had been equally dry, not to mention a bit overdone. Apparently the man was so new at cooking, he couldn't tell that much himself. She ate the brownie in silence and washed it down with the bottled water Evan had also supplied. When she was done, Lorna climbed onto her bike. "We'd better go. I hear the best pizza in town is at Mama Mia's!"

# Chapter 6

Lorna slid into a booth at the pizza parlor, and Evan took the bench across from her. When their waitress came, they ordered a large combination pizza and a pitcher of iced tea.

As soon as the server was gone, Evan leaned forward on his elbows and gave Lorna a crooked smile. "You're beautiful, you know that?"

She gulped. No one but Ron had ever looked at her as if she were the most desirable woman on earth. Lorna leaned back in her seat and slid her tongue across her bottom lip. "Now it's your turn to tell me about Evan Bailey," she said, hoping the change in subject might calm her racing heart and get her thinking straight again.

She watched the flame flicker from the candle in the center of the table and saw its reflection in Evan's blue eyes. "My life is an open book, so what would you like to know?" he asked.

*I'd like to know why you're looking at me like that.* "You told our group in class that your major is psychology, but you never said what you plan to do with it once you graduate," she said, instead of voicing her thoughts.

The waitress brought two glasses and a pitcher of iced tea to the table. As soon as she left, Evan poured them both a glass. "I'm hoping to land a job as a school guidance counselor, but if that doesn't work out, I might go into private practice as a child psychologist."

Lorna peered at him over the top of her glass. "Let me guess. I'll bet you plan to analyze kids all day, and then come home at night to the little woman who's been busy taking care of your own children. Is that right?"

He chuckled. "Something like that."

"How come you're not married already and starting that family?"

He ran his fingers through his short-cropped, sandy brown hair. "Haven't had time."

"No?"

"I was born and raised in Moscow, Idaho, and I'm the only boy in a family of three kids. I enrolled in Bible college shortly after I graduated high school, but I never finished."

"I take it you're a Christian, too?"

He nodded. "My conversion came when I was a teenager."

"How come you never finished Bible college?" she questioned.

"I decided on a tour of duty with the United States Air Force instead." A muscle jerked in his cheek, and he frowned slightly. "I had a relationship with a woman go sour on me. After praying about it, I figured the best way to get over her was to enlist and get as far away from the state of Idaho as I could."

In the few weeks she'd known Evan, this was the first time Lorna had seen him look so serious, and it took her completely by surprise. She was trying to decide how to comment, when the waitress showed up with their pizza. Lorna was almost relieved at the interruption. At least now she could concentrate on filling her stomach and not her mind.

After a brief prayer, Evan began attacking his pizza with a vengeance. It made Lorna wonder when his last good meal had been. By the time she'd finished two pieces, Evan had polished off four slices and was working on another one. He glanced at Lorna's plate. "Aren't you hungry?"

"The pizza is great. I'm enjoying every bite," she said.

He swiped the napkin across his face and stared at Lorna. It made her squirm.

"Why are you looking at me that way?"

"What way?"

"Like I've got something on my face."

He chuckled. "Your face is spotless. I was thinking how much I enjoy your company and wondering if we might have a future together."

Lorna nearly choked on the piece of pizza she'd just put in her mouth. "Well, I—uh—don't think we're very well suited, and isn't it a little soon to be talking about a future together?"

"I'm not ready to propose marriage, if that's what you're thinking." His eyes narrowed. "And please don't tell me you're hung up about our age difference." Evan looked at Lorna so intently she could feel her toes curl inside her tennis shoes.

"That doesn't bother me so much. We're only talking about four years."

"Right." Evan raised his eyebrows. "You couldn't be afraid of men, or you wouldn't have been married before."

"I am not afraid of men! Why do you do that, anyway?"

"Do what?"

"Try to goad me into an argument."

He chuckled behind another slice of pizza. "Is that what you think I'm doing?"

"Isn't it?"

He dropped the pizza to his plate, reached across the table, and took hold of her hand.

She shivered involuntarily and averted her gaze to the table. "I wish you wouldn't do that, either."

"Do what? This?" He made little circles on her hand with his index finger.

She felt warmth travel up her neck and spread quickly to her cheeks. "The way you look at me, I almost feel—"

"Like you're a beautiful, desirable woman?" He leaned farther across the table. "You are, you know. And I don't care about you being four years older than me. In fact, I think dating an older woman might have some advantages."

She pulled her hand away. "And what would those be?"

He crossed his arms and leaned back in his seat. "Let's see now. . . You'd be more apt to see things from a mature point of view."

"And?"

"Just a minute. I'm thinking." Evan tapped the edge of his plate with his thumb. "Since you're older, you're most likely wiser."

She clicked her tongue. "Sorry I asked."

"Would you be willing to start dating me?" he asked with a hopeful expression.

She shook her head. "I'm flattered you would ask, but I don't think it's a good idea."

"Why not?"

Something indefinable passed between them, but Lorna pushed it aside. "I have my heart set on finishing college, and nothing is going to stop me this time."

He gave her a quizzical look. "This time?"

Lorna ended up telling him the story of how she'd sacrificed her own career and college degree to put her husband through school. She ended it by saying, "So, you see, for the first time in a long while, I'm finally getting what I want."

"That's it? End of story?"

She nodded. "It will be when I graduate and get a job teaching music in an elementary school."

"Why not teach at a junior or senior high?"

"I like children—especially those young enough to be molded and refined." She wrinkled her nose. "The older a child is, the harder to get through to his creativity."

"Does that mean I won't be able to get through to your creative side?" he asked with a lopsided grin.

"Could be." She folded her napkin into a neat little square and lifted her chin. "I really need to get home. I've got a lot of homework to do, and I've wasted most of the day."

Evan's sudden scowl told her she'd obviously hurt his feelings. "I didn't mean *wasted*. It's just that—"

He held up his hand. "No explanations are necessary." He stood, pulled a few coins from his back pocket, and dropped them on the table. "I hope that's enough for a tip, 'cause it's all the change I have."

She fumbled in her jacket pocket. "Maybe I have some ones I could add."

"Please don't bother. This will be enough, and I sure don't expect you to pay for the tip."

"I don't mind helping out," she insisted.

"Thanks anyway, but I'll take care of it." With that, Evan turned and headed for the cash register.

Lorna stood there with her ears burning and her heart pounding so hard she could hear it echoing in her ears. The day had started off so well. What had gone wrong, and how had it happened?

Evan was already up front paying for the pizza, so Lorna dug into her pocket and pulled out a dollar bill, which she quickly dropped to the table. Maybe she'd made a mistake thinking she and Evan could be friends. He obviously wanted more, but she knew it was impossible. In fact, he was impossible. Impossible and poor.

Evan said good-bye to Lorna outside in the parking lot. He was almost glad they had separate cars and he wouldn't have to drive her home. He didn't understand how a day that had started out fun and carefree could have ended on such a sour note. From all indications, he'd thought Lorna was enjoying their time together, but when she said she'd wasted most of the day, he felt deflated, even though he hadn't admitted it to her. That, plus the fact that she seemed overly concerned about his not having enough tip money, had thrown cold water on their time together.

What had turned things around? Had it been the discussion about their age difference? Children? Or maybe it was the money thing. Lorna might think he'd been too cheap to leave a decent tip. That could be why she'd climbed into her little red car with barely a wave and said nothing about hoping to see him again. Of course, he hadn't made the first move on that account, either.

"I thought she might be the one, Lord," Evan mumbled as he opened the door to his Jeep. Remembering the look on Lorna's face when she'd eaten the treat he'd given her earlier that day, he added, "Maybe I should have followed the recipe closer and added some chocolate chips to the top of those brownies."

# Chapter 7

The following Monday morning in Anatomy, Evan acted as though nothing were wrong. In fact, he surprised Lorna by presenting her with a wedge of apple pie he said he'd made the night before.

"It's a little mushy, and the crust's kind of tough," he admitted, "but I sampled a slice at breakfast, and it seemed sweet enough, at least."

Lorna smiled politely and took the plastic container with the pie in it. It was nice of Evan to think of her, but if he thought the dessert would give him an edge, he was mistaken. Lorna was fighting her attraction to Evan, and to lead him on would sooner or later cause one or both of them to get hurt.

*Probably me,* she thought. *I'm usually the one who makes all the sacrifices, then loses in the end.* What good had come out of her putting Ron through college and med school? He'd been killed in a senseless accident, leaving Lorna with a broken heart, a mound of bills, and no career for herself. It was going to be different from now on, though. She finally had her life back on track.

"You look kind of down in the mouth this morning," Evan said, nudging her arm gently with his hand. "Everything okay?"

She shrugged. "I'm just tired. I stayed up late last night trying to get all my homework done."

He pursed his lips. "Guess that's my fault. If you hadn't wasted your Saturday bike riding and having pizza with me, you'd have had lots more time to work on your assignments."

So Evan had been hurt by her comment about wasted time on Saturday. Lorna could see by the look in the man's eyes that his pride was wounded. She felt a sense of guilt sweep over like a cascading waterfall. She hadn't meant to hurt him. As a Christian, Lorna tried not to offend anyone, although she probably had fallen short many times since Ron's death.

"Evan," she began sincerely, "I apologize for my offhanded remark the other day. I had a good time with you, and my day wasn't wasted."

He grinned at her. "Really?"

She nodded.

"Would you be willing to go out with me again—as friends?"

Lorna chewed on her lower lip as she contemplated his offer. "Well, maybe," she finally conceded.

"That's great! How about this Saturday night, if you've got the evening off from working at Farmen's."

"I only work on weeknights," she said.

"Good, then we can go bowling, out to dinner, to the movies. . .or all three."

She chuckled softly. "I think one of those would be sufficient, don't you?"

"Yeah, I suppose so. Which one's your choice?"

"Why don't you surprise me on Saturday night?"

"Okay, I will." Evan snapped his fingers. "Say, I'll need your address so I can pick you up."

Lorna felt as though a glass of cold water had been dashed in her face. There was no way she could allow Evan to come by her in-laws' and pick her up for what she was sure they would assume was a date. She couldn't hurt Ann and Ed that way. It wouldn't be fair to Ron's memory. Maybe she should have told Evan she was busy on Saturday night. Maybe. . .

"You gonna give me your address or not?"

Lorna blinked. "Uh—how about we meet somewhere, like we did last Saturday?"

His forehead wrinkled. "Are you ashamed for your folks to meet me?"

"I live with my in-laws, remember?"

"So?"

"They might not understand about my going out with you," she explained. "They're still not over the loss of their son."

Evan stared at her for several seconds but finally shrugged his shoulders. "Okay. If that's how you want it, we can meet at Ivar's along the waterfront. I've been wanting to try out their famous fish and chips ever since I came to Seattle."

Lorna licked her lips. "That does sound good."

Evan opened his mouth to say something more, but their professor walked into the room. "We'll talk later," he whispered.

She nodded in response.

Lorna entered the choir room a few minutes early, hoping to get her music organized before class began. She noticed Evan standing by the bulletin board across the room. She hated to admit it, but he was fun to be around. Could he be growing on her?

When she took a seat at the piano and peeked over the stack of music, she saw Vanessa Brown step up beside Evan. "Are the names posted for the choir solos yet?" the vivacious redhead asked. "I sure hope I got the female lead." She looked up at Evan and batted her lashes. "Maybe you'll get the male lead, and then we can practice together. Our voices would blend beautifully, don't you think?"

*Oh, please,* Lorna groaned inwardly. The omelet she'd eaten for breakfast that morning had suddenly turned into a lump in the pit of her stomach. She didn't like the sly little grin Evan was wearing, either. He was up to something, and it probably meant someone was in for a double dose of his teasing.

Evan stepped in front of Vanessa, blocking her view of the board. She let out a grunt and tugged on his shirtsleeve. "I can't see. What's it say?"

Evan held his position, mumbling something Lorna couldn't quite understand.

"Well?" Vanessa shouted. "Are you going to tell me what it says or not?"

He scratched the back of his head. "Hmm. . ."

"What is it? Let me see!"

Evan glanced over at Lorna, but she quickly averted her gaze, pretending to be absorbed in her music.

When she lifted her head, Lorna saw Vanessa slide under Evan's arm, until she was facing the bulletin board. She studied it for several seconds, but then her hands dropped to her hips, and she whirled around. "That just figures!" She marched across the room and stopped in front of the piano, shooting Lorna a look that could have stopped traffic on the busy Seattle freeway. "I hope you're satisfied!"

Lorna was bewildered. "What are you talking about?"

"Professor Burrows chose *you* for the female solo!" Vanessa scowled at Lorna. "Just because you're older than the rest of us and play the piano fairly well shouldn't mean you get special privileges."

Lorna creased her forehead so hard she felt wrinkles form. "Why would you say such a thing?"

"The professor doesn't think you can do any wrong. She's always telling the class how mature you are and how you're the only one who ever follows directions."

Lorna opened her mouth to offer some kind of rebuttal, but before she got a word out, Evan's deep voice cut her off. "Now wait a minute, Vanessa. Lorna got the lead part for only one reason."

Vanessa turned to face Evan, who stood at her side in front of the piano. "And that would be?"

"This talented woman can not only play the piano, but she can sing. Beautifully, I might add." He cast Lorna a sidelong glance, and she felt the heat of a blush warm her cheeks.

Vanessa's dark eyes narrowed. "Are you saying *I* can't sing?"

"I don't think that's what he meant," Lorna interjected.

Vanessa slapped her hand on the piano keys with such force that Lorna worried the Baldwin might never be the same. "Let the man speak for himself!" She whirled around to face Evan. "Or does the cute little blond have you so wrapped around her finger that you can't even think straight? It's obviously you're smitten with her."

Evan opened his mouth as if he was going to say something, but Vanessa cut him off. "Don't try to deny it, Evan Bailey! I've seen the way you and Lorna look at each other." She sniffed deeply. "Is she trying to rob from the cradle, or are you looking for a mother figure?"

Evan's face had turned crimson. "I think this discussion is over," he said firmly.

"That's right, let's drop it," Lorna agreed.

Vanessa glared at Evan. "Be a good boy now, and do what Mama Lorna says."

He drew in a deep breath. "I'm warning you, Vanessa. . ."

"What are you going to do? Tell the teacher on me?" she taunted.

Lorna cleared her throat a couple of times, and both Evan and Vanessa turned to look at her. "We're all adults here, and if getting the lead part means so much to you, I'll speak to the professor about it, Vanessa."

"I'll fight my own battles, thank you very much!" Vanessa squared her shoulders. "Unlike some people in this class, I don't need a mother to fix my boo-boos." She turned on her heels and marched out of the room.

Evan let out a low whistle. "What was that all about?"

Lorna shook her head slowly. "You don't know?"

He shrugged. "Not really. She said she wanted the solo part, you offered to give it to her, and she's still mad. Makes no sense to me." He snickered. "But then I never was much good at understanding women. Even if I did grow up with two sisters."

Lorna pinched the bridge of her nose. How could the man be so blind? "Vanessa is jealous."

"I know. She wants your part," Evan said, dropping to the bench beside Lorna. "She can't stand the fact that someone has a better singing voice than she does."

"I think the real reason Vanessa's jealous is because she thinks you like me, and she's attracted to you."

Evan looked at Lorna as though she'd lost her mind. "I've done nothing to make Vanessa think she and I might—"

"That doesn't matter. You make people laugh, and your manner is often flirtatious."

Evan rubbed his chin and frowned. "What can I say? I'm a friendly guy, but that doesn't mean I'm after every woman I meet."

Lorna reached for a piece of music. "Tell that to Vanessa Brown."

# Chapter 8

Evan moved away from the piano, wishing there were something he could say or do to make Lorna feel more comfortable about the part she'd gotten. The scene with Vanessa had been unreal, but the fact that Lorna was willing to give up the solo part she'd been offered was one more proof that she lived her Christianity and would make a good wife for some lucky man. It just probably wasn't him.

He took a seat in the chair he'd been assigned and studied Lorna. She was thumbing through a stack of music, her forehead wrinkled and her face looking pinched. Was she still thinking about the encounter with Vanessa, frustrated with Evan, or merely trying to concentrate on getting ready for their first choir number?

Lorna was not only a beautiful, talented musician, but she had a sensitivity that drew Evan to her like a powerful magnet. Anyone willing to give up a favored part and not get riled when Vanessa attacked her with a vengeance made a hit with Evan. Lorna had done the Christian thing, even if Vanessa hadn't. Now if he could only convince her to give their relationship a chance. Maybe their Saturday night date would turn the tide.

Lorna had just slipped on her Farmen's apron when Chris came up behind her. "How was school today?"

"Don't ask."

"That bad, huh?"

"Afraid so."

"You've been back in college for a couple of weeks. I thought you'd be getting used to the routine by now."

Lorna grabbed an order pad from the back of the counter and stuffed it in her apron pocket. "The routine's not the problem."

Chris's forehead wrinkled. "What is, then?"

Lorna rubbed the back of her neck, trying to get the kinks out. "Never mind. It's probably not worth mentioning."

"It doesn't have anything to do with Evan Bailey, does it?"

"No! Yes. Well, partially."

Chris glanced at the clock on the wall above the serving counter. "We've still got a few minutes until our shift starts. Let's go to the ladies' room, and you can tell me about it."

Lorna shook her head. "What's the point? Talking won't change anything."

Chris grabbed her arm and gave it a gentle tug. "Come on, friend. I know you'll feel better once you've opened up and told me what's bothering you."

"Oh, all right," Lorna mumbled. "Let's hurry, though. I don't want to get docked any pay for starting late."

Lorna was glad to discover an empty ladies' room when she and Chris arrived a few moments later. Chris dropped onto the small leather couch and motioned Lorna to do the same. "Okay, spill it!"

Lorna curled up in one corner of the couch and let the whole story out, beginning with her entering the choir room that morning and ending with Vanessa's juvenile tantrum and Evan's response to it all.

Chris folded her hands across her stomach and laughed. It wasn't some weak, polite little giggle, like Lorna offered her customers. It was a genuine, full-blown belly laugh.

Lorna didn't see what was so funny. In fact, retelling the story had only upset her further. "This is no laughing matter, Chris. It's serious business."

Her friend blinked a couple of times, and then burst into another round of laughter.

Lorna started to get up. "Okay, fine! I shouldn't have said anything to you, that's obvious."

Chris reached over and grabbed hold of Lorna's arm. "No, stay, please." She wiped her eyes with the back of her hand. "I hope you know I wasn't laughing at you."

"Who?"

"The whole scenario." Chris clicked her tongue. "I just don't get you, Lorna."

"What do you mean?"

"Evan Bailey is one cute guy, right?"

Lorna nodded and flopped back onto the couch.

"From what you've told me, I'd say the man has high moral standards and is lots of fun to be with."

"Yes."

Chris leaned toward Lorna. "If you don't wake up and hear

the music, you might lose the terrific guy to this Vanessa person. If I'd been you today, I don't think I could have been so nice about things." She grimaced. "Offering to give up the part—now that's Christianity in action!"

Lorna crossed her legs and swung her foot back and forth, thinking the whole while how tempted she had been to give that feisty redhead a swift kick this afternoon. She'd said what she felt was right at the time, but it hadn't been easy.

"From all you've told me, I'd say it's pretty obvious the woman has her sights set on Evan Bailey." Chris shook her finger at Lorna. "You need to put this whole age thing out of your mind and give the guy a chance."

Lorna cringed. "That's not really the problem. I think Evan is as poor as a church mouse."

"What gives you that idea?"

Lorna quickly related the story of her and Evan's bicycle ride and how when they'd had pizza, he didn't have enough money to leave a decent tip.

Chris groaned. "Don't you think you're jumping to conclusions? Maybe the guy just didn't have much cash on him that day." She squinted her eyes. "And even if he is dirt poor, does it really matter so much?"

"It does to me. I don't want to get involved with another man who will expect me to give up my career and put him through college."

Evan was excited about his date with Lorna tonight. He'd been looking forward to it all week and had even tried his hand at making another online sweet treat, which he planned to give Lorna after dinner this evening. It was called Lemon Supreme and consisted of cream cheese mixed with lemon juice, sugar, eggs, and vanilla. Graham cracker crumbs were used for the crust, and confectioner's sugar was sprinkled over the top. He hadn't had time to sample it, but Evan was sure Lorna would like it.

At six o'clock sharp, Evan stood in front of Ivar's Restaurant along the Seattle waterfront. He was pleased when he saw Lorna cross the street and head in his direction. He'd been worried she might stand him up.

"Am I late?" she panted. "I had a hard time finding a place to park."

"You're right on time," he assured her. "I got here a few minutes ago and put my name on the waiting list at the restaurant."

"How long did they say we might have to wait for a table?"

"Not more than a half hour or so," he said.

"Guess we could go inside and wait in the lobby."

Evan nodded. "Or we could stay out here awhile and enjoy the night air." He drew in a deep breath. "Ah, sure does smell fresh down by the water, doesn't it?"

She wrinkled her nose. "Guess that all depends on what you call fresh."

"Salt sea air and fish a-frying. . .now that's what I call fresh," he countered with a wide smile.

She poked him playfully on the arm. "You would say something like that."

He chuckled. "Ah, you know me so well."

"No, actually, I don't," she said with a slight frown.

"Then we need to remedy that." Evan gazed deeply into her eyes. "I'd sure like to know you better, 'cause what I've seen so far I really like."

Lorna gulped. Things were moving too fast, and she seemed powerless to stop them. What had happened to her resolve not to get involved with another man, or even to date? She had to put a stop to this before it escalated into more than friendship.

Before she had a chance to open her mouth, Evan took hold of her hand and led her to a bench along the side of the building. It faced the water, where several docks were located. "Let's sit awhile and watch the boats come and go," he suggested.

"What about our dinner reservations?"

"They said they'd call my name over the loudspeaker when our table's ready. Fortunately, there's a speaker outside, too." Evan sat down, and Lorna did the same.

The ferry coming from Bremerton docked, and Lorna watched the people disembark. She hadn't been to Bremerton in a long time. She hardly went anywhere but work, school, church, and shopping once in a while. What had happened to the carefree days of vacations, fun evenings out, and days off? *Guess I gave those things up when I began working so Ron could go to school.* Working two jobs left little time for fun or recreation, and now that Lorna was in school and still employed at one job, things weren't much better. *I do have the weekends free,* her conscience reminded. *Maybe I deserve to have a little fun now and then.*

"You look like you're a hundred miles away," Evan said, breaking into her thoughts.

She turned her head and looked at him. "I was watching the ferry."

He lifted her chin with his hand. "And I've been watching you."

Before Lorna could respond, he tipped his head and brushed a gentle kiss against her lips. As the kiss deepened, she instinctively wrapped her arms around his neck.

"Bailey, party of two. . .your table is ready!"

Lorna jerked away from Evan at the sound of his name being called over the loudspeaker. "We—we'd better get in there," she said breathlessly.

"Right." Evan stood up, pulling Lorna gently to her feet.

She went silently by his side into the restaurant, berating herself for allowing that kiss. *I'll be on my guard the rest of the evening. No more dreamy looks and no more kisses!*

# Chapter 9

Farmen's Restaurant was more crowded than usual on Monday night, and Lorna's boss had just informed her that they were shorthanded. With God's help, she would get through her shift, although she was already tired. It had been a busy weekend, and she'd had to cram in time for homework.

Lorna thought about her date with Evan on Saturday, which hadn't ended until eleven o'clock, because they'd taken a ride on one of the sightseeing boats after dinner. She'd thoroughly enjoyed the moonlight cruise around Puget Sound, and when Evan walked Lorna to her car, he'd presented her with another of his desserts. This one was called Lemon Supreme, and she had tried it after she got home that night.

Lorna puckered her lips as she remembered the sour taste caused by either too much lemon juice or not enough sugar. *I doubt Evan will ever be a master baker,* she mused.

She glanced at her reflection in the mirror over the serving counter, checking her uniform and hair one last time, as she contemplated the way Evan had looked at her before they'd said good night. He'd wanted to kiss her again; she could tell by his look of longing. She had prevented it from happening by jumping quickly into her car and shutting the door.

"I only want to be his friend," Lorna muttered under her breath, as she strolled into the dining room.

She got right to work and took the order of an elderly couple. Then she moved across the aisle to where another couple sat with their heads bent over the menus.

The woman was the first to look up, and Lorna's mouth dropped open.

"Fancy meeting you here," Vanessa Brown drawled.

Before Lorna could respond, Vanessa's companion looked up and announced, "Lorna works here."

Lorna's hand began to tremble, and she dropped the order pad. Evan Bailey was looking at her as though nothing was wrong. Maybe his having dinner with Vanessa was a normal occurrence. Maybe this wasn't their first date.

Forcing her thoughts to remain on the business at hand, Lorna bent down to retrieve the pad. When she stood up again, Vanessa was leaning across the table, fussing with Evan's shirt collar.

Lorna cleared her throat, and Vanessa glanced over at her. "What's good to eat in this place?"

"Tonight's special is meat loaf." Lorna kept her focus on the order pad.

"Meat loaf sounds good to me," Evan said.

"You're such a simple, easy-to-please kind of guy," Vanessa fairly purred.

Lorna swallowed back the urge to scream. She probably

shouldn't be having these unwarranted feelings of jealousy, for she had no claim on Evan. He'd obviously lied to her the other day, when he denied any interest in Vanessa. A guy didn't take a girl out to dinner if he didn't care something about her. *He took me to dinner on Saturday. Does that mean he cares about both me and Vanessa? Or could Evan Bailey be toying with our emotions?*

Lorna turned to face Vanessa, feeling as though the air between them was charged with electricity. "What would you like to order?"

"I'm careful about what I eat, so I think I'll have a chicken salad with low-cal ranch dressing." Vanessa looked over at her dinner partner and batted her eyelashes. "Men like their women to be fit and trim, right, Evan?"

He shrugged his shoulders. "I can't speak for other men, but to my way of thinking, it's what's in a woman's heart that really matters. Outward appearances can sometimes be deceiving."

He cast Lorna a grin, and she tapped her pencil against the order pad impatiently. "Will there be anything else?"

Evan opened his mouth. "Yes, actually—"

"Why don't you bring us a couple of sugar-free mocha-flavored coffees?" Vanessa interrupted. She gave Evan a syrupy smile. "I hope you like that flavor."

"Well, I—"

"Two mochas, a meat loaf special, and one chicken salad, coming right up!" Lorna turned on her heels and hurried away.

Evan watched Lorna's retreating form. Her shoulders were hunched, and her head was down. Obviously she wasn't at her best. He could tell she'd been trying to be polite when she took their orders, but from her tone of voice and those wrinkles he'd noticed in her forehead, he was certain she was irritated about something.

*Probably wondering what I'm doing here with Vanessa. Wish she had stuck around longer so I could have explained. Maybe I should have gone after her.*

"Evan, are you listening to me?"

Evan turned his head. "What were you saying, Vanessa?"

"I'm glad I ran into you tonight. I wanted to ask your opinion on something."

"What's that?"

Vanessa leaned her elbows on the table and intertwined her fingers. "All day I've been thinking about that solo part I should have had."

"You're coming to grips with it, I hope."

She frowned. "Actually, I've been wondering whether I should have taken Lorna up on her offer to give the part to me. What do you think, Evan? Should I ask her about it when she returns with our orders?"

Evan grunted. "I can't believe you'd really expect her to give you that solo. Professor Burrows obviously feels Lorna's the best one for the part, or she wouldn't have assigned it to her."

Vanessa wrinkled her nose. "And I can't believe the way you always stick up for that little blond. She's too old and too prim and proper for you, Evan. Why don't you wake up?"

Evan reached for his glass of water and took a big gulp, hoping to regain his composure before he spoke again. When he set the glass down, he leaned forward and looked Vanessa right in the eye. "I'm not hung up on age differences, and as far as Lorna being prim and proper, you don't know what you're talking about."

Vanessa blinked and pulled back like she'd been stung by a bee. "You don't have to be so mean, Evan. I was only trying to make you see how much better—"

She was interrupted when Lorna appeared at the table with their orders. Evan was glad he could concentrate on eating his meat loaf instead of trying to change Vanessa's mind about a woman she barely knew.

As Lorna placed Evan's plate in front of him, she was greeted with another one of his phony smiles. They had to be phony. No man in his right mind would be out with one woman and flirting with another. For that matter, most men didn't bring their date to the workplace of the woman he'd dated only two nights before. *Dated and kissed,* she fumed.

Lorna excused herself to get their beverages, and a short time later she returned with two mugs of mocha-flavored coffee. She looked at Evan sitting across from Vanessa, and an unexpected yearning stirred within her soul. Why couldn't she be the one he was having dinner with tonight? All this time Lorna had been telling herself that she and Evan could only be friends, so it didn't make sense to feel jealousy over seeing him with Vanessa Brown.

*Maybe I don't know my own heart. Maybe. . .*

"This isn't low-cal dressing. I asked for low-cal, remember?" Vanessa's sharp words pulled Lorna's disconcerting thoughts aside. "I think it is," she replied. "I turned in an order for low-cal dressing, and I'm sure—"

"I just tasted it. It's not low-cal!"

Lorna drew in a deep breath and offered up a quick prayer for patience. "I'll go check with the cook who filled your order."

She started to turn, but Vanessa shouted, "I want another salad! This one is drenched in fattening ranch dressing, and it's ruined."

Lorna was so aggravated her ears were ringing, yet she knew in order to keep her job at Farmen's she would need to be polite to all costumers—even someone as demanding as Vanessa. "I'll be back with another salad."

As she was turning in the order for the salad, Lorna met up with her friend, Chris.

"You don't look like the picture of happiness tonight," Chris noted. "What's the problem—too many customers?"

Lorna gritted her teeth. "Just two too many."

"What's that supposed to mean?"

Lorna explained about Evan and Vanessa being on a date and how Vanessa was demanding a new salad.

Chris squinted her eyes. "I thought you and Evan went to Ivar's on Saturday."

"We did."

"Then what's up with him bringing another woman here on a date?"

Lorna leaned against the edge of the serving counter and groaned. "He's two-faced. What can I say?"

"Want me to finish up with that table for you?"

Lorna sighed with relief. "Would you? I don't think I can

face Evan and his date again tonight."

Chris patted Lorna's arm. "Sure. What are friends for?"

Lorna peered into the darkening sky, watching out the window as Evan and Vanessa left the restaurant. She thought it was strange when she saw them each get into their own cars, but shrugged it off, remembering that she and Evan had taken separate vehicles on Saturday night. Maybe Evan didn't have time to pick Vanessa up for their date. Maybe she'd been out running errands. It didn't matter. Lorna's shift would be over in a few hours, and then she could go home, indulge in a long, hot bath, and crash on the couch in front of the fireplace. Maybe a cup of hot chocolate and some of Ann's famous oatmeal cookies would help soothe her frazzled nerves. Some pleasant music and a good inspirational novel to read could have her feeling better in no time.

Lorna moved away from the window and sought out her next customer. She had a job to do, and she wouldn't waste another minute thinking about Evan Bailey. If he desired someone as self-serving as Vanessa Brown, he could have her.

Determined to come up with a way to win Lorna's heart, Evan had decided to try another recipe from his online cooking class. This one was called Bodacious Banana Bread, and it looked fairly simple to make. Between the loaf of bread and the explanation he planned to give Lorna tomorrow at school, Evan hoped he could let her know how much he cared.

Whistling to the tune of "Jesus Loves Me," Evan set out the ingredients he needed: butter, honey, eggs, flour, salt, soda, baking powder, and two ripe bananas. In short order he had everything mixed. He poured the batter into a glass baking dish and pulled it off the counter. Suddenly, his hand bumped a bowl of freshly washed blueberries he planned to have with a dish of vanilla ice cream later on. The bowl toppled over, and half the blueberries tumbled into the bread pan, on top of the banana mixture.

"Oh, no," Evan moaned. "Now I've done it." He tried to pick the blueberries out, but too many had already sunk to the bottom of the pan.

"Guess I could bake it as is and hope for the best." Evan grabbed a wooden spoon and gave the dough a couple of stirs, to ensure that the berries were evenly distributed. He figured it couldn't turn out any worse than the other desserts he'd foiled since he first began the cooking class. That Lemon Supreme he'd been dumb enough to give Lorna without first tasting had been one of the worst. He'd sampled a piece after their date on Saturday night and realized he'd messed up the recipe somehow, because it wasn't sweet enough.

Two hours later the bread was done and had cooled sufficiently. Evan decided to try a slice, determined not to give any to Lorna if it tasted funny.

To Evan's delight, the bread was wonderful. The blueberries had added a nice texture to the sweet dessert, and it was cooked to perfection. "I think I'll call this my Blueberry Surprise," he said with a chuckle. "Sure hope it impresses Lorna, because I'm not certain I have any words that will."

# Chapter 10

Going back to school the following day—knowing she would have to face both Evan and Vanessa—was difficult for Lorna. She didn't know why it should be so hard. Evan had made no commitment to her, nor she to him.

When she arrived at school, Lorna was surprised to see Evan standing in the hall, just outside their anatomy class. He spotted her, waved, and held up a paper sack. "I have something for you, and we need to talk." His voice sounded almost pleading, and that in itself Lorna found unsettling.

"There's nothing to talk about." Lorna started to walk away, hoping to avoid any confrontations and knowing if they did talk, her true feelings might give her away.

Evan reached out and grabbed hold of her arm. When she turned to face him, he lifted his free hand and wrapped a tendril of her hair around his finger. He leaned slightly forward—so close she could feel his breath on her upturned face. If she didn't do something quickly, she was sure she was about to be kissed.

Evan moved his finger from her hair to her face, skimming

down her cheek, then along her chin.

Lorna shivered with a mixture of anticipation and dread, knowing she should pull away. Just as Evan's lips sought hers, the floor began to move, and the walls swayed back and forth in a surreal manner. Lorna had heard of bells going off and being so much in love that it hurt, but if this weird sensation had anything to do with the way she felt about Evan, she didn't want any part of loving the man.

Evan grasped Lorna's shoulders as the floor tilted, and she almost lost her balance. Knowing she needed his support in order to stay on her feet, Lorna leaned into him, gripping both of his arms. "What's happening?" she rasped.

"I believe we're in the middle of a bad earthquake." Evan's face seemed etched with concern. It was a stark contrast from his usual smiling expression.

Lorna's eyes widened with dread. She looked down and thought she was going to be sick. The floor was moving rhythmically up and down. It reminded her of a ship caught in a storm, about to be capsized with the crest of each angry wave.

"This is a bad one!" Evan exclaimed. "We need to get under a table or something."

She looked around helplessly; there were no tables in the hall and none in the anatomy class, either. The room only had opera-style seats. "Where?"

Evan pulled her closer. "A doorway! We should stand under a doorway."

The door to their classroom was only a few feet away, but it took great effort for them to maneuver themselves into position. Lorna's heart was thumping so hard she was sure Evan could hear each radical beat. She'd been in a few earthquakes during her lifetime, but none so violent as this one.

A candy machine in the hallway vibrated, pictures on the wall flew in every direction, and a terrible, cracking sound rent the air as the windows rattled and broke. A loud crash, followed by a shrill scream, sent shivers up Lorna's spine. There was no one else in the hallway, which was unusual, considering the fact that classes were scheduled to begin soon. Where was everybody, and when would this nightmare end?

Another ear-piercing sound! Was that a baby's cry? No, it couldn't be. This was Bay View Christian College, not a day care center.

"I think the scream came from over there," Evan said, pointing across the hall. He glanced down at Lorna. "Did that sound like a baby cry to you?"

She nodded and swallowed against the lump lodged in her throat.

"Stay here. I'll be right back." Evan handed Lorna the paper sack he'd been holding.

"No, don't leave me!" She clutched the front of his shirt as panic swept through her in a wave so cold and suffocating, she thought she might faint.

"I think you'll be okay if you wait right here," he assured her. "Pray, Lorna. Pray."

The walls and floor were still moving, though a bit slower now. Lorna watched helplessly as Evan half crawled, half slid on his stomach across the hall. When he disappeared behind the door, she sent up a prayer. "Dear God, please keep him safe."

At that moment, the truth slammed into Lorna with a

force stronger than any earthquake. Although she hadn't known Evan very long, she was falling in love with him. In the few short weeks since they'd met, he had brought joy and laughter into her life. He'd made her feel beautiful and special, something she hadn't felt since Ron's untimely death. They had a common bond. Both were Christians, interested in music, and each had a desire to work with children.

*Children.* The word stuck in Lorna's brain. She had always wanted a child. When she married Ron, Lorna was sure they would start a family as soon as he finished med school. That never happened because her husband had been snatched away as quickly as fog settles over Puget Sound.

She leaned heavily against the door frame and let this new revelation sink in. Was going back to school and getting her degree really Lorna's heart's desire? Or was being married to someone she loved and starting a family what she truly wanted? *It doesn't matter. I can't have a relationship with Evan because he doesn't love me. He's been seeing Vanessa.*

"Lorna! Can you come over here?" Evan's urgent plea broke into her thoughts, and she reeled at the sound of his resonating voice.

The earthquake was over now, but Lorna knew from past experience that a series of smaller tremors would no doubt follow. She made her way carefully across the hall and into the room she'd seen Evan enter only moments ago.

She stopped short inside the door. In the middle of the room lay a young woman. A bookcase had fallen across her legs, pinning her to the floor. Lorna gasped as she realized the woman was holding a crying baby in her arms. The sight brought tears to Lorna's eyes. Covering her mouth to stifle a sob, she raced to Evan's side and dropped down beside him. She noticed beads of perspiration glistening on his upper lip. "Is she hurt badly? What about the baby?" Tears rolled down Lorna's cheeks as she thought about the possibility of a child losing its mother, or the other way around. *Please, God, let them be all right.*

"The woman's legs could be broken, so it wouldn't be good to try to move her. The baby appears to be okay." He pointed to the sobbing infant. "Could you pick her up, then go down the hall and find a phone? We need to call 911 right away."

Lorna nodded numbly. As soon as she lifted the child into her arms, the baby's crying abated. She stood and started for the door. Looking back over her shoulder, she whispered, "I love you, Evan, even if you do care for Vanessa Brown."

The next few hours went by in a blur. A trip to the hospital in Evan's car, following the ambulance that transported the injured woman. . . Talking with the paramedics who'd found some identification on the baby's mother. Calling the woman's husband on the phone. Pacing the floor of the hospital waiting room. Trying to comfort a fussy child. Waiting patiently until the father arrived. Praying until no more words would come. Lorna did all these things with Evan by her side. They said little to each other as they waited to hear of the mother's condition. Words seemed unnecessary as Lorna acknowledged a shared sense of oneness with Evan, found only in a crisis situation.

The woman, who'd been identified as Sherry Holmes, had

been at the college that morning, looking for her husband, an English professor. He'd left for work without his briefcase, and she'd come to deliver the papers he needed. Professor Holmes wasn't in his class when she arrived. He'd been to an early morning meeting in another building, as had most of the other teachers. Why there weren't any other students in the hallway, Lorna still did not understand. She thought it must have been divine intervention, since so much structural damage had been done to that particular building. Who knew how many more injuries might have occurred had there been numerous students milling about?

Lorna felt a sense of loss as she handed the baby over to its father a short time later. She was relieved to hear that the child's mother was in stable condition, despite a broken leg and several bad bruises.

"You look done in," Evan said, taking Lorna's hand and leading her to a chair. He pointed to the paper sack lying on the table in the waiting room, where Lorna had placed it when they first arrived. "You never did open your present."

She nodded and offered him a weak smile. "Guess I've been too busy with other things." She pulled it open and peeked inside. A sweet banana aroma overtook her senses, and she sniffed deeply. "I'm guessing it's a loaf of banana bread."

Evan smiled. "It started out to be, but in the end, it turned out to be a kind of blueberry surprise."

She tipped her head and squinted her eyes. "What?"

Evan chuckled. "It's a long story." He motioned to the sack. "Try a hunk. I think you'll be pleasantly surprised."

Lorna opened the bag and withdrew a piece of the bread.

She took a tentative bite, remembering the other treats he'd given her that hadn't turned out so well. To her surprise, the blueberry-banana bread was actually good. It was wonderful, in fact. She grinned at him. "This is great. You should patent the recipe."

He smiled and reached for her hand. "I don't know what surprises me the most. . .the accidental making of a great-tasting bread or your willingness to be here with me now."

"It's been a pretty rough morning, and I'm thankful the baby and her mother are going to be okay," she said, making no reference to her willingness to be with Evan.

"The look of gratitude on Professor Holmes's face will stay with me a long time." Evan gazed deeply into Lorna's eyes. "Nothing is as precious as the life God gives each of us, and I don't want to waste a single moment of the time I have left on this earth." He stroked the side of her face tenderly. "You're the most precious gift He's ever offered me."

Lorna blinked back sudden tears. "Me? But I thought you and Vanessa—"

Evan shook his head and leaned over to kiss her. When he pulled away, he smiled. Not his usual silly grin, but an honest "I love you" kind of smile. "I came to the restaurant last night to talk to you," he said. "I was going to plead my case and beg you to give our relationship a try."

"But Vanessa—"

"She was not my date."

"She wasn't?"

He shook his head.

"You were both at the same table, and I thought—"

"I know what you thought." He wrapped his arms around Lorna and held her tightly. "She came into Farmen's on her own, saw me sitting at that table, and decided to join me. The rest you pretty well know."

She shook her head. "Not really. From the way you two were acting, I thought you were on a date."

Evan grimaced. "Vanessa Brown is a spoiled, self-centered young woman." He touched the tip of Lorna's nose and chuckled. "Besides, she's too young for someone as mature as me."

Lorna laughed and tilted her head so she was looking Evan right in the eye. "In this life we don't always get second chances, but I'm asking for one now, Evan Bailey."

He smiled. "You've got it."

"I think it's time for you to meet my in-laws."

"I'd like that."

"And I don't care how poor you are, either," she added, giving his hand a squeeze.

"What makes you think I'm poor?"

"You mean you're not?"

He shook his head. "Not filthy rich, but sure no pauper." He bent his head down to capture her lips in a kiss that evaporated any lingering doubts.

Lorna thought about the verse of scripture Ann had quoted her awhile back. *"Delight yourself in the Lord and he will give you the desires of your heart."* Her senses reeled with the knowledge that regardless of whether she ever taught music or not, she had truly found her heart's desire in this man with the blueberry surprise.

## Recipe for Blueberry Surprise:

$\frac{1}{3}$ cup butter
$\frac{2}{3}$ cup honey
2 eggs
$1\frac{1}{4}$ cups all-purpose flour
2 teaspoons baking powder
$\frac{1}{2}$ teaspoon salt
$\frac{1}{4}$ teaspoon baking soda
2 mashed, ripe bananas
1 cup blueberries

Cream butter and sugar until fluffy. Add the eggs, beating well after each. Add the bananas and mix well. Combine the dry ingredients and add to the creamed mixture, mixing thoroughly. Gently fold in the blueberries. Pour into a 9x5-inch loaf pan that has been lined with waxed paper. Bake at 350 degrees for 50 to 60 minutes, or until a wooden toothpick comes out clean. Cool, remove from pan, and gently pull away the waxed paper. (Makes 1 loaf.)

## WANDA E. BRUNSTETTER

Wanda E. Brunstetter lives in Central Washington with her husband, Richard, who is a pastor. They have been married forty-one years and have two grown children and six grandchildren. Wanda is a professional ventriloquist and puppeteer, and she and her husband enjoy doing programs for children of all ages. Wanda's greatest joy as a Christian author is to hear from a reader that something she wrote has touched that person's heart or helped in some special way.

Wanda has written nine novels with Barbour Publishing's Heartsong Presents line, three novellas, and her collection of four previously published Amish novels, *Lancaster Brides*, was a bestseller. Wanda believes the Amish people's simple lifestyle and commitment to God can be a reminder of something we all need.

Visit her web page at: www.wandabrunstetter.com

# Bittersweet Memories & Peppermint Dreams

## by Pamela Griffin

# Dedication

A special thank you to my crit buds on this project,
and to Lena—who gave me permission to use
the tartar sauce/cake incident, based on the real-life
experience of one of her family members.
As always, this is dedicated to my Lord, Jesus,
who sweetens all the flops in my life,
making masterpieces from the messes.


"Taste and see that the LORD is good."
PSALM 34:8

# Chapter 1

"W"ait! Don't leave without me!"

Frantically waving her arm, Erica Langley darted through the icy drizzle, jumped a puddle, and just made it to the bus as the huge door closed. She pounded on the glass with gloved fingers. The driver opened the door again and raised bushy gray brows as he watched her clomp up the steep metal stairs and produce her ticket.

"Almost missed the bus, lady," he grumbled.

"Sorry." She attempted a smile, one he didn't return.

Clutching her shoulder bag to her hip, Erica caught her breath and eyed the seats on either side of the narrow aisle. The front and middle ones were full. Toward the back she spotted two empty rows, but she didn't think her shaky legs would carry her that far. Six rows down she spotted an empty seat on the left and moved toward it.

"May I?" she asked the elderly woman by the window, wondering why no one had claimed the coveted spot. Places close to the door were usually first to go.

"That seat is taken, but you can sit here, if you'd like." The deep masculine voice came from Erica's right. "The passenger who was sitting beside me just got off."

She turned. Gentle brown eyes—puppy-dog eyes—smiled up at her. The hint of a crease in his right cheek suggested a boyish grin when his smile was full-blown. His auburn hair was cut short but unkempt, as if he'd run his fingers through the damp twirls a few times. Beads of moisture sparkled in the strands as if he, too, had made a recent dash into the cold rain. He moved a couple of magazines and a leather briefcase off the aisle seat next to him.

Erica hesitated, uncertain whether she wanted to be in such close proximity to this attractive stranger. He must be uncomfortable with his long, trim build folded into that confined space. His jeans-clad knees hit the upholstered back of the seat in front of him. And he wasn't slouching.

"I promise, I don't bite." His sober expression didn't match his light words.

Embarrassed to feel all eyes on her—even the driver's, who impatiently looked at her in his long mirror above the wheel—Erica sank to the seat. As the bus rumbled out of the parking lot, she wished she had removed her coat first. To stand up now would be awkward. But judging from the warmth, the heater must be on full blast. Deciding she didn't want to bake, even in such frigid weather, she pulled off her gloves and shrugged her right shoulder out of the coat sleeve. Twisting from side to side, she tried to rid herself of the rest of the red wool garment. A large hand touched her shoulder.

"Allow me." Brown Eyes took her black furry collar and helped her remove her other arm from the sleeve. Then he pulled the coat from under her while she braced her hands on the chair arms and lifted herself a few inches. "Are you sure you want to take this off? You're shaking like a leaf."

*Which has nothing to do with the cold. Get a grip, Erica. You're twenty-three, not thirteen.* "Thanks, I'm fine." Fully seated again, she reclaimed her coat, laying it over her lap. She leaned forward, lifting her waist-length dark hair away from her back so it wouldn't pull, and brought the thick swathe to rest over one shoulder. With jerky movements she straightened her cable-knit sweater, pulling the hem farther down over her jeans, and settled back for the long ride.

"Nasty weather to be out." *Duh!* She mentally struck her forehead, realizing how stupid that sounded.

"Yeah," he agreed. "But at least we're not getting sleet and snow like they are about fifty miles northeast of here. So what brings you out on a night like this?"

Erica hesitated. How could she answer such a simple getting-to-know-you question when her reasons were anything but basic? Should she relay her desire to find the missing piece of her life's puzzle and explain the driving curiosity that compelled her to brave January's bleak weather for a nine-hour bus trip? Or the curiosity that drove her to find out if too much time and distance would hamper the reunion for which she so desperately yearned? And so anxiously feared.

As Erica studied his face—a strong, dependable face—she realized she could tell him none of these things. How could she speak of her heart's hopes and fears when she herself didn't understand them? He was only a stranger, someone who would pass in the night like the fabled ship. Still, there was something about his easy manner that invited confidence.

"Difficult question?" His words came out amused.

She settled for a standard answer. "I bought my ticket early to get the discount price. Since it's nonrefundable, I didn't want to lose out. You?"

"Going home. I had a business conference, and I'm not crazy about plane travel, especially on a day like today." He held out his hand. "I'm Ryan Meers."

She hesitated, taken aback by his open friendliness, then took the hand and offered a returning smile. "Erica Langley."

He gave her hand a little shake. "Pretty name. Nice to meet you, Erica."

Their conversation was interrupted as the lady who had the opposite aisle seat returned—a young pregnant woman with a tot wrapped in a pink baby sling around her. The child looked as if she couldn't be more than a year old. The woman looked exhausted.

"Here, let me help." Erica reached for the strap of the bulky diaper bag, which was sliding off the woman's arm.

"*Gracias.*" Her lips pulled up in a faint smile at Erica. She wriggled her way into the confined space, one hand over the child lying against her protruding belly, the other clutching the chair back as she dropped to her seat.

"You certainly have your hands full," Erica said sympathetically. "How old is your baby? And when are you due?"

"*No hablo ingles.*" Brow creased, the woman shook her head with an apologetic look.

"Oh." Erica's smile faded. She knew no Spanish.

Ryan leaned across Erica and began speaking in what

sounded like fluent Spanish. Indeed, the words poured from his lips as if he'd been born to them. The woman's face brightened, and she nodded with a huge smile, offering a stream of words in reply.

"Baby Elita is ten and a half months old, and Carmen is due in two months, though she hopes little Pablo comes sooner," Ryan explained to Erica.

She cast him an incredulous stare. "With a name like Ryan and the auburn hair to match, you speak Spanish?"

He gave her another one of his lopsided grins. "Actually several languages, though I'm not fluent in all of them. My mother is a French teacher, I took Spanish in high school, and I had a roommate in college whose family transferred here from Germany. I also know some sign language. My aunt signs at her church."

"What? No Gaelic?" Erica felt her own lips turn upward.

He chuckled, a pleasant sound that sent a rumbly sort of tremor straight to the pit of her stomach. "No, no Gaelic." He settled back in his seat. "So tell me, Erica, where are you headed?"

She liked the way he said the syllables of her name. Soft, not harsh as she often heard them. "A small, pin-dot town on the map. From what I understand, if you blink you'll pass it by."

"One of those, huh? I'm from a town like that myself. Population 942. Wait, I take that back. Mindy Jacobs had a baby last week. Make that 943."

Erica laughed. "I've always thought small-town life would be so charming. Close-knit families, friendly neighbors, everyone knowing everyone else."

"And everyone else's business," Ryan filled in wryly. "So what's the name of this pin-dot, small town?"

"Preston Corners."

"You're kidding! That's where I'm headed."

Erica's eyes widened. "Really?" A flicker of something akin to nervous energy lit inside her. "Any chance you know Wes Beardsley?"

"Do I! My nemesis and best buddy all through high school. We played sports together."

"Oh?" Her heartbeat quickened. "What's he like?"

"What's he like?" Ryan repeated the question, as if he didn't understand it. "I don't know. . .he can be a regular card at times. A real ham when it comes to the spotlight. Other times he can be stone-dead serious."

Erica moistened her bottom lip, mentally storing the information. "And what's he look like now? Is he tall? Short? Heavy? Thin? Does he have wavy hair like yours or. . .or is it straight?" She fumbled with the last words when Ryan's brows gathered in a suspicious frown, and she realized how odd her questions must seem.

"His hair's straight. He's shorter than I am. Huskier, too." He fixed her with a sober stare. "He's married, you know. Has a great wife—Stacey—and three kids. He married his high school sweetheart, as a matter of fact. They dote on each other."

"Three kids?" Erica knew about the wife but not the kids. Wes hadn't mentioned them during their phone conversation. A firewood peddler had come knocking on her door, cutting the call short. "What does he do for a living?"

"Why do you want to know so much about him?"

Her gaze fell to her lap. "I haven't seen him in a while. I'm just curious."

"Really. . . Curious?" He crossed his arms and leaned against the bus wall, eyeing her as if she were the typical other woman out to steal his buddy from the family who loved him. "So, what are you to Wes? An old girlfriend he met on summer vacations? A pen pal? A college chum?"

Erica tried to swallow the lump that had risen to her throat. Might as well tell him. Since he lived in Preston Corners, he'd know soon enough anyway.

"I'm his sister."

"His sister?" Ryan's disapproving tone changed to shock then grew wary. "Wes doesn't have a sister. We've been buddies for over fifteen years, so I should know."

Erica released a whisper-soft breath and forced herself to hold his gaze. "I didn't know he had a sister, either. Not until several weeks ago. Actually, he has two of them. Me and. . ." She mentally searched for the name. "Paula. Yes, that's it. Paula Rothner. She's my sister, too."

Ryan only stared. Erica offered a thin smile.

"You're putting me on," he said at last.

"No. It's kind of a long story."

"I'm not going anywhere for the next nine hours. The bus isn't due to pull into Preston Corners until tomorrow morning."

"Okay." She repeatedly smoothed her hand down her leg, as though to remove a stubborn wrinkle in her jeans that wasn't there. Anxiety was written all over her. "I don't remember much about life before first grade," she began slowly, her soft, Texas drawl becoming more pronounced. "Just hazy recollections. But I was never sure if they stemmed from something that actually happened or if they came from a recurring dream I've had for as long as I can remember." She cast a worried glance his way. "Does that sound crazy?"

"No. I've read that a child doesn't reach memory stage until six years of age, though I disagree. I remember my dad tossing me up in the air before I hit kindergarten." He tugged at his ear. "The article went on to say that every part of our existence, from babyhood on, takes deep root in a part of our brain that stores that information. Some people never retrieve the events of their first years. But, depending on the memory, especially if it's a traumatic one, our subconscious mind remembers. And it may revisit us in our dreams."

Erica looked surprised. "You sound well informed on the subject."

"I read that in a psychology magazine. I'm a professional counselor."

"Oh." Her eyes took on a wary respect. "I guess that would explain why you know so much about it."

Erica looked away, and Ryan frowned. Why was it that when people found out what he did for a living, they tensed up? As if afraid he might dive into their personal history, asking them to expose their deepest and darkest secrets.

The swishing of wheels on wet pavement and the tapping of light rain on the window were the only sounds heard in their row. Erica began to twist a strand of long hair around her index finger. As tightly as she wound it, Ryan was surprised her fingertip didn't turn blue.

"If you want to talk about it, I promise I won't make you stretch out and lie down on the empty seats in back."

"What?" Her startled gaze met his.

"Like a psychiatrist's couch. People seem to expect me to suggest such a thing. Though I think that mode of analysis is ancient history for the therapist. I wouldn't know, since I'm only a high school counselor."

"A high school counselor?"

"Yes. We have our own methods. We use candy as a bribe to get the kids to talk." Ryan gave her a teasing grin then dug in his jacket pocket and pulled out a red foil-wrapped candy kiss.

Her eyebrows lifted in amusement as she took it. "Thanks." She opened the foil with a crisp rustle and popped the chocolate drop into her mouth. "Mmm. I love these."

"That one's on the house. But if you want another. . ." He pulled a silver piece of candy from his pocket and held it by its white tag, moving his hand to make it sway like a pendulum in front of her face. "Zin you must tell me your dreeem."

Erica laughed at his mad hypnotist-doctor impersonation. "You know, you're easy to talk to."

"Thanks. That's probably the nicest compliment I've gotten all week." He set the candy kiss in her hand. "And just to put your mind at ease, I was only teasing. I don't force confidences."

"That's okay. Like I said, I feel comfortable talking to you."

"So it's not my profession that makes you nervous?" he asked when she averted her gaze to the seat in front of her and was quiet a little too long.

"Not really. I think your profession is great. Necessary for all the troubled youth our world has today. I've just been a bundle of nerves since I woke up this morning, after having had that dream again last night." She released a tired sigh. "I don't know the particulars—how or why—but I can guess what happened. In my recurring dream or memory or whatever it is, there's a cabin in the woods with a porch along the front. I'm about four years old. Two older children and I are crying and screaming as a woman and a man in uniform pull us down the porch steps. I'm struggling to get away. I keep crying for something, but they won't listen. They put us in their car. I turn to look out the rear window at a young woman standing on the porch, watching as the car drives off. She just stands there and doesn't make any move to stop them from taking us." Erica's eyes closed.

Ryan knew Wes was a foster child. But he'd never supposed him to have blood siblings, since he rarely brought up his past when they were kids and never mentioned having sisters. Two weeks before Christmas, Wes expressed a desire to talk to Ryan, seeming eager about something, but had been interrupted by Peggy and the demand that he pull her loose tooth. After that, the kickoff of the football game took precedence. The subject was never brought up again, since Ryan left a few days later to visit one of his sisters for the holidays.

"Do you think the woman was your mother?" he prodded gently.

"After talking to Wes, I'm sure of it. He called, you know. Said he'd been trying to locate me for years. The couple who adopted me moved around a lot." She frowned. "No one told me about my parents when I was old enough to ask. After I'd been in the state's custody a year, Margaret and Darrin 'came to my rescue,' as they put it—"

"Margaret and Darrin?"

A lonely look filtered over Erica's face, exposing her vulnerability. "My adoptive parents. They didn't want me calling them Mama and Daddy. They said it made them feel old."

Ryan experienced a strong urge to reach out and hold her hand, but stopped just short of doing so by lacing his fingers tightly across his stomach. "That must've hurt."

She shrugged as if it weren't all that important, but he could see evidence of the pain in her tense mouth and downcast eyes. "I learned not to let it bother me."

"So Wes told you that you had a brother and sister and that he wanted to meet you?"

She nodded. "I can't begin to describe how I felt. I think he said a retired social services worker helped him uncover my new last name and that he'd found me through the Internet. I don't remember—I was pretty much in a daze after his first few sentences when he introduced himself. But I did feel such a strong relief to know I wasn't alone in the world. Margaret and Darrin were off on another cruise, and I was lonely. Wes invited me to his home for Christmas 'to spend time getting to know one another again,' as he put it, and I felt as if something clicked into place. It felt strange, too, as if I were in a dream and I'd wake up to find the conversation hadn't been real. But I had his voice on my answering machine to prove it!"

Her eyes lit up and she giggled, making Ryan smile.

"I went out that night and bought gifts for him and Stacey.

I had no idea what their tastes were. I was just thrilled to discover I had a family. Silly of me, I know." She turned a self-conscious glance toward the back of the seat in front of him.

"No, not silly," Ryan corrected. "Generous and thoughtful, but not silly." This time he followed the impulse to lay his hand over hers and give it an encouraging squeeze. Shock, then pleasure, filled her eyes. Cinnamon-colored eyes that warmed him to his soul. "So why weren't you able to visit Wes at Christmas?"

Her expression clouded, and he wished he could retrieve the question as quickly as he did his hand. "I got laid off a few days later. I was a secretary for a corporation that makes kitchen appliances. They had to cut corners and started with people most recently hired."

"That must have been a blow, especially right before the holidays." Ryan reached for his thermos of coffee. He didn't want her to think he was making any moves.

"It was. I wallowed in self-pity for a while. Then I got a postcard from Margaret, telling me they'd met some friends on the cruise and were extending their vacation. I decided it was time to stop feeling sorry for myself and go and meet my brother." Erica cocked her head as if puzzled. "You know, I've always been a fairly private person. I can't believe I'm sitting here, opening up to you like this."

"It's not so surprising. I'm your one link with Wes right now. You feel closer to him by talking to me. My profession might have something to do with it, too, though sometimes people clam up when they discover I'm a counselor. Others talk to me about their problems and have ever since I was a kid. It influenced my career choice. That and a lot of prayer."

"You're a Christian, too?"

"I wouldn't have made it without God in my life, though I didn't find Him until I was sixteen."

"I probably wouldn't have made it without Him, either." She averted her gaze.

Ryan changed the subject, noting how somber she'd become. "How long are you staying in Preston Corners?"

"Until Wes gets tired of me, I guess."

"I can't see that happening." His soft remark brought color to her cheeks, and he admired her fresh beauty. Thick, sable lashes framed her expressive eyes. Besides the frosty pale lipstick she wore, he could see no evidence of other makeup.

A soft grunt from Carmen's seat brought their attention her way. She was attempting to get out of the chair, baby in tow.

"Is everything okay?" Ryan asked in Spanish.

She shook her head and put a hand to her stomach. "I need to go to the restroom again. Every fifteen minutes or so! This baby kicks a lot—he will be a good fighter. Or maybe a soccer player. But Pablo does no good for his mother's poor bladder. Nor does his sister, Elita."

Ryan chuckled then interpreted for the mystified Erica. "Tell her I'll hold the baby," Erica said, pushing up Ryan's estimation of her by several notches. "It can't be easy for her to juggle the girl and tend to her needs, too."

Ryan related the offer. Carmen turned eyes full of surprise Erica's way, hesitated, then carefully lifted the sling from around her neck and placed Elita in Erica's open arms.

"Oh, isn't she just precious?" Erica cooed as she set the

bundle on her lap and looked down at the girl once Carmen waddled off. "She's got eyes like big semisweet chocolate drops, just like her mama. Don't you, sweetheart?" She grabbed one small dusky-colored hand and smiled at the tot, who stared up at her, perfectly content to be in this stranger's care.

Ryan watched as Erica continued to play with and talk nonsense to the child. She would make a good mother some-day. He turned his gaze toward the rain-streaked glass and the traffic whizzing by in the next lane. Why that thought popped into his head, when he had little to base it on, Ryan had no idea. But one thing he did know: As tempting as Erica was, as sweet as she seemed, he would keep his vow and not get involved with her. Not with any woman.

# Chapter 2

Near midnight, the bus rumbled to a stop by a motel. An all-night café stood nearby. Everyone turned curious eyes toward the driver as he stood and awkwardly faced them. By the expression on his craggy face, Erica sensed the news wasn't good.

"Sorry, folks. The winter storm took an unexpected turn and has hit the next two towns on our route. We might be gettin' some ugly weather here, too. I talked to my supervisor, and he advised me to wait 'til daylight when the bridges and overpasses are clear of ice. By then the sand trucks will've made their runs over the freeway. You're welcome to sleep on the bus—we got plenty o' blankets and pillows—or if you want a bed, there's a motel over yonder." That said, he quickly reclaimed his seat, as if relieved that his brief ordeal at public speaking was over.

Several passengers grumbled, and some got out their cell phones, but no one complained too loudly. Who could argue with someone who wanted to protect lives?

Erica sighed and settled back in her seat. Texas was like

that. Not many knew how to drive in winter weather, so the least amount of snow or sleet shut things down fast. Earlier today, she'd been thankful to learn the bus company hadn't canceled this trip since the storm wasn't forecast for their route. She'd watched the news last night to be sure. But then, Texas weather was so unpredictable.

"Treat you to a midnight snack?" Ryan asked.

Erica smiled, deciding to make the best of things. "Only if we have separate bills."

As they left the bus, she focused on the electric, red vacancy sign broadcasting its message from the motel's office window "over yonder," as their hillbilly driver had put it. She wished she could afford a room, but with the loss of her job, she should watch her money. Her lease would soon be up on her apartment, and she might have to find a cheaper place to live. Regardless, Erica couldn't let Ryan pay for her meal when they were only strangers.

They sat tucked away in a cozy booth of the warm restaurant. Pictures of cartoon armadillos wearing cowboy hats and toting six-shooters in gun belts covered the gray board wall near their window. The table itself bore an old-fashioned newspaper print décor with headlines about bandits, cattle drives, and cowboys mixed in with ads sporting everything from men's hair tonic to ladies' corsets.

They munched on longhorn cattleburgers and tater sticks, and downed a pot of hot, decaffeinated coffee labeled Thick-as-Mud Brew. Afterward, Erica was surprised when Ryan motioned the grandmotherly waitress over to their table a second time and ordered a batch of chocolate-chip pancakes, also asking Erica if she wanted anything more. Grinning, she shook her head, wondering where Ryan stowed all his food. When the waitress brought his order to the table, Erica couldn't hold back a laugh and noticed amusement flicker in the waitress's eyes, too.

A whipped cream smiley face with white bushy eyebrows decorated the top of the chocolate-dotted stack of four pancakes, and a maraschino cherry nose sat in its middle.

Ryan lifted his eyebrows and looked at the waitress.

She grinned. "Normally, I'd just do it up like the picture on the menu, but I couldn't resist. Since you ordered what the little tykes usually do."

Ryan puckered his mouth, as if holding back a laugh at the joke played on him, and the crease mark in his cheek deepened. "Well, you pegged me right, ma'am. I'm a boy at heart, with an insatiable sweet tooth to match. Got any chocolate syrup to go over these?" His golden-brown eyes gleamed as the smile stretched across his face.

"For you, sugar, anything." The waitress moved away, soon returning with the requested item.

"You know," Erica mused, "staring at that work of art makes me wish I'd learned how to cook. I live off microwave dinners, and any time I have a craving for a sweet, there's a bakery down the street from where I live. Still, it must be nice to be able to just whip up something whenever you feel like it."

Ryan doused his pancake stack in a river of semisweet dark syrup and cut off a big bite with his fork. He soaked it in the sweet liquid pool and, wearing a teasing smile, offered it Erica's way. "Want a sample before I demolish this?"

His manner was friendly, as if she were his kid sister,

nothing more. Yet to Erica the gesture seemed almost intimate, as if they were boyfriend and girlfriend and not merely strangers sharing a bus seat. Heat warmed her cheeks, and she wished she hadn't spoken.

"No, that's okay."

"You sure? I hate to eat all this in front of you." A chocolate dribble slipped from the pancake and hit the table. Another drip looked well on its way to following it.

Deciding it would be better to just take that one bite than make a bigger mess, or draw any unwanted attention their way, Erica leaned on her elbows toward him and snipped the bite off the fork with her teeth. Despite her caution, she felt the syrup coat the skin outside her mouth. Embarrassed, she hastily licked the chocolate away from the corners, then settled back in her seat and blotted her mouth with a napkin, afterward wiping up the spill on the table. Ryan hadn't moved a muscle, only stared at her. His fork, now empty, was still extended.

"Thanks," she managed. "It's good."

Her words seemed to snap him out of whatever trance held him bound, and he dove into his dessert as though he hadn't just eaten a three-course meal. They made small talk about food, the café, and the area, but Erica sensed a peculiar tension now lingering in the air. Ryan paid to have his thermos refilled with hot coffee for the trip, and then, to Erica's dismay, plucked up both bills from the table before she could reach for her purse.

"Ryan, I said—"

"Please," he interrupted, his gaze gentle. "Let me do this for Wes's little sister. As a welcome to Preston Corners?"

"We're not there yet," she countered dryly. His answering smile disarmed her and made her forget the reason she didn't want him to pay for her meal.

After they both took a quick restroom break, Erica pulled the faux fur collar of her wool coat around her ears. Ryan did the same with his jacket, and they braved the bitter cold wind on their hurried trek back to the bus. The disgruntled driver gave them a nod as they boarded but offered nothing by way of communication.

"I'm beginning to think he's a mountain hermit moon-lighting as a bus driver," Erica whispered.

Ryan chuckled but didn't answer.

"So, tell me about yourself," Erica said once they'd settled in their seats. She noticed many chairs throughout the bus were empty, including the row next to theirs, and the rows ahead of them and behind. She and Ryan were sequestered in their own private world, made even more private with the now dim lighting. As though reading her mind, he clicked on the small light overhead.

He turned in his seat until he faced her better. His knees almost brushed hers. Crossing the arm nearest her over his waist, he propped the back of his head against the plastic window shade. "About me, huh? Okay. . . I grew up the only male sibling in a house of five females, all who went through varying degrees of emotional traumas. At different times, of course. Dad was the smart one; he practically lived in his study."

"And I'm sure you were always calm, never once raising your voice or getting emotional?" Erica gave him a mock reproving stare, trying to hold on to the light mood that revisited them.

Still, she couldn't help feeling envy that he'd had a true home and what she detected as a good relationship with his family, despite his teasing words.

"Nope, never," he said with a straight face. "I was a perfect saint."

"Yeah, right. I'd love to hear your sisters' versions."

"You may just get the chance. Most of them still live in Preston Corners."

His reply made her feel awkward, as though he might think she were asking for an invitation to get to know him better. Flustered, she reached for her handbag, unzipped it, and fumbled inside for what she wanted. She pulled out a brush, her makeup bag, and a crumpled wad of lipstick-stained tissues.

"Looking for something?" Ryan asked, clearly amused.

Her fingertips located a thin box. "Be nice, or I might not share." She opened the cardboard flap and tipped a white square into her palm then handed the box to him. "Want one?"

"I'm not sure." Ryan eyed the offering as if it were poison pellets. "What is it?"

"Cyanide gum," she quipped.

"In that case, I'll take one. I haven't had my quota for the day." He popped a square into his mouth with a grin, and she rolled her eyes.

"Actually, it's a gum you chew in place of brushing your teeth."

"Does it work?"

"I don't know, but it better. I almost missed the bus from standing in line to buy it. 'But for white teeth and fresh breath, I'll do anything.'" She mimicked a commercial she'd heard for the gum and gave him a toothpaste ad smile while fluttering her lashes.

The late hour must be getting to her. Or nervousness. Or insanity. Or all three. Aware she was acting ridiculous, she self-consciously tucked her hair behind one ear.

Ryan's grin faded, and the expression in his eyes softened. "You know what, Erica? I think Wes is going to love you."

Unable to sleep, Ryan studied Erica's closed eyes. He remembered how they'd widened at his last words, an hour ago, about Wes loving her. As if fearful that he actually might.

Conversation between them grew stilted after that. Erica went in search of a pillow and blanket, claiming she was tired. Once she'd taken her seat, also bringing back with her a pillow and blanket for him, she turned slightly away with a soft "G'night, Ryan."

Had Erica misinterpreted his words and thought he was making a pass? A better question might be why he felt so comfortable with her, as if he'd known her all his life. Was it because she was Wes's kid sister, and he saw some of his buddy in her?

Looking down at her slightly plump form and the dark crescent of lashes resting against her rosy cheek, Ryan rejected that idea. Except for the fact that they had similar eye color and both had straight hair, she looked little like Wes. And her lips were bowed, not thin. Slightly parted as they were now, they looked entirely too kissable. The second time he'd thought about kissing her. The first time was at the café when she'd eaten the pancake bite and he'd experienced a strong urge to kiss the chocolate from her mouth. That had been a mistake. He shouldn't have offered her a sample, though his intention had only been friendly.

He wrenched his gaze from her face and looked over the darkened bus, listening to snores rumbling through the area, the driver's the loudest. Sleet tapped the windows. Ryan shouldn't have drunk so much coffee, either—another item to add to his list of "shouldn't have dones"—or at least a wise choice would have been to have his thermos filled with decaf.

Hearing a soft whimper, he looked at Erica. A vee had formed between her brows, as if a dream troubled her. She whispered something he couldn't understand. He brought his ear closer to her lips, hoping she'd say it again.

"Mama, don't let them take me. . ."

At the faint gasp of words that bubbled out, something powerful clenched his gut. Before he could question his actions, Ryan shifted his pillow and lifted the armrest. He wrapped a protective arm around Erica's shoulders, gently moving her so that her pillow rested against his side. Then, reaching above, he turned out the light.

Daylight streamed through the window, beckoning Erica awake. She rested against something solid and warm. Opening her eyes, she saw that her pillow was a blue patterned sweater. A blue patterned sweater that moved up and down with each breath of its owner, and something equally solid and warm looped around her upper back.

Gasping, she straightened and looked into Ryan's amused eyes.

"Good morning," he said. "We should be nearing Preston Corners soon."

Her face going hot, Erica pulled away, and he moved his arm from around her. Slowly he pumped it up and down, as if lifting a ten-pound weight, and massaged his elbow, obviously trying to remove the stiffness. To cover her embarrassment, Erica plucked her pillow from the floor and smoothed her tangled hair with her fingers. She couldn't believe she'd ended up cuddled against his side. By the sun's position in the sky, she'd slept for a while. She vaguely remembered waking up for a few blurry moments around dawn, when the motel passengers boarded and the bus started back up, but she'd drifted off to sleep again. Had she lain against Ryan the entire night?

Carmen gave her a knowing smile, flustering Erica all the more. Ryan's words hit her then.

"Did you say we're nearing Preston Corners?"

"In less than an hour, I expect, though we're traveling slower than normal because of the weather. We passed Little Rock not long ago." He smiled. "Welcome to Arkansas."

She swallowed, her gaze going to the window and the hilly terrain with its masses of snow-flocked pine and hardwood trees flying past. Much different than the flatlands of central Texas. Like a whole new world. Had it been a mistake to follow her heart on a whim? Had she acted rashly once again—something Margaret often accused her of doing?

"Anything wrong?" Ryan asked.

She shook her head no, then nodded yes. "What if he

doesn't like me?" she murmured. "What if I'm nothing like he remembers?"

"If my calculations are accurate, you were four and Wes was nine at the time. Besides, what's not to like? I've enjoyed having you as a seatmate, Erica. You're a lot of fun to be with. I've known Wes a long time, and like I told you last night, I'm sure he'll love you."

This time Ryan's encouraging words didn't rattle her. Last night, when he'd said them, she imagined they were coming straight from Ryan's heart and hadn't been about Wes at all. A foolish thought. Why she was drawn to this man on such short acquaintance, she had no idea.

Her gaze went to the winter land scenery flashing by the window. Soon a good chunk of her history would be settled forever. Yet now, Erica wasn't sure she was ready to face it.

# Chapter 3

At the bus depot, Ryan looked for Wes's blue truck and frowned. "I can't understand why he's not here yet. He would've called the bus company to find out the new arrival time."

Erica's gaze flitted to the pavement, around the nearly empty parking lot, then back to him. She seemed agitated. "I didn't expect him to come. I sort of came without telling him."

"He didn't know you were coming?" Ryan asked, incredulous. "The bus originally wasn't scheduled to arrive until three-thirty this morning. What were you planning to do when you got here?"

"I thought I'd just hang around the depot until a decent time, then look him up in the phone book." She shrugged self-consciously. "Look, I jumped into this without thinking ahead, a foolish habit of mine. If you could just tell me where he lives, I'll phone for a taxi."

Ryan shook his head in amused exasperation. "No taxi. You can ride with me. My car's parked in that lot over there. The transmission was acting up, which was one reason I didn't want to risk driving it all the way to Dallas. But it should make it to Wes's house all right."

Uncertainty crossed her features, and Ryan thought he knew the reason. To go with him would pair them alone together for the first time. She only had his word that he was Wes's friend.

"Tell you what. I'll give Wes a call, tell him you're here, and he can verify that I'm not the big bad wolf out to accost pretty girls wearing red coats." He grinned at his Red Riding Hood joke.

She rolled her eyes but nodded for him to go ahead.

He pulled out his cell phone and dialed. Wes wasn't home, but Stacey was. After filling her in, Ryan handed the phone to Erica, who took it with a trembling hand.

"Hello? Yes, I'm Erica," she said in a squeaky voice. She listened awhile, glanced at Ryan, and nodded. "I met him on the bus." A flicker of a smile played with her lips, and she looked away. "No, but he did tell me that he wasn't a wolf. . . . Really. . ." She drawled, then giggled and shot another look Ryan's way.

Just what was Stacey telling her?

"Thanks. I will. I'm looking forward to meeting you, too. You and Wes both. Bye." She handed the cell phone back to him. "She seems nice."

"Yeah, she's great. What'd she say about me?"

She appeared amused. "Just that I'm safe in taking you up on your offer for a ride."

"Is that all she said?"

"All you need to know." Grinning like a kid with a juicy

secret, Erica grabbed her suitcase and overnight bag and moved toward his car.

With a wry smile, Ryan turned off his phone, shut it, and picked up his own suitcase. He was glad she'd relaxed but wished it hadn't been at his expense. Knowing Stacey as he did, he had a feeling a lot more was said about him.

An hour later, Erica willed herself not to start pacing again. Stacey was a regular fireball—and as sweet as they came. After Erica's arrival, she gave Erica a warm hug, then hurried back to the kitchen to finish preparing Wes's lunch. He'd be home from his job at his construction firm any minute. The older kids were at school, so Erica hadn't had a chance to meet them yet, and baby Lance was taking his nap. Ryan thumbed through some books in a walnut built-in bookcase, having stated that he wanted to see Wes's face when his buddy caught sight of Erica. She didn't mind. She preferred having Ryan there. His presence calmed her, at the same time stimulating her in a way she didn't understand. For the past eight years she'd dated on and off, but had never found Mr. Right. Had she met him on a bus?

The sound of wheels crunching up the rocky drive alerted her. Erica clutched the armrests in a death grip, her gaze fastened to the front door. She didn't breathe as boots clomped up the porch and the door swung open, revealing a husky, dark-haired man with a beard.

"Ryan!" he greeted. "I didn't know you were back in town. How was the convention?"

"As conventions go, all right, I suppose. I got back today. And I brought someone with me." Ryan looked at Erica where she sat in a far corner of the room. The newcomer followed suit.

"Hello," he said, his expression curious as he rubbed his whiskered jaw. "So, you're a friend of Ryan's?"

Erica only sat and stared, as if she'd been cast in cement. Yet inside, her emotions exploded like sticks of dynamite.

Ryan put his hand to the newcomer's shoulder. "Wes, surely you recognize your baby sister?" he said quietly.

For a moment Wes only stood there. Then his eyes widened, and he dropped the rolled-up newspaper he held. It fell to the glossy hardwood floor. "Erica?" His voice deepened to a low rumble.

Unable to stand, she managed the briefest of nods. He took a few uncertain steps her way, sudden moisture glistening in his eyes, the same cinnamon color as hers with the same flecks of dark red. "I'm your brother," he said, kneeling on one leg before her. "I'm Wes."

The earnestness on his rugged face, the longing for acceptance answered Erica's own deep need. "I know," she whispered, tears filling her eyes.

They reached for each other at the same time. Softly crying and laughing, brother and sister held to one another tightly, and the wound that came about when they were torn apart as children began slowly to mend.

After dinner, the family and Ryan sat in the living area around a blazing fire. The tenseness of the unknown had eased, and

Erica now felt relaxed.

"If she's Daddy's sister," round-eyed Peggy asked, "what does that make her to me?"

"Our aunt, stupid," Peggy's nine-year-old brother replied. "Same as Aunt Paula."

"I'm not stupid! Just because you're a year older doesn't mean you know everything, Billy Beardsley!" She stuck out her tongue at him.

"Kids," Stacey warned, "if you two don't stop this bickering, you're going to bed. And there's no name-calling in this house, either." Her green gaze pierced her son, who was a miniature of her in looks and coloring, whereas Peggy favored her father and had the same cinnamon-colored eyes. Eight-month-old Lance looked up from a nearby playpen, his hair surprisingly blond and his eyes light brown.

Stacey's gaze sailed to the clock above the mantel, and her brows rose. "Oops, my mistake. It's already past bedtime."

"Aw, Mom," Billy complained, "can't we stay home from school tomorrow, since Aunt Erica came to visit?"

"You'll have plenty of chances to spend time with her. Now, tell everyone good night, and then it's off to bed with both of you."

Two sets of grumbles met her demand, but one stern look from Stacey silenced them. After depositing hugs and kisses to both men, Peggy whispered something in her father's ear. His eyes glistened and he nodded.

Shyly, the girl approached Erica. "Can I hug you good night, too—I mean since you're my new aunt and all?"

Pain shot through the bridge of Erica's nose at the sudden

onslaught of tears. "Of course you can."

Peggy tentatively slipped her arms around Erica but moved away before Erica could reciprocate, as if a sudden case of bashfulness had hit. Billy held out his hand. "I'm too old for all that mushy stuff. Night."

Holding back a laugh, Erica managed as serious a face as Billy's and shook his hand. "Night."

"Hope you have lots of peppermint dreams," Peggy added with a smile.

"Peppermint dreams?" Erica asked.

"That's what I call sweet dreams from God," Peggy explained. "Dreams Jesus gives to make us happy."

After the kids scrambled giggling from the room, Stacey spoke. "Back to Christmas; I'm so sorry you weren't able to contact us." Her gaze flew to Wes, who lay stretched out in an easy chair, his stocking feet propped on the matching ottoman. "But trust my husband to omit necessary information, like our phone number."

He shrugged. "Hey, I was nervous, too. Give a guy a break." He winked conspiratorially at Erica, and she felt a pleasant tingle at the bond they now shared. "I guess I should've called back when we didn't hear from you, but I got to thinking maybe you didn't want to have anything to do with us after all, and I didn't want to push. Just so you know it, Paula's planning to visit again sometime before spring. She's a Realtor in Florida and is married to a pilot. They have six kids, so she won't be able to get away anytime soon. I hope you can stay with us awhile."

"I don't know. My lease *is* almost up on my apartment. I guess I could call Margaret and ask if she would send someone to collect my things. But are you sure I won't get in the way?"

"Never," Wes assured. "We've got a lot of lost years to make up for."

"And we have a nice guest room with its own bath," Stacey inserted. "Consider it yours."

"Thank you." Erica smiled, touched by their kindness. She was glad to be connected to such a family. "Can I ask you a question, Wes?"

"Sure, honey. Ask away."

The endearment warmed Erica. "I've had a disturbing dream since as early on as I can remember. I was wondering if you could enlighten me about any of it." She told them her dream, noticing how sober Wes grew.

"Red Baby," he said gruffly.

"What?" The words sounded familiar, though Erica didn't know why.

"The name of your Raggedy Ann doll. You took it everywhere. Wouldn't part with it. I don't know why they wouldn't let you take it with you that day, unless they couldn't find it. That's what you were crying out for. That and Mama."

"Then my dream really did happen?"

He nodded. "Exactly as you told it."

Silence permeated the room. Erica, now somber, stared into the dancing fire. Her gaze wandered to Ryan's sympathetic one and locked.

Stacey cleared her throat and stood. "Well, those dishes won't wash themselves."

"I'll help." Erica started to rise, but Stacey waved her back down. "No, this is your first day here. I had someone else in mind." She looked directly at her husband.

Wes interlaced his fingers and cupped his hands behind his head. "You could ask Mrs. Warner next door. She's got time on her hands now, with her family out of town and all."

Stacey's eyes narrowed. "Mrs. Warner, huh? I don't know, Erica, he looks mighty comfortable, don't you think?" Stacey's lips twisted in a grin as she grabbed a nearby pillow and flung it at her husband's flat stomach. "To work, O mighty king. Before we ate, you offered to help serve your queen in yonder castle kitchen after the festive banquet—remember?"

Wes groaned. "Actually, I'd forgotten."

"Good thing I've got a great memory then," she replied sweetly. Stacey shot a look between Ryan and Erica then back to her husband, her eyes widening in emphasis. She couldn't have been more obvious if she'd pulled Erica out of her chair and shoved her down on Ryan's lap.

"Oh, all right," Wes grumbled with a soft wink at Erica as he followed his wife to the kitchen. "A monarch's work is never done."

An uneasy silence filled the room, broken only by baby Lance's gurgling conversation with a stuffed giraffe in his playpen.

"Mommy!" A call came from the hall. "Are you coming to tuck us in?"

"In a minute, sweetie," Stacey's voice sailed from the kitchen, and she giggled. "Wes, stop that!"

Ryan abruptly stood. "Well, it's back to the old grindstone for me tomorrow. Tell Wes and Stacey I had to leave, would you? I'll let myself out."

"Sure. Good night." Erica wondered if she should walk him to the door anyway. Would he try to kiss her if she did? Somehow, she doubted it. Except for yesterday when he'd taken her hand for a few, brief seconds—and later, when she'd fallen asleep all over him—Ryan had kept his distance and hadn't touched her. Maybe Erica was reading more into the situation than was there.

The thought discouraged her. Was she falling for him?

# Chapter 4

Erica cut another heart from the red foil to glue on the poster that would hang in the children's hospital playroom. She'd been at Preston Corners almost four weeks now, each day bringing her closer to her new family. The one bee in her honey had to do with Ryan.

Though he'd come over on Monday nights to watch football with Wes and on Sundays to eat dinner with the family, he'd never once asked her out. Erica knew she hadn't imagined the interested look in his eyes when she'd caught him watching her—many times. Nor his embarrassed flush and uneasy grin before he turned away.

"Stacey, what's wrong with me?" Erica tossed the scissors aside.

Stacey quit sprinkling silver tinsel bits on the glue covering some pink construction paper. "Wrong with you? There's nothing wrong with you. You're a born artist, and these decorations are sure to make every child at the hospital smile. I like the goofy faces you drew on the heart people."

"I'm not talking about this." Erica waved a hand over the

214

kitchen table covered with craft supplies. "I'm talking about Ryan."

"Ahh," Stacey said and nodded sagely. "Let me guess. He hasn't made a move yet?"

Erica fidgeted. "That sounds as if I *expect* him to think of me as more than a friend." She frowned. "But what else am I to assume? He comes over all the time, and we talk. A lot. He acts interested in me, and I've caught him watching me a number of times."

"Want big brother Wes to ask his intentions?" Stacey lifted her brows in a teasing way.

Erica blew out a frustrated breath. "Thanks a lot, Stacey." She didn't need banter right now. She needed advice.

Stacey dusted off her hands, producing a shower of shiny silver particles that floated to the table. "Okay, all kidding aside. Remember what I told you on the phone the day Ryan brought you here? That he could in no way be classified as a wolf, and a more apt description would be a meek lamb?"

"Yes, but I thought you were joking."

"Well, to a certain degree I was. But it's a known fact that Ryan's never made the first move when it comes to women, though it wasn't always like that. In the conversational department, he's in his element. When it comes to anything else, he backs off. Fast. After his junior year in high school he quit dating, though I'm not sure why. Believe me, Erica, you're not the first woman I've heard complaints from."

"He's had a lot of admirers, huh?"

"Scads. With a face and body like that, and the fact that he's a lovable ex-jock with a sympathetic heart and a penchant for listening to problems—for listening at all, for that matter—is it any wonder?"

"I suppose not." Erica concentrated on cutting another heart from shiny paper, determined not to let Stacey's revelation upset her. "So he's Mr. Perfect. Like in that old Milton Bradley Mystery Date Game where you open the door, hoping to get the smiling guy in the tux?"

Stacey laughed. "Hardly! I've known Ryan as long as I've known Wes. He's a dear, but his place is a wreck. Takeout containers all over the room, discarded clothes slung over chairs. He makes an effort to do a quick cleanup when company calls, but it's obvious he doesn't live that way. He needs a woman to pick up after him. His sisters cleaned up his messes while he was growing up. Didn't do him any good, if you ask me."

"I've heard bachelors can be messy," Erica defended him.

"Maybe, but there's more. Sometimes his discussions on psychology can be about as effective as going under anesthesia. Really mind-numbing."

Erica didn't think they were all that bad, and she'd heard a number of them.

"Basically all I'm saying, Erica, is if a woman weighs the good with the bad and finds she's willing to put up with all of it, then she's also going to have to be willing to make the first move."

"The first move?" Erica had no experience in that area. Her dates had been simple, usually ending with a kiss at her front door. But she'd never initiated any of them.

"Yep," Stacey said with a decisive nod. "The first move."

Troubled, Erica lowered her gaze to the table. She noticed a piece of paper lying atop a stack of magazines. A Web site was scrawled underneath the caption "The Lion Cooks."

"What's this?" she asked.

"Hmm?" Stacey looked up from spreading more glue on construction paper. "Oh, an online cooking course I thought about taking. It offers dessert-making classes. I˙can't now, of course. Not since they called me back to work at the hospital because Janine is going on maternity leave. The drive there is one hour both ways. I won't have any extra time for cooking classes. But I'm glad the adoption finally went through for Janine. She's waited a long time for that baby."

Erica hoped the unknown Janine treated her child with more love and kindness than Erica had received from her adoptive parents. She fingered the paper, and her mind returned to the Ryan situation. How hard could it be to learn to bake and whip up a few scrumptious desserts with which to tempt him? Margaret had never allowed Erica in the kitchen during her childhood, claiming she didn't want her to make any messes. Yet at the memory of how enthusiastically Ryan devoured the chocolate-chip pancakes at the restaurant, Erica was ready to give baking a try. Maybe this could be considered a "first move."

"Mind if I sign up for the course?"

"Be my guest." Stacey smiled. "My great-granny always said, 'A way to a man's heart is down his gullet and through his belly.' And Ryan has a big sweet tooth."

Erica smiled at how well Stacey read her true intentions.

"Auntie Erica? Are you sure you're s'posed to put that in there?" Peggy's voice was doubtful. "That's not what Mommy uses when she makes cookies."

Drawing her brows together, Erica studied the empty can in her hand, then gave the child a confident smile. "My online cooking instructor said it's okay to substitute ingredients we don't have. So I don't see why not."

Erica felt more at ease with her new family every day, but not enough so that she was going to ask them to buy the required ingredients for her homework recipes. With no car at her disposal, a solo trip to the supermarket was out of the question, as well. Anything she needed and didn't have she would locate an adequate substitute for, since Stacey had given her free rein in the kitchen. Erica's high school teachers once labeled her "creative." Now was the time to put some of that creativity to use.

She hesitated, feeling as if she'd forgotten something. Had she put in salt? Oh, well. A little more wouldn't hurt, even if she had. Ryan liked things salty, too—like chocolate-covered pretzels. But where was the teaspoon she'd used?

She looked all over the counter. No measuring spoon. Nor did it show up in the silverware drawer. Which must mean that she hadn't used the salt yet. Cupping her palm, she studied its middle. That seemed about right for a teaspoon-sized amount. She poured the white grains into her hand and tossed them onto the dough in the bowl.

Noting Peggy's uncertain expression, Erica smiled. "It'll be fine. Wanna stir?"

Eagerly Peggy nodded and reached for the wooden spoon. After a number of rotations with the utensil, she relinquished the blue ceramic bowl to Erica, who scraped the lumpy batter into miniature mounds on a greased cookie sheet and slid it onto the top rack of a preheated oven. Erica couldn't help noticing that Peggy didn't ask to lick the spoon or the bowl. Wasn't that the first thing kids usually wanted to do?

A few minutes later, Billy sauntered into the room, a St. Louis Cardinals baseball cap on his head. "Yuck! What's that smell?"

Erica frowned. Obviously the kid didn't like oatmeal. "I'm baking cookies. Don't worry, you don't have to eat any."

"Good!" The boy grabbed a baseball mitt from the counter and a ball, tossing it in the air as he headed out the back door.

Peggy tugged on Erica's sleeve. "Billy's just mad 'cause he got in trouble today at school and has detention tomorrow."

Erica smiled. "I'm not upset. Not everyone likes the same things. And that'll leave more cookies for us to enjoy."

Peggy wrinkled her brow, as though she wasn't so sure, then walked over to pick up her doll that was sitting in the chair "watching" them. "Will you play house with me?" she asked.

"Later, okay? I don't want to risk the chance of me not hearing the timer and having these burn." Erica looked at the rag doll. "You know. . .I used to have a doll something like that when I was a little girl."

"What happened to her?"

Erica stared at the painted cloth face a moment, feeling uneasy, as if an old unwanted memory were trying hard to resurface. Hurriedly she looked away and stared through the oven window at the baking lumps of dough. "I don't know." Her voice came out hoarse.

Peggy was quiet for so long that Erica looked over her

shoulder. The child had left the kitchen, leaving Erica to her thoughts. She wasn't ready to face the details of her past, whatever they might reveal, and forced herself to think of something more pleasant—like the pleased, adoring look that was sure to be on Ryan's face when he tasted the cookies she'd spent an hour making for him.

The doorbell rang, and she smiled.

# Chapter 5

R yan—what's wrong?" Erica leaned across the table. "Are you okay?"

The most peculiar look was on his face, as if he'd been frozen in time. His eyes had widened, and he slowly chewed the large bite of cookie in his mouth as if it were concrete and not crumbs.

"Nothing," he mumbled between slow chews, barely moving his lips as he spoke. "Can I, uh, have some water?"

"Sure."

Erica retrieved a small tumbler, filled it, and handed it to him. He slugged it down like a man who'd just spent a week traveling through the desert and had come to his first oasis.

"Is anything wrong?" she asked when he lowered the cup.

"No, everything's fine." His voice still came out raspy. He set the rest of his cookie on a napkin, walked over to the sink, refilled the glass, drank it down, and refilled it again. "Uh, Erica, what kind of nuts did you use?"

"The recipe called for walnuts, but we didn't have any. I read it was okay to substitute pecans, but we didn't have any of those, either. So I, um, used peanuts."

"Ahh. Salted ones?"

She nodded. "I figured with oatmeal it would work, and you do like salty foods, right?"

He gave her a strange look. "Sometimes." He drank down the rest of the water.

Erica studied her hands clasped on the table. Maybe she *had* put in too much salt. The teaspoon she'd used had been found on the floor earlier, hidden by the throw rug partially covering it. And the peanuts probably made the cookies even worse.

"Feel like going to the Dairy Drizzle?" Ryan set the empty cup on the counter. "We could drive down for a couple of large chocolate shakes. My treat."

"In the wintertime?"

He grinned. "That's the best time of year for ice cream desserts."

The man had just downed three glasses of water and was still thirsty for a shake? Those cookies must have really been bad!

Erica gave him the best good sportsmanlike smile she could muster. "Make mine a hot chocolate, and I'm with you 100 percent."

Once outside, Erica took a deep breath of the bracing air. It sparked a feeling of playfulness in her. "Let's walk. It's only two blocks."

Ryan agreed. They moved along the wet sidewalk, which had been brushed free of the powdery snow that dusted the ground. The setting sun was magenta-pink, glowing like a tropical disk that just touched the uppermost tips of the greenish-black pines. Layers of rose-tinged, ivory clouds moved in long, gentle waves around and below the neon sun. To Erica, it looked as if a foretaste of summer filled the sky, while the earth stubbornly retained winter. Just ahead, the forested Ozarks produced a picturesque backdrop, and a church steeple could clearly be seen nestled midway up the snowy hill.

"I love this place," she enthused, her breath misting in the cool air. "It's so small-town Americana, like a Norman Rockwell painting. It's as if time passed by this small corner of the world and left it ageless."

Ryan looked up at the wooded mountains. "We've gone so far as to put a computer in the library, but in many respects, Preston Corners hasn't changed all that much in fifty years. You should have been here for the tree-lighting ceremony at Christmas. It's a big event the whole town turns out for, and the mayor awards the honors of pulling the switch to the most outstanding citizen of the year. This past December, the privilege was given to sixteen-year-old Twila Miller, for saving a child she was babysitting from his burning home."

"Have you ever been given the honors?"

"Once." He seemed embarrassed to say it.

Smiling wide, Erica tugged at her furry coat collar, bringing the edges together. She closed her eyes, absorbing the scent and feel of her surroundings. "I wish I could've seen it. In fact, I wish I could stay in Preston Corners forever."

"You like it that much?"

"Oh, yes! I've lived in many states, but here. . .well, I feel like I've come home."

"Maybe you should stay then."

Ryan's quiet words startled her, and she spun to face him.

The snow muffled sound, making it easy to hear a voice, even one spoken in low tones. But she'd heard his words clearly enough, whether he'd meant them to be heard or not.

"Do you want me to stay, Ryan?"

He shoved his hands into his jacket pockets. "Sure, if that's what you want."

They were alone on the sidewalk, no neighbors in sight. Feeling suddenly daring but a little anxious, too, Erica closed the distance between them until she was within touching distance. "But what do you want?" she insisted softly.

"Whatever you want." He looked beyond her, avoiding her eyes.

Clamping a tight lid over her fear of being rejected, Erica spoke. "Well then, if you really mean that, what I want is for you to stop treating me like I'm nothing more than Wes's kid sister—when I think what you really want is to kiss me as much as I want you to."

Sudden flames burned within his eyes, rivaling the heat she felt in her face at blurting the bold words. Yet after weeks of his coming around to see her, and not always Wes, what was Erica to think? Especially considering the longing in his eyes when she'd caught him looking at her, time and again.

"So now you're playing counselor?" His voice sounded as if he needed to clear it.

She'd already stepped over the line of embarrassment. Might as well rush all the way in and hope she wasn't acting too much the fool. "I'm just telling you how I feel, Ryan. I think you like me as much as I like you. But for some reason you don't want to admit it."

He inhaled a swift breath, and she wondered if she'd made a mistake. What if she'd misread his actions?

An eternal moment stretched between them. Just when Erica was ready to escape back to the house, he gently brushed his gloved fingertips across her jaw, pushing back a thin strand of long hair that had connected with the corner of her mouth.

"I do like you, Erica. But let's take this slow and easy. Please?"

How slow was slow? And easy? Patience was never an easy virtue for Erica, but she nodded, trying to understand his point of view. Okay, maybe she *was* trying to push things between them too fast. She'd never had any real and lasting relationships with either her adoptive parents or her few former boyfriends. Maybe her desire to experience the joy of a truly loving relationship spurred her into jumping in the middle of love's shining sea, when she should just carefully wade out through its shallow waters. The waters beyond could be tumultuous if one wasn't prepared—hadn't her school chums told her that? She didn't want an icy and unexpected wave to overtake her before she could get a grip on her life or her feelings. She wanted the waters to ease around her, warm and inviting, like being immersed in the hot springs up to her neck.

Wes and Stacy had taken her for a daylong trip to the hot springs weeks ago, and Erica loved them. That's what she wanted her experience with Ryan to be like—a love that was warm, tender, and soothing, like the springs. But one that was bubbling up, effervescent, and alive, too! Until then, she would just have to be patient. Too bad they didn't offer a course on patience online, like they did cooking classes.

"How about we get that hot chocolate?" Ryan asked, breaking Erica from her thoughts. He held out his hand for her to take.

Confused, Erica studied him, caught his faint smile, then returned it and clasped his gloved hand. "You're on."

The lighthearted mood back, they strolled down the sidewalk. Feeling silly, Erica swung their clenched hands between them in exaggerated arcs as if they were two young kids, until she had him laughing and they were both bantering again.

Later that night, once Ryan left, Erica jotted an e-mail to Cynthia, her online cooking instructor.

> *I blew it, Teacher—I really blew it. I don't think I'm cut out to be another Sara Lee or Betty Crocker. Just call me Butterfingers—or better yet—The Cookie Cremator. This "substitute queen" really blew it.*

She went on to type out all that happened then sent the post. She was surprised when the computer bell dinged not five minutes later, telling her she had mail. It was from Cynthia.

> *Erica,*
>     *First rule of baking, and one that will save you a great deal of embarrassment in the future: always sample your creations before serving them to guests.*

Erica felt the blush heat her face. She should have known

better. Ryan had walked into the kitchen at the same time the cookies came out of the oven, and Erica was so excited about her treat for him, she'd offered them without taste-testing first. She read the remainder of the post.

> *Don't feel bad. Every cook—especially one so new to baking as yourself—has her moments. I could tell you of a few embarrassing mistakes that I made when I first started, like the time I lifted the beaters while the mixer was still going. But I better not say more, lest you lose respect for your teacher. And I do understand your reasons for needing to substitute, but try not to do too much of that if you possibly can. If you're unsure about the suitability of your substitute, please contact me. I would be more than happy to help or offer any suggestions I can.*
>
> *Happy cooking! (And it will get better. I promise.)*
> *Cynthia Lyons*

Erica smiled. The woman was such an encourager. Maybe Erica would make it through this course, if not with flying colors, then with crawling ones. She groaned at her lame joke and punched out a reply to Cynthia.

# Chapter 6

Hearing a knock at the door, Ryan pushed the mute button on the TV remote and went to answer. "Wes," he said with some surprise when he saw his visitor, whom he'd seen only that morning. "Everything okay?"

Wes walked into Ryan's apartment, hands in his jacket pockets, and eyed the place as if he'd never seen it before. Ryan moved to pick up his jacket that he'd tossed over the chair and shoved his shoes under the coffee table with his socked foot. Empty, food-speckled cardboard containers from Ming-Lee's Chinese Restaurant were strewn over the coffee table from dinner, and he swiped them together, walking with his armload to the kitchen trash.

"What's up?" he asked once he returned. Wes still hadn't taken the seat Ryan cleared for him. Ryan looked at the brown vinyl cushion to make sure nothing else was there. He was no housekeeper, as all his friends knew, and generally picked up around the apartment once a week since he was rarely home. His sisters jokingly called him a hopeless slob, but he didn't think he was as bad as all that.

"I need to talk with you about Erica." Wes remained standing a few feet inside the door. He seemed uncomfortable, and Ryan thought he understood. Wes must need counseling. Maybe things between him and his newfound sister weren't as smooth sailing as Ryan had assumed from seeing them together these past weeks.

Ryan adopted his understanding, counselor expression. "Come on in the rest of the way and sit down." He reclaimed his sunken spot on the vinyl couch.

Wes finally moved and took a seat on the matching chair. He leaned forward, elbows on his knees. "You've been over to see Erica a lot lately."

"Yeah?" Taken aback, Ryan copied Wes's sitting position, waiting to see where this conversation was going.

Wes compressed his mouth. "I'm just wondering where all this is leading and what you've got in mind."

In disbelief, Ryan stared at his old friend some seconds before he answered. "Let me get this straight. You're asking me what my intentions are toward your sister?"

"That about sums it up."

"Wes, this is me you're talking to. Your best buddy from high school." Ryan tried to remain calm, though he felt justifiably upset. "We've known each other since we were in Little League together. We go to the same church, and for the past five years, I've come to your house every Sunday to eat dinner with your family. And now you're telling me that you don't *trust* me?"

"It's not that I don't trust you." Wes began to bounce one leg in his nervousness. "It's just that I care about Erica. Stacey said she's uncertain about everything right now and is trying so hard to fit in with our family. I feel sorry for the poor kid. I know she's scared to face the past. Whenever I bring it up, she cuts me off and changes the subject." A trace of a smile lifted his thin lips. "She's trying hard to please you, too, what with those awful desserts she makes. No one wants to hurt her feelings and tell her she's no cook. So we force the food down anyway. But she does it all—the cookies, the pastries, the pies—for you. Stacey told me that's the only reason Erica enrolled in the cooking class. To please you."

Ryan squirmed. He hadn't known that. He remembered the tart, stringy rhubarb concoction that followed last Sunday's meal and his polite comment that he was too full, after taking the first awful bite that made his lips pucker. In the future, he resolved to be a more gracious guest. Even if he had to get his stomach pumped afterward, he didn't want to hurt Erica's feelings.

"Normally I wouldn't have told you and risk embarrassing Erica should she find out. But I don't want her hurt, Ryan. You haven't exactly dated anyone since high school, so your sudden interest in Erica has caused Stacey concern. I confess, I'm at a loss, too. You were a regular Fonz in our sophomore and junior year, dating a different girl every weekend. The sudden switcheroo from wildly popular with the chicks to sworn off them for good confused me."

Ryan's face heated. He didn't like to be reminded of his past. "So what you're saying, basically, is that for you to see me with Erica sets off all sorts of mental alarms because you think I may have resorted to my old ways? The big bad wolf's waiting for his chance to gobble up your little sister?" Ryan was unable to keep the bitter sarcasm from his voice. Again, he forced himself to maintain self-control. After all, Wes didn't know the entire story. Ryan never told him.

"Wes, I'm a practicing Christian now. I wasn't then. I'm also a high school counselor and need to keep my reputation squeaky clean. If I didn't abide by what I tell those kids, then I wouldn't be much of an example, would I?"

Wes placed his palms on his knees and stood, evidently tense. "I know all that, but you're confusing Erica. Stacey's had a number of talks with her, and Erica doesn't know how you feel about her or even where the relationship is going, if there is one. Her words, not mine."

"So what do you want me to do about it?"

"Tell her."

The answer was so obvious Ryan should have figured it out himself. Yet to tell Erica would mean to break a confidence, to share a secret. And the only way he would do that was to seek permission first, obtained through a long-distance phone call. The thought made him suddenly tired.

"You're right. I should've said something long ago."

Wes chuckled, and Ryan looked up from staring at the faded ring on the coffee table. "What's so funny?" Humor escaped him at the moment.

"I do believe this is the first time I've ever counseled you, old buddy."

Ryan grinned. "Even counselors need advice sometimes."

"No hard feelings?"

"None taken."

"Good." Wes moved to the door and put his hand on the knob. He looked over his shoulder. "See you at dinner Sunday?"

"Not this time around. I need to take care of some things."

"I understand."

Once Wes left, Ryan sank back into the cushions and stared at the ceiling. It would be better for Erica if he made himself absent for a while. He enjoyed her company, but after learning what he had, he didn't feel right about continuing his visits. She evidently wanted them to be more than friends, and Ryan couldn't allow that to happen.

Erica moved through the small crowd flocking the bake sale tables of the church cafeteria and spotted Stacey. "Have you seen Ryan?"

"No." Stacey's gaze fell to the plate of brownies in Erica's hand. "Just find any old spot to put those down."

"Oh, these aren't for the sale. The ones I made for the fund-raiser are over there already. I put these aside for Ryan."

Stacey's brow wrinkled. "Erica, Wes and I think there's something you should know. . . ."

Erica looked past her, catching sight of a tall auburn-haired man in a beige polo shirt near the glass doors. "There he is. Sorry, Stacey, but I need to catch him before he leaves." She weaved through the hungry buyers and hurried out the door, catching up to Ryan on the sidewalk.

"Oh—hey, Erica."

Wasn't he glad to see her? He seemed tense. "Are you coming over for dinner?" she asked. "I haven't seen you in weeks."

"I suppose I could. I do need to talk to you about something. Or we could talk now."

"Now's not a good time." If they talked now, he wouldn't come for dinner, Erica somehow knew. "I should go collect the kids from children's church. Stacey has her hands full with the bake sale. So, I'll see you later." She gave him a bright smile and hurried away, then realized she still held his plate of brownies. She would just give them to him after dinner.

The next few hours plodded by for Erica, but Ryan did come to dinner. He was quieter than usual, though he laughed at Billy's corny jokes and gave the proper amount of interested admiration to the new dress on the doll Peggy shoved toward his face. After the dishes were cleared away, the family scattered, leaving Erica and Ryan alone. Sure their absence was intentional, Erica suddenly felt nervous. Quickly, she retrieved the plate of brownies from the counter and set it in front of him.

"I made these for you," she explained.

He looked at the dark squares beneath the pink cellophane for so long Erica wondered if he'd heard her. Finally, he lifted a corner of the plastic wrap and picked up the smallest brownie. Substitutions had been necessary again, but this time Erica was pleased with the results.

Ryan took a nibble and chewed. Surprise lifted his eyebrows, and he took a much bigger bite. "These are all right." He sounded as if he didn't quite believe it.

"Oh, I'm so glad you think so!" Erica smiled in relief. "I had to substitute again. We didn't have vegetable oil, so one of the girls in my online cooking class told me that applesauce works just as well."

Ryan took another bite and stared at the brownie as if puzzled. He sniffled softly, as though his nose was starting to run. "It doesn't have any apple taste to it. But it does have a flavor that's unique."

"That's probably the carrots."

"Carrots?" Slowly, Ryan lowered the brownie. He sniffled again, harder this time.

"Stacey didn't have applesauce, either—the baby ate it all. And since this recipe was for an assignment, I had to bake it this week. So, because Lance's baby food is like the consistency of applesauce, I figured a jar of carrots would work just as good. Carrot cake is delicious, so I thought it would work okay. . . ." Her words trailed off, uncertain.

The strangest expression came over his face. "It did work, except for one thing. I'm allergic to carrots."

"Allergic?" Years ago, a former classmate of Erica's had been rushed to the emergency room because of a severe reaction to shellfish. Erica knew food allergies were nothing to tamper with. "Oh, Ryan, I'm so sorry! Do you need me to take you to the hospital?"

"No, I'm okay." He pushed the plate of brownies far from him, as if even being near the dark squares could make it worse. "The reactions I've had have never been severe. Just annoying."

His voice sounded funny, as if his nasal passages or throat were getting clogged. Were his eyes watering?

"Maybe if you drank some water it would help? And if you went outside, maybe the fresh air would help clear your sinuses?"

"Maybe." Ryan rose from the table to fill a glass with

water. He drank it down and refilled it two more times.

Spring warmed the days, though it was still cool enough for a sweater. Erica excused herself to grab one, then joined Ryan in the spacious backyard. An abundance of green-leafed oaks, maples, and gum trees filled the surrounding area. Instead of a fence, a high row of bushes acted as a boundary line all around. Ryan stuck his hands in his pockets and moved across the grass. Erica walked beside him.

"Have you decided what you're going to do yet?" Ryan asked. "About living here?"

At least he sounded a little better. "I thought, for now, I might apply at Jewel's Mini-mart. They're looking for a cashier."

"Then you've decided to move to Preston Corners?"

"Yes. Wes and Stacey want me to, and I do, too. When I'm ready to dig deeper into the past, if I'm ever ready, I want them nearby. It'll only take a week or so to make arrangements to move my things here. When I can afford it, I saw the most darling apartment complex near Wes's." She looked at him and gasped. "Oh, no!"

"What's wrong?"

"Your face!" She stood within a foot of where he was standing and reached out to touch his jaw. "You've got a patch of little pink bumps on your cheek."

"A rash," he said weakly and lifted his fingers to scratch it. "Sometimes it happens when I accidentally ingest carrots or any member of the parsley family. Avocados, too."

"You don't know how sorry I am about all this." Before she could think twice, Erica moved to place a sympathetic kiss on the unaffected area at the corner of his mouth near the growing rash. She felt him startle, but otherwise he didn't move. She pulled back to look at him. "Forgive me for poisoning you?"

"Erica, that's a little harsh. Besides, there's nothing to forgive. You didn't know."

They were standing so close she had to tip her head back to see his face. She lifted her hand to his opposite cheek. "At least this side's okay," she whispered.

"That's good." His reply came low. They stared at each other a long moment before his head began to lower. At the brush of his lips across hers, her heart jumped. As he allowed them to linger, an electric-like warmth tingled through her. Suddenly he jerked back, as if the physical contact now alarmed him.

"Ryan?" She felt confused. "What's wrong?"

"Nothing's wrong." His voice sounded angry as he moved a short distance away.

Feeling duly rebuffed, she snapped, "So it's me you don't like? I'm sorry. I guess I had it all wrong."

"I do like you, Erica—too much. That's the problem. And please stop saying you're sorry." He briskly rubbed his pink cheek with his fingertips.

"Maybe you should go put something on that," Erica suggested, pity taking the sharp edge off her anger. She felt bad for her outburst. Anyone suffering as he was wouldn't have kissing on his mind.

"It can wait. There's something I need to say." He stood, uneasy, as if trying to figure out how to begin. "My sister got pregnant when she was a senior in high school. It was a secret closely guarded by our family, even in this small town. Wes didn't even know about it."

Erica drew her brows together. So why was he telling her?

"She moved to the city to stay with friends of my mom's until the baby came. Then she gave her away in an open adoption. Once Susan returned home, her boyfriend—a guy I'd idolized—didn't want anything to do with her, so she tried to commit suicide. My parents put her in a mental hospital a hundred miles away and told everyone she was off visiting relatives. My sister screwed up her life in more ways than one, though I could never call Taylor a mess. She's in high school missions now. Her adoptive family sends Susan pictures each birthday and keeps her informed, which is how I know all that."

Erica frowned during Ryan's awkward spiel. So Ryan's sister had given away her daughter, too, though the circumstances were much different than Erica's. Still, Erica didn't understand what this had to do with the present. "Why are you telling me this, Ryan?"

He shoved his hands in his pockets and studied the bushes nearby. "When Susan snapped and I saw the bandages on her wrists, I swore I'd never end up in a situation like hers. I'm ashamed to admit it, but I treated the girls I dated in high school just as badly as Susan's boyfriend treated her. Using them to get what I wanted and not giving any thought to what could happen next. When I thought my sister was going to die, and I saw how badly her heart was broken over the jerk, I wondered how many girls I might have hurt, too. I became a Christian during that time, and I vowed to myself and to God that I'd never date again. That I would wait until He shows me who to marry, if I'm to marry." He looked at her again. "I was wrong to have kissed you, Erica. I don't want to complicate things between us."

"There's no need to make a federal case of it, Ryan. It was just a simple kiss."

His eyes were sober. "Was it?"

So he had felt the connection, too. Yet she was determined not to let him see how he'd hurt her. "Why didn't you tell me this before today?"

"I had to call Susan and get permission to tell her story. She's happily married now and living in Tennessee, but she's not at home much and is hard to get ahold of."

"But—when you told me that you wanted to take it slow and easy. . ."

"You're right. I shouldn't have put it like that." He sneezed.

She looked at his jaw and frowned. "The rash is spreading. You really should go take care of it."

"I need to get home anyway. I'll put something on it then and take some antihistamines, too. But before I go, please tell me things are still okay between us. I never meant to hurt you, and I certainly never meant to lead you on."

"I know. The fault's as much mine as it is yours. I shouldn't have jumped to conclusions."

Erica smiled through her disappointment. Yet she couldn't help envying the unknown woman Ryan would one day marry.

# Chapter 7

R yan pulled his car into Wes's drive, noticing Erica peek out the window then quickly draw back. He couldn't blame her for not wanting to see him. Not after last week.

When he was a teenager, it had been difficult to keep his self-made vow to God. As the years progressed and any temptation arose, he learned to take it to the Lord in prayer and forget about it. Until this past January, when he'd met Erica on the bus, he'd been successful. Now Erica taunted his thoughts daily. Nor had he been able to get their sweet kiss erased from his memory bank.

Ryan left the car and knocked on the front door. "Hey," he said, when she opened it a short time later.

"Hey back." Her words sounded uncertain. Obviously she wondered what he was doing there.

"Ready to go?"

Surprise touched her eyes. "You're coming with us?"

"Actually, I'm taking you. Wes couldn't get off work, so I offered."

"Oh." She hesitated before sending a wisp of a smile his way. "Then I guess I'm ready."

Ryan wished there were something he could say or do to smooth things between them, but it was probably best to say nothing. Hopefully, any tension would ease up soon.

The forty-five-minute drive passed with little said. Using Wes's directions, Ryan found the place and pulled into a clearing in the woods. An abandoned cabin stood there. Erica clutched the door handle, though she made no attempt to get out.

"It's just like I remember in my dream," she said, her voice faint. "When Wes told me our old cabin wasn't far, I knew I had to come. To see for myself. I thought I was ready for this. . .now I'm not so sure."

"You going to be okay?" Ryan asked, noticing how she had paled.

She gave a faint nod. "I had the ministry team pray with me Sunday. For courage to face whatever I might find and for God to help me put any missing pieces together."

"Then He will."

She sucked in her lower lip, her doubtful gaze still on the ramshackle building.

He reached over to squeeze her hand. "Sometimes we have to confront our pasts to be able to go on in the present and live fulfilling lives. But remember, Erica, it's only the past. It can't hurt you. Not unless you let it."

"I know." She took a deep breath and held it. "I never told anyone this, but I had a friend in fourth grade. Before we moved, I used to pretend her parents were mine. . .that when her mother baked cookies, it was for me—her little girl. And when her father played softball with us, that he was my daddy, too. I even called them by those names, though I sensed it made them uncomfortable."

Raw pain filled the eyes she turned his way. "Margaret and Darrin never loved me. They adopted me to do a good deed and be elevated in their social circle of the community. Oh, they saw to every material need I had. I went to elite private schools and had the best education money could buy. The nicest clothes, a roomful of expensive toys—everything a child could possibly want. At least that's what I was told often enough." Her words were mocking, bitter.

Before Ryan could respond, Erica wrenched open the door and got out. He followed suit, coming around to her side of the car. She turned tormented eyes his way.

"Why'd she do it, Ryan? Why'd she sign away her own children?"

"I thought Wes told you—"

Erica gave an impatient wave of her hand. "Oh, yeah, sure. He told me that when he found her years ago, she told him she did drugs. I know all that. But it doesn't excuse the fact that my mama gave us away to strangers! Like unwanted secondhand shoes!"

Erica rushed toward the porch. Before reaching it, she picked up a good-sized rock and hurled it at the cabin. Thankfully, her aim wasn't the greatest. It just missed the window. Ryan hurried to stop her before she could try again.

"Erica, listen! You have every right to be angry—I understand. Believe me, I do. But this isn't the way to deal with your anger."

"Take your hand off my arm, Ryan," she seethed between her teeth. "I want to break every window in that horrible place, then watch it burn to the ground!"

She struggled to get away. He wasn't getting through to her, so he did the only thing he knew to do, the only thing he wanted. He drew her close and held her tightly. At first she fought—hard. Finally, when she saw she wasn't getting anywhere, she wilted against him. Her agonized sobs pierced the air, making painful stabs at his heart.

"Shh, it's okay," he murmured, planting a few kisses atop her head until she stilled. He pulled back, wishing he had a handkerchief. With his thumbs he wiped away her tears. "Feel any better?"

She shrugged.

"Let's sit down." Once they settled on the top porch step, he looked at her. "I know that right now all you feel is the pain. But, Erica, deep down I think your mama loved you."

"Yeah, right." She grew rigid, but he put up a hand to stop the rest of her terse words.

"Let me finish. She told Wes that on one occasion—when she woke from her drug stupor and realized two days had passed—that during that time anything could've happened to you and the others without her knowledge. She realized then that she wasn't fit to raise you. She thought she could get over her drug habit the first time someone called social services. But after two years and countless failures she gave up and signed the papers."

Erica's hands on her lap tightened into fists. He didn't know if it would do much good to continue, or even what he could say to get through her self-made blockade. But he tried again. "I think she must have felt what Moses' mother felt when she put him in that reed basket and sent him down the Nile for his own good. Like Moses' mother, your mother knew that life with her was dangerous to her children. She made the ultimate sacrifice, Erica. For you."

"Sure she did." Erica compressed her lips and blinked, as if trying to keep more tears at bay. "I wish I could believe that. I really, really do. But I can't." She shot to her feet and wandered down the porch steps to the periphery of tall pines circling the mountain cabin.

Ryan longed to know what was on her mind. *Please, God,* he sent up a silent prayer. *Show her what it is that she so desperately wants to know, and reassure her as only You know how.*

After a time of walking near the fringe of trees, Erica retraced her steps to the house. Before turning at the south corner, she looked at Ryan, as if about to say something, then stopped. Her brows came together, and she lowered her gaze to the bottom of the porch. All of a sudden, she fell to her knees on the grass and dropped down on all fours.

"Erica?" Puzzled, Ryan moved her way. When he reached her, she had wriggled halfway under the crawl space of the porch, only her jean-clad legs showing.

"Oh! It's here. Oh, Ryan. . ."

She backed out, holding a misshapen grayish clump of material with a scrap of faded red around its middle. One black button eye remained, the painted smile from the circular doll face barely discernible. Only a few pinkish-white pieces of yarn were still attached to the cloth head.

"Red Baby." She said the name as if it were a coveted treasure she held and not a mildewed scrap of rags. Sitting back on her legs, she brought it to her chest and stared at the trees, her eyes going distant. The gentle breeze played with her long hair, lifting the top strands as if in a caress. Suddenly she turned wide eyes his way. Ryan knew he'd never forget the expression on her face as long as he lived.

"I remember," she said in awe. "Mama told us that some nice people were coming to take us to better homes. I cried and told her I didn't want to go. She held me on her lap and cried with me, then pushed me away and ordered me not to cry, that she was only doing it for my own good. I ran out of the house, angry, and hid under the porch with my doll. I was determined no one would find me. But I got hungry and sneaked into the kitchen for an apple. That's when they came."

Tears trickled from her lashes. "Oh, Ryan, you must be right. Mama cried with me and held me. She didn't want me to go, either. So she must've loved me some. . ."

Emotion clutched Ryan's throat. He crouched beside her and laid a gentle hand on her shoulder. "I'm sure she did, Erica. After all, how could she keep from it?"

At his quiet words, shock filled her eyes. He stood to his feet, wishing he could retrieve the hasty comment. He knew he loved her. But it didn't matter what he wanted. He'd made a vow.

"Are you ready to go?" he asked gruffly. "We have a long drive ahead."

She nodded. "I think I'm finally laying my ghosts to rest." A soft smile lit her face. "I'm going to make it, Ryan. I'm truly going to make it."

"Of course you are." He helped her up and squeezed her hand, allowing the contact to last no more than a second. Then he turned and walked to the car.

After a silent and uncomfortable drive, they finally approached Wes's house. Erica noticed a shiny red car in the driveway. She watched the front door to the house fly open, and a chic woman with short, frosted blond hair came hurrying down the steps. Erica had no more than opened her car door and stepped out when the woman—shorter than her by almost a foot—gave her a breathless smile.

"Erica?" she asked. "But of course, you're Erica! You and Wes have the same eyes."

Before Erica could reply, she found herself engulfed in a heartfelt hug, surprisingly strong coming from such a petite woman. Stunned, Erica shot a look at Ryan, but he only shrugged.

"I'm Paula Rothner," the woman laughingly explained as she pulled back. "Your long-lost sister."

Tears pricked Erica's eyes. "Paula?"

The woman nodded, clasping Erica's upper arms. "I was ten last time I saw you. Oh, but you still have the same sweet face!"

"Paula. . ." This time Erica returned the tight hug. Any lingering gray clouds that had revisited her at the return of Ryan's emotional distance blew away from her heart. "We weren't expecting you until day after tomorrow, but I'm so glad you came early."

Paula's shining eyes surveyed Erica from head to foot, then darted to the faded clump of material she held. Her brows drew together in puzzlement. "What is that?"

Erica looked at the dilapidated doll. "I found it under the porch of our old cabin. It's my old doll."

"Red Baby? To think it was there all that time. . ." Paula's expression sobered. "Stacey told me you went to the cabin."

"I had to see it."

"I understand. Let's talk over coffee. Stacey and Wes went for some takeout fried chicken." Paula looked at Ryan for the first time. "You must be Wes's friend—Ryan, isn't it? I've heard a lot about you."

"All good I hope."

"Let's just say that I never knew someone as 'meek as a lamb' could look so strong."

Ryan groaned. "Maybe I don't want to know the rest. Stacey's always loved to tease me, ever since high school. I never knew if it was because she was an only child or if it's because she's two years older than me."

Paula's eyes twinkled. "She ordered me to tell you to stay for dinner."

He hesitated as though he might accept, then shook his head. "I can't. Saturdays are laundry days, and I have plenty. I'm sure you have a lot of catching up to do, without me around."

Erica felt a stab of disappointment and managed what she hoped was a dazzling farewell smile, as if she didn't care whether he stayed or not. "Okay, then. Thanks for the ride, Ryan. See you around." She turned her back on him and walked toward the house, ignoring Paula's curious upraised brow.

"Yeah, see you. . ." Erica couldn't help hearing the confusion in his voice. Knowing she'd behaved immaturely, and remembering how sweet he'd been at the cabin when she was falling apart, she looked his way. He hadn't moved from his spot.

"Thanks, Ryan." She gave him a genuine smile this time. "For being the best friend a girl ever had."

He stared at her a few seconds before replying. "Any time, Erica." His smile was faint as he turned to go.

She had tried to make amends for her bad behavior. Why did he still seem upset?

Once inside, Erica put water on the stove to heat. Paula spotted a pan on the counter, and with a spoon she reached for a messy dessert square. One small chunk had already been taken out.

"Don't eat those!" Erica blurted, startling Paula into snatching back her hand. "I forgot to throw them away," she meekly added.

"Throw them away?" Paula eyed the yellow, white-powdered topping in confusion.

"I'm taking an online cooking class," Erica explained, feeling the blush rise to her face. "And I didn't have a lemon, so I substituted lemon juice. Only I didn't know that when it's concentrated you're only supposed to use a little. Three tablespoons are equal to one lemon, I found out. Only I didn't know that at the time, because Peggy had torn off the label, and all I had to look at was a green bottle."

Paula raised her brows at Erica's haphazard explanation. "So how much did you put in?"

"Um. . .one cup for each lemon." The words were reluctant. "And the recipe called for two lemons, so the bars are really tart, not to mention runny."

Paula tried to suppress a smile, but it ended in a laugh. She put her arm around Erica's shoulders. "Don't feel bad. I'm no cook, either."

"Really?"

"Yeah. It must be an inherited trait or something."

Both women giggled, and Erica set about making some raspberry herb tea. "Do you use sweetener?"

"Just a teaspoon of honey. Not the jar." Paula winked to take the sting off her joke.

Erica rolled her eyes and grinned. She prepared both cups, taking them to the table. "Now that we're finally together, I have no idea where to start."

"Tell me about what happened today," Paula suggested. "And how you found Red Baby."

Erica sobered. "Okay. Maybe you can help fill in the blanks."

For the next several minutes, Paula listened, her eyes sympathetic. "How hard it must have been for you, not knowing! I was older so I remember more than either you or Wes do." Paula looked down at her tea and stirred it. "Mama not only had a drug problem, she drank. Sometimes she was so wasted she couldn't do the simplest things. I took care of you and Wes when Mama would pass out." Her lips lifted in a slight smile, and she stretched her hand across the table to cover Erica's. "You were my live baby doll; I loved you so much."

Erica returned the smile.

After a moment, Paula withdrew her hand. "Twice, someone

called social services, and they came. I was so glad to get out of there and live a normal life with normal people, even if it was only a foster family. But they were nice."

Erica's mouth dropped open. "You were glad Mama gave us away?"

"No, sweetie, maybe glad is the wrong word. Relieved might fit better, though I missed you and Wes a whole lot. It would've been perfect if we could've stayed together. Just the three of us. I guess I loved Mama, too, but even at ten, I knew something was wrong with her and with the way we lived."

Paula released a soft breath. "Mama got married young, she told me once. When Daddy ran out on her, it's like she completely folded. She never finished high school and couldn't get better work than to sack groceries. With her drug habit, the money went fast, and we never had enough food on the table. Then there were those weird, perverted boyfriends of hers that always came around." Paula shuddered. "Let's just say, sometimes it's better not remembering."

Erica stared at her flowered mug. "But she did love us?"

"I don't know. I guess. She never physically abused us, though she slapped my face on a few occasions when I sassed her. She just never was able to take care of herself, much less three kids." Paula shook her head, as if to dispel her thoughts. "I learned long ago not to think about those days. Even the Bible mentions something about not looking behind and only looking forward."

"If I'd done that, I wouldn't be here," Erica argued.

"Maybe. But I believe God had a hand in all of us finding one another again. We're all Christians—thankfully all raised by Christian families—and God is our Father and leads us. He's the One who brought you home, Erica. All I'm saying is that I don't think we should look too closely at what happened before. Let's just live in the present and forget the rest."

Erica thought about Paula's words. Margaret and Darrin could hardly be called Christians. Erica had accepted the Lord through their maid's counsel. Yet her sister was right. Now that the past had been dug up and laid bare, it was time to lay it to rest.

"Paula, have you talked to Mama since Wes found her?"

Her sister fidgeted with the handle of her mug, looking at it as she ran one coral fingernail up and down the curve. "No. Why?"

"Wes has her number in New Mexico, and I'd like to call her. Do you want to get on the extension?"

Paula's expression was one of surprise.

"I think you're right and we do need to let go of what happened," Erica admitted softly. "But I want to talk to Mama again. I never had much of a home life, so this is important to me."

"But why involve Mama? We have each other now."

"Wes's pastor said that a big part of forgetting is forgiving. He's right. How can I carry a grudge about the past and forget it at the same time? There's no way. Wes has already forgiven Mama. Let's you and I do the same."

Paula's brow creased. "I hadn't realized I still had any bad feelings toward her until today. But I'm not sure I'm ready to talk to her yet, either."

"Will you at least try? Or, if you can't, will you just listen to what she has to say?"

"You realize that could be painful?"

"Yes. But how will we know if we don't try? I'd like for us to call her together. That way we'll be here to support one another if it doesn't turn out well."

Paula was quiet a moment. "I guess you're right. It's time."

Erica hurriedly located the number written in the address book by the wall phone and made the long distance call. Now that she'd reached this decision, she didn't want to delay. Cowardice might set in if she did. Paula might change her mind. Erica could almost hear the rapid beats of her heart as she waited. One ring. . .two. . .then three. . .

Disappointed, she was about to hang up on the fifth ring when a woman's husky voice answered. "Hello?"

Erica froze, her mind reeling. She sank to a nearby chair.

"Hello?" The woman seemed perturbed now. "Is anyone there?"

"Mama?" Erica croaked.

A pause. "Who is this?" The woman sounded almost angry.

*Oh, dear God. . .did I made a mistake and dial a wrong number?*

Resisting the impulse to slam the receiver back on its hook, she clutched the phone more tightly. "It's, um, it's Erica. And—and Paula's here, too. We're at Wes's house."

She impatiently nodded toward Paula, who'd moved to the family room, staring at the cordless as if it were a live snake ready to strike. Finally, she picked up the receiver. "Hello, Mama." Her voice came out in a flat monotone.

"Paula?" the woman said in a raspy breath. "And Erica?"

Erica nodded then realized what she was doing. "Yes."

"*My* Paula and Erica?" The woman was clearly crying.

251

"Yes, Mama. It's me." This from Paula, who sounded subdued.

"Oh, my babies. I'm so sorry. You'll never know just how sorry. . ."

Erica smiled through her tears. She knew.

# Chapter 8

Three weeks later Erica watched as Wes pulled up to the bus station. "You're sure about this?" he asked with a frown. "You're welcome to stay."

She forced a smile. "It's time I went home. I can't impose on you and Stacey forever."

"But I don't understand why you changed your mind about living here. The job at the mini-mart probably wasn't the greatest anyway—I'm sorry that they'd already found someone. But, like I said, they're looking for a secretary at the church. That's right up your alley." He cast a studied glance around the parking lot.

"I know, but after talking with Mama, I realize I need to have a heart-to-heart with Margaret and Darrin, too. Maybe their reasons were wrong for adopting me, but they did take care of me all those years. I need to at least thank them for that. I never did." There was another reason for her sudden getaway, one Erica didn't want to voice. Her heart was tied to Ryan's, and living in Preston Corners had become too difficult. She admired Ryan's decision to wait for the wife that God handpicked for him, and she loved him too much to try to change his mind. Every time he came to Wes's house—twice a week for the baseball game and Sunday dinner—was bittersweet torture for Erica. What was worse was when he stayed away, as he'd done this past week. Maybe, in time, she would consider living in Preston Corners. But not yet.

Wes helped her with her luggage, making sure the bus employee stowed it properly. He asked her if she had her ticket for the fourth time and generally treated her like the big brother he was. And she loved every bit of it.

"You're coming back for Thanksgiving and Christmas?" Wes asked. "It's the earliest Mama can get here with her husband. He sounds like a nice guy. He's the one who helped her get into the drug rehabilitation program, you know. Now they both head a drug support/help group in their community. You really have to come back, Erica. Christmas in Preston Corners isn't something to miss. Peggy and Billy can take you sledding on the hill behind our house, if we have snow. And Stacey makes one mean turkey with all the trimmings. You can even make a dessert to go with it, if you really want to."

He seemed edgy, talking more than usual and about things she already knew. She studied him curiously. "Wes, you're acting weird. Is everything okay?"

"Sure. Except that my little sister is leaving us."

Erica accepted his tight bear hug. "I'll be back," she said into his shoulder. "Now that you've found me, you'll have a hard time getting rid of me."

"As if I'd want to try." His smile was wide in his beard. "You know, Erica, Ryan wasn't too happy when I told him you were leaving. I thought there might be something between you two. . ."

"No. Please, tell him good-bye for me." So Ryan wasn't too happy? Still, that hadn't stopped him from keeping his distance.

"You have my number?" Wes asked as they walked to the bus door. He shot another look around the parking lot.

"I think Stacey wrote it on every available piece of paper she could find and stuck them all in my luggage. I'm surprised she didn't embroider it on the throw pillow you guys gave me for a birthday present."

He grinned and scratched his beard. "If you'd have put the idea in her head, she probably would have."

"I never knew my birthday was in June until Paula told me. Margaret always gave me a party in August, the month they adopted me."

"Erica, did they abuse you?" Wes's voice grew gruff. "You never said much about your life with them."

She let out a long sigh. "No, not physically, anyway. More like emotional neglect. It's in the past, and I'd rather not talk about it. I've forgiven them, too."

Admiration shone in his eyes. "Ryan was right. It's awful you had to grow up living with those people, but it's helped to shape you into a woman of character. I'm proud to call you my sister."

Wes's words floated through Erica's head minutes later as she sat on the half-empty bus, waiting for it to depart. She put her carryall on the seat beside her, not wanting company. For Wes she had been brave, but now, with no one around to see, she slipped into the doldrums.

Oh, how she would miss Ryan! He, on the other hand, was probably breathing a huge sigh of relief that he wouldn't have to sample any more of her cooking disasters. Her last flop two weeks ago had been her worst. No wonder he hadn't come around last Sunday.

The chocolate cake layers had turned out flat—like pancakes—and she'd used two containers of fudge icing to try to give them a lift. Erica had laid her fork down after the first strange-tasting bite. Surprisingly, Ryan continued to eat the cake, though with a martyred expression on his face. Halfway through, when he asked what she'd substituted this time, she told him she'd had all the ingredients for once, then named each one. His face seemed to turn a little green on the last item she mentioned, and Stacey laughed outright. Erica felt the blush rise to her cheeks again. How was she supposed to know that cream of tartar wasn't the same thing as tartar sauce? To make matters worse, she'd confused the recipe amount with the ingredient above it and had put in a half cup instead of a teaspoon.

Sighing, she propped her elbow on the armrest and laid her cheek in one hand, turning her head to stare out the window for a last glimpse of Preston Corners. From her place in the sixth row, she heard the pressurized sound of the door shut, then several seconds later, open again. Footsteps clomped up the metal stairs. Obviously the latecomer had almost missed the bus, as she had that long-ago day in January. Had it really been five whole months since she'd sat beside Ryan on a seat much like this one and admired his gentle brown eyes?

"Excuse me. Is this seat taken?"

Erica's heart skipped a beat. With disbelief, she turned to face the tardy passenger.

"No?" Ryan smiled, took her carryall off the aisle seat, and sank onto it, setting down the sack he carried. "At least we have better traveling weather today. Sunny. Warm. Though it's a bit humid, isn't it? Probably because of all that rain we got last night."

"What are you doing here?" Erica managed.

He pulled a wrapped box from his sack. "I missed your birthday and wanted to get this to you. Happy birthday."

Tears clouded her eyes. She blinked them away as he laid the box on her lap. When she didn't move, he pulled the yellow ribbon holding the flower-sprigged wrapping paper together.

"You really shouldn't have, Ryan."

"Hush and open your present."

With trembling fingers, she undid the flaps at both ends and slid a shirt box from the confines. She offered him a puzzled look, but he only nodded. "Go on."

Erica lifted the box top, pulled back the tissue, and stared. A tear escaped and fell to the pinafore covering the green calico dress of the Raggedy Ann doll in her lap.

"Interesting thing about those dolls," Ryan said close to her ear. "They come with a message printed on their chests."

Erica didn't remember that. "They do?"

"Go ahead and take a peek. I don't think your new Red Baby would mind."

Feeling incredibly foolish as well as strangely anticipatory, Erica lifted the dress over the doll's white bloomers. Emotion catching her throat, she cupped a hand over her mouth at the embroidered message that met her eyes: A red heart held the words "I love you."

Suddenly she heard the sound of tires crunching over gravel. Her gaze jerked to his expectant one. "Ryan! The bus is moving. You need to tell the driver to let you off."

He blew out a short breath and shook his head with a wry grin. "Not quite the response I was hoping for. Maybe this will prod you into saying the right thing." He lifted the doll—to reveal a black velvet box nestled in the tissue.

Erica's eyes widened as she looked from the box to Ryan then back again. She swallowed. Did this mean what she thought it did?

His fingers went to her chin, gently forcing her gaze to meet his serious one. "Erica, I was a fool. All along the Lord was showing me His will regarding you, but I'd been so accustomed to running away I couldn't see it. Not until our kiss. That really started me seeking Him. Then when you called me your best friend that day we went to the cabin, well, I knew I wanted much more than to just be friends with you. Still, God had to show me the truth."

Erica felt dazed. "The truth?"

"That you're the one He handpicked for me. Maybe your personal quest brought you to Preston Corners, but God had a hand in it all along. For my benefit, as well as yours." He clasped her hands, his expression tender. "I love you, Erica Langley."

"Really?"

Ryan nodded. *"Je T'aime. . ."* He brought her hand to his

mouth and kissed the back of her fingers. "*Te amo. . .*" He kissed her other hand. "*Ich liebe dich.* . .and if you want me to say it in sign language, I'll tell you I love you that way, too. Just please tell me I'm not too late, and you'll be my wife."

Erica never knew joy could produce itself in so many tears.

"Erica?" he prompted, as if concerned.

"Before I give you my answer, I think I do want you to say it in sign language," she said staunchly, though she felt deliriously giddy. "I'm not convinced yet."

With a wide grin, Ryan took her in his arms and kissed her breathless.

Loud clapping and wolf whistles filled the bus, breaking them apart. They cast self-conscious glances at the smiling people in the seats around them. Then they looked at each other. Erica stared up into Ryan's gentle brown eyes, knowing she could gladly look into them a lifetime. "Okay, Ryan, you've convinced me," she whispered. "I'll marry you."

Ryan gave her another kiss, this one brief but tender. Erica giggled, swiping one hand over her tear-wet cheek. "When you make up your mind about something, you don't collect dust, do you?" she asked.

"I've waited a lifetime for you, Erica. How could I wait another moment?"

The words warmed her soul, but reality beckoned. "Shouldn't you get off the bus before it leaves the city limits? I'll come back to Preston Corners soon." Nothing could keep her away now.

"I made arrangements to take some time away, though I'll bet Wes thought I'd never get here. He flagged the driver to wait when he saw my car careen around the corner."

"Wes?" she said incredulously, then remembered his extreme interest in the parking lot while they were saying good-bye. "So, he knew all along you'd show!" She grinned. "The weasel. Playing it up and making me think we wouldn't see each other again for a very long time."

"He probably was beginning to wonder when I was so late. I had to go through the third degree when I told him of my feelings for you several days ago. But we now have his blessing." Ryan smiled. "I'm going back with you to help you pack and get your affairs settled. I have a friend in the area I'll stay with. Then I'm personally escorting you back to Preston Corners, where you belong."

Erica didn't argue. She'd felt this place was home almost since the moment she saw it.

"Don't you want to see your ring?" Ryan asked.

"Oh, of course I do!"

Ryan popped open the jeweler's box. He pulled out the diamond solitaire and slid it onto her extended finger. Awed, Erica looked at the beautiful token of his love, then tightly interlaced her fingers with his—though what she really wanted was to throw her arms around him and kiss him again. Yet they'd given the other passengers enough of a show for one day. She lifted his strong hand clasped with hers and contented herself with kissing one of his knuckles.

"Ryan Meers, I love you," she whispered, certain no one could be as happy as she.

# Epilogue

With winter's breeze chilling her face, Erica stood beside Ryan at the front door and watched their guests leave. Paula herded her troop into a minivan, then slid inside, next to her husky husband. Their mother hesitated beside a silver Buick's car door, which her tall, dignified-looking husband held open for her, and looked over her shoulder once more to wave. Erica smiled and waved back at the beautiful brunette, whom she'd been surprised to see she so strongly favored at their first face-to-face meeting—the day before Erica's wedding.

This past year, after three weeklong visits and countless phone calls between them, Erica and her mother had grown close. Erica was happy to see that even Paula was loosening up around their mother, though she still seemed sullen at times. But for the most part, they were all friends.

"You'll see them tomorrow," Ryan teased, tightening his arm around her waist. "They'll be here another week."

"I know," Erica sighed happily. "It's just that every moment is so precious. Sometimes you don't know how blessed you are until it's all taken from you. But thankfully, what got ripped away from me was restored." She looked up at him, her gaze adoring. "And you've been such a rock of support through it all. I've loved every moment of our married life together, Ryan."

He grinned and brushed his lips against hers. "Care to go for a few more rounds, Mrs. Meers?"

"I'm game if you are. At least sixty more years or so. This has been a wonderful first anniversary."

The baby started crying, and both Ryan and Erica turned to look. Margaret, with her perfectly coiffed hair and expensive clothes, appeared totally out of her element with little Charla.

"I don't think she likes me." Margaret awkwardly held the bald-headed baby up in the air a foot away from her.

"Sure she does," Erica said. "Just jiggle her against your shoulder. She loves that."

Margaret did so. The baby stopped crying and nestled her head against Margaret's neck. Erica smiled at the look of surprised contentment that crossed Margaret's face. During their heart-to-heart talk over a year ago, Erica learned some things about her adoptive mother. Margaret had been abused as a child and struggled with low self-esteem all her life; she didn't know how to show love to others. In an uncharacteristic emotional moment, Margaret assured Erica that, despite Margaret's inability to show it, Erica had been loved and wanted.

The baby fell asleep, and Darrin moved toward Margaret. "Put her in the bassinet. It's time to leave these kids alone."

Ryan lifted his eyebrows in Groucho Marx style at Erica, and she giggled.

At the door, she turned to Margaret. "I'm so glad you could

come. Of course, you must also come to Christmas dinner at Wes's tomorrow. We're eating at one o'clock and then later we're all going to the tree-lighting ceremony together. Wes has been elected to light the tree this year for all the volunteer work his construction firm has done for the community."

Margaret seemed uncertain. "Are you sure we won't be imposing?"

"Oh, no! Stacey asked me to remind you. After all, you're family, too."

Ryan agreed as he picked up his plate from a nearby table, where a tabletop fiber-optic Christmas tree rotated in its stand. He took a bite of the last piece of anniversary cake.

Tears glistened in Margaret's eyes. "Thank you for inviting us. Your entire family is wonderful. It's amazing to see how much good has come about in all of your lives, despite everything that's happened. In fact. . ." She looked at her husband, and he gave a nod. "Would you mind very much if Darrin and I went to church with you tomorrow? I'd like to learn more about this God of yours that you said made it all possible."

Erica's heart felt near bursting with joy. "Oh, I'd love for you to come!" She stepped forward to hug the astonished Margaret, who still wasn't accustomed to physical displays. Margaret gave an uncertain smile then walked away with Darrin, who also got a quick hug first.

"I think she's coming around," Ryan said as he moved beside Erica and observed them drive away in their Lincoln Towncar. "I think they both are."

"Oh, I hope so." Erica closed the door against the cold and watched Ryan fork another bite of dessert into his mouth. "I'm glad you like the cake. I just wish it wouldn't have fallen. It was supposed to look like a pinwheel. Not a broken wheel. I guess a cake decorating class will be the next course I take. I wonder if Cynthia's offering one."

"Well, no matter how it looks, it tastes great! You've improved a lot over the year, hon. But it sure is different. It looks like a child's cake with all that carnival-like festivity on top—but Christmassy, too."

"Didn't I once hear you say something about being a kid at heart?" Erica teased and looked at the slice on his plate. "The semisweet chocolate pieces remind me of the bittersweet memories I had of my childhood. And the crushed peppermint glaze on top?" She snapped a good-sized bit off the red-and-white speckled dark chocolate triangle perched atop the fudge icing.

"Hey!" Ryan laughed in mock protest.

Smiling, she continued her explanation, holding up the chocolate piece. "It reminds me of something Peggy once said about God giving us peppermint dreams—what I think of as a bright future. This cake is symbolic of His sweetening my life and bringing good out of the bad. And giving me His best, when I met you." She gave him a peck on the lips then popped the huge chunk of melting chocolate into her mouth, hitting the outside of her lips and making a mess of herself, giggling.

"All right, you!" Ryan set his plate down and grabbed her hands before she could wipe away the streaks. He bent toward her, trying to dart light licks to her cheeks to get the chocolate off her face—while she shook her head from side to side to evade his silly efforts, laughing like a child being tickled. A few hit their mark—when suddenly, his mouth targeted hers, and he gave her a long, delicious kiss that made Erica forget all about childish games.

"The baby's asleep," he murmured.

"Mmm," she agreed with a smile, her arms still looped around his neck.

Ryan kissed the sensitive spot near her ear. "One last thing, before I forget all about that cake, Mrs. Meers. What were those nuts you used? They had a strange flavor I've never tasted before."

Erica let out a nervous, uncertain giggle, and Ryan straightened to look at her. She lifted her brows sheepishly. "Um. . .nuts?"

He released a heartfelt groan. "Never mind. I don't want to know."

She let out another giggle, and bending down, Ryan captured it with a kiss.

# DARK CHOCOLATE 'N' PEPPERMINT DREAM CAKE

A fun "cake makeover" to add zip to any plain cake, Erica and Ryan's anniversary cake is good for all occasions. A chocolate-lovers' dream, it's been a favorite in our family for years.

Cake mix (chocolate or white)
1 box semisweet baking chocolate pieces (8 ounces)
Chocolate fudge frosting
Several pieces hard peppermint candy—crushed
1/2 cup slivered or sliced almonds (optional)

Bake cake according to directions on box. Cool and frost. Sprinkle with nuts if desired. Melt semisweet chocolate using low heat. Spread evenly over cookie sheet covered with waxed paper and freeze. After 5 minutes check chocolate. You want it firm enough to score, but not totally solid. Using a round inverted cake pan as a guide, cut a circle in the chocolate toward end of cookie sheet, then score the circle as if cutting a pie, making 8 triangular "pieces."

Score remaining chocolate by making 2 parallel lines approximately 5 inches apart (or height of cake). Within those lines, make cuts 2–3 inches apart, so that you end up with a row of rectangles. Repeat above steps for next row. When all chocolate is scored, refreeze.

Once chocolate is solid, carefully break along scored lines. Spread triangles on top of cake at slight angle, to resemble a pinwheel, with only one long edge digging into frosting.

Use rectangles to "fan" around side of cake, anchoring edges into frosting. You should end up with a 3-D effect. If chocolate begins to melt, freeze until solid, then resume decorating. Sprinkle crushed peppermint over top and sides of cake.

Cover cake and store in refrigerator. (The peppermint will slightly melt to give a glazed effect.)

*Warning: This cake mysteriously disappears overnight when chocolate-lovers are in the house.

## GRANDMA VERA'S YUMMY OATMEAL COOKIES
### (Just don't use salted peanuts. *grin*)

1 cup shortening
1 cup granulated sugar
1 cup brown sugar
2 eggs
1 teaspoon vanilla
1½ cups flour
1 teaspoon baking soda
1 teaspoon salt
3 cups quick-cooking oats
¼ cup to ½ cup chopped walnuts (optional)

Cream shortening and sugars. Add eggs and vanilla. Beat well. Mix flour, soda, and salt in separate bowl. Add to creamed mixture. Stir in oats and walnuts. On waxed paper, shape dough into rolls 1 to 1½ inches in diameter. Wrap rolls in waxed paper. Chill thoroughly. . .slice cookies about ¼ inch thick. Bake on ungreased cookie sheet at 350 degrees for 10 minutes or until lightly browned. Yield: 5 dozen mouthwatering, scrumptious cookies. Enjoy!

## PAMELA GRIFFIN

Pamela Griffin lives in Texas and divides her time among her first loves, God and family—with writing coming in as a close second. She also loves to bake sweet things, and every Christmas, especially, the house is filled with mouthwatering scents. Like the heroine in her story, Pamela is a bit of a creator and enjoys being inventive if she doesn't have the usual ingredients on hand. Thankfully, she's never experienced the major flops that Erica had, and no medical assistance was required for the eaters of her sweet treats. Pamela's main goal in writing Christian romance is to encourage others through entertaining, hard-to-put-down stories that also heal the wounded spirit. Please visit Pamela at: http://users.waymark.net/words_of_honey.

# Cream of
# the Crop

by Tamela Hancock Murray

# *Dedication*

**To Daddy**
**A sweet man who loves sweet treats**

# Chapter 1

Gwendolyn Warner opened the heavy door to the office marked Executive Suite. She was greeted by a large desk situated toward the back of a plush room. Each wall was decorated with framed ads for DairyBaked Delights' products. On either side of the desk and behind it were doors labeled with the names of the president, CEO, and vice president. The chief executive officer's door remained ajar.

She looked at the business card in her hand. *Rhoda Emerson, Chief Executive Officer, DairyBaked Delights.* The person she was supposed to see. She looked at the sign once more and confirmed she was in the right place. Good. At least she wouldn't be late for her interview. This job was too important. She couldn't blow her chances by being late. She had to appear smart, creative, self-assured, and capable.

No one was sitting behind the desk, so Gwendolyn decided to settle in one of the two red upholstered chairs with a magazine and wait to be called. She had arrived fifteen minutes early, as was her usual method.

In her best effort to look nonchalant, she retrieved a woman's magazine from her black leather tote. The cover promised articles revealing how to drop ten pounds in two weeks and how to create fabulous desserts, along with photos of the latest celebrity hairstyles. None of these items interested her. Gwendolyn wanted to study the photographs inside. Besides, she had to do something except sit on the edge of the seat, legs crossed at the ankles, hands holding on to her knees for dear life. No, she couldn't afford to look too anxious.

Absorbed in her magazine, Gwendolyn startled when a male voice boomed from behind the president's door.

"I never authorized hiring a new photographer for our ad campaign! We could save money by using file photos."

Save money? She clenched her teeth. Uh-oh. Maybe she wouldn't get this job after all.

A calm, steady reply came from a female voice. "But this photographer comes to us with fine references, education, and credentials. And since she's just started her own studio, her fees should be very reasonable."

"Using file photos would be even more reasonable," the man snapped.

Shaking her head, Gwendolyn decided she would vote this man least likely to suffer a stomach ulcer from suppressing his emotions.

"I'd like to know who decided to override my authority in this matter. I thought I was supposed to oversee all ad campaigns," he bellowed.

Gwendolyn's chest tightened. *What is this? With my*

background, I thought that I'd be a shoo-in to photograph the new *DairyBaked Delights ad campaign.* Anxiety clenched its ugly grip around her midsection.

"Sebastian, I suppose I did. But I wanted a new photographer, and so I made the decision," the female voice answered, still maintaining calm.

*Sebastian. Where have I seen that name?*

She looked around the room and read the name on the door in the back of the room. Sebastian Emerson, Vice President.

A small gasp escaped her lips. So the VP didn't want anything to do with her? How could she conquer such a formidable adversary? Her interview prospects for this job seemed to be waning quickly.

*Heavenly Father, I pray it's Your will for me to get this job. If it is, let this Sebastian man see that he needs to support me in my work. In the precious name of Your Son, amen.*

She knew her prayer was selfish, but she felt that such a desperate petition was needed. If she didn't get this high-paying assignment, Gwendolyn would have to admit to her brother that she couldn't make a living on her own as a photographer.

Through years of hard work and sacrifice, Bruce, who was fifteen years her senior, had established a successful photography studio. Gwendolyn had been his assistant since high school. At first, Bruce was proud that his kid sister was part of his business. Gwendolyn was a miracle baby, born in her mother's forty-fifth year. By that time, Bruce was a teenager and had become accustomed to his status as an only child. With so many years between them, Bruce had always been protective of her, but he never related to her as an equal.

Still, she had imagined he would be proud when, after discovering a love for photography in his studio, she announced that she wanted to follow in his professional footsteps. But when she left Northern Virginia to earn her degree in photography at a small college in the southwestern part of the state, Virginia Intermont College, his lack of enthusiasm was palatable. He preferred not to talk about her studies, except to remind her how many years he had worked to establish himself in a brutally competitive field. He was worried about how she would pay back the college loans. A reasonable worry, to be sure, since her field was so uncertain. But he had succeeded without a university degree. She had hoped that, in time, he would come to consider her an asset, someone who could partner with him in his work. Instead he regarded her as a rival, sending her on the least desirable assignments and booking her portrait sessions on the times he knew she had a Bible study or a church choir rehearsal scheduled. After three years of trying to prove herself, she knew she had no choice but to strike out on her own. Her decision magnified Bruce's feelings that she was nothing more than a competitor to be squelched. If Gwendolyn failed and had to beg him to take her back, he would be sure to make her life even more miserable.

Failing was not an option she wanted to contemplate. She had to succeed.

A female voice brought her back into the present. "I'm the one who authorized the new hire."

Gwendolyn glanced again at the sign on the door and

confirmed that the office belonged to the CEO. Rhoda Emerson, the woman she was scheduled to see.

"And your father agrees with me," Mrs. Emerson said.

*Your father? So Sebastian is Mrs. Emerson's son. Maybe I can win this one after all.* She felt a smile of triumph form on her lips.

She could sense from his persistence that Sebastian wasn't going down without a fight. "I thought we would just use the outtakes from our last photo shoot. The ones that Ebba took."

"No. I let you have your way last time, but not now. Even the best of Ebba's remaining pictures aren't what she would want to appear in any DairyBaked Delights ad. I won't hear of it."

"Ebba was the only one who could handle Pansy," Sebastian pointed out.

*Pansy. That must be the name of the cow.*

"I'm sure this photographer will do just fine with Pansy," Mrs. Emerson argued. "I've been assured there will be no problem."

Gwendolyn swallowed. Her experience with animals was limited to the pets little children would bring in to Bruce's portrait studio to be photographed. Their owners usually took care of them.

*Lord, please help me!*

"He'd better be good with animals. Pansy has been our symbol since the company started." Even though she'd never met him, Gwendolyn could almost see Sebastian folding his arms over his chest. "I'm not giving Pansy up for anybody."

"No one is asking you to. And you may as well know now, the photographer is not a he. It's a she. Gwendolyn something or another," Mrs. Emerson answered.

Gwendolyn wrinkled her nose. Some ally, if she couldn't remember her last name.

"And I'm sure she'll know what it takes to reach the next generation," her ally continued. "When I was young, there weren't so many choices. Now everyone has so many options in every area of life. That includes what type of commercial baked goods to buy. Not only do we have to compete with traditional bakeries, but many grocery stores have their own top-notch bakeries as well. Not to mention the big mail order bakeries. And all of them use every possible medium to remind consumers how many choices they have."

"You forgot to mention the biggest new kid on the block— the Internet," he reminded her. "Why do you think I recommended that you ask for Internet rights to the photos?"

"Oh, the Internet. Yet another thing I have to worry about." Gwendolyn heard Mrs. Emerson sigh. "How will I ever reach kids today?"

"You can start by not referring to young adults as kids." Sebastian retorted. "I know this is a new generation. But must we be like everybody else and use blatant sex appeal to sell our product? The people who buy our products respect us for not pandering to the lowest common denominator. We don't want to lose our base of established customers!"

*Blatant sex appeal?* No one had told Gwendolyn that the shoot would have anything to do with sex appeal. All she knew was that the ads would involve a cow and some baked goods. Even though creativity was her business, Gwendolyn had a hard time picturing an ad with a cow and a cake as being sexy.

A feeling of grudging admiration for Sebastian welled up inside her. At least he tried to hold on to some standards.

At that moment, a chubby matron who Gwendolyn surmised was the executive secretary entered from the hallway. Spotting Gwendolyn, she hurried to close Mrs. Emerson's door before setting a stack of paperwork on her desk. "May I help you?"

She stood. "I'm Gwendolyn Warner. I have an appointment with Rhoda Emerson."

"Oh. So you're the photographer. Sorry to keep you waiting. I had to step out of the office." The matron looked more embarrassed than the situation warranted. Perhaps she knew Gwendolyn had overheard an argument. "Uh, I'll let her know you're here."

"Thanks." Still wanting to appear calm, Gwendolyn returned to her seat.

The secretary quickly entered the CEO's office and then emerged a few moments later. She gave Gwendolyn a brief nod. Gwendolyn's heart began to hammer. *What will I do if they decide not to hire me? Oh, I can't think of that now.*

Fixing her face into a pleasant mask, Gwendolyn set her shoulders straight, smiled politely, and swept into the CEO's office with the confidence that had served her well during many interviews and difficult photo shoots.

Gwendolyn had taken care to appear in dressy pants, flat shoes, and a crisp white cotton shirt that bespoke a healthy pride in appearance yet told onlookers that her clothes wouldn't encumber her work.

Gwendolyn knew she had made the right decision to wear her favorite gray wool trousers when she saw Mrs. Emerson attired in a soft but businesslike suit the color of charcoal. Short but loose bleached blond curls and soft makeup gave her a youthful appearance but did not quite camouflage the fact that she qualified for senior citizens' discounts. Though Gwendolyn had heard Mrs. Emerson could be tough, she sensed the older woman possessed a gentle side behind her businesslike veneer.

Gwendolyn scanned the office, in search of her antagonist. He was nowhere in sight. An interior door offered a clue as to how he had made his escape.

*Coward!*

Mrs. Emerson broke into her thoughts. "Thank you for meeting with us today," she said, extending her hand.

"Us?"

"Yes. My son, Sebastian, will be in momentarily," Mrs. Emerson assured. "In the meantime, I've already looked over your sample photos. I must say, they are quite impressive."

"Thank you, Mrs. Emerson. I do my best to create memorable photographs." She handed the older woman a formal portfolio of her best photos. "I also have examples of my most recent work here, if you care to see them."

"Certainly." Mrs. Emerson took the portfolio. "Please, call me Rhoda." She sat down in the executive chair behind a large desk, but not before motioning for Gwendolyn to take her seat in a nearby leather chair. Gwendolyn watched as Rhoda flipped through the book. "Hmm," she said.

"You have a question?"

"I notice that your professional portfolio includes weddings and portraits, but no commercial ads."

Gwendolyn swallowed. She knew when she agreed to the interview that Rhoda might mention her lack of commercial experience, but this woman cut right to the chase! "I was an assistant at Bruce Studios for five years," she answered.

At that moment, the young photographer was glad to see that Rhoda apparently didn't make the connection that Gwendolyn and Bruce shared the same last name. "You might know us. I mean, them." Calling the people at Bruce's studio "them" instead of "we" seemed strange. "They" were her work family. And her friends. She cleared her throat.

"Yes, I am familiar with them. Your association was one of the main reasons why I was willing to give you a chance."

*Oh, great. I'll never get out from under his shadow.*

Rhoda flipped through to the last picture. "And, I do like the artistic shots you included."

Rhoda's compliment gave Gwendolyn courage. Maybe she did have a grain of talent, after all. "Thank you, ma'am."

"Oh, don't 'ma'am' me." She waved at Gwendolyn as if the gesture would cause the offending reference to disappear. She shoved a box in her direction. Gwendolyn's inspection revealed that it contained individually wrapped brownies.

"All right, Rhoda." Gwendolyn selected a tempting piece of cake loaded with frosting and chocolate chips. "Thank you." She nodded toward her portfolio as Rhoda continued to flip through the pages. "My education is mentioned on my résumé. College gave me an opportunity to take artistic photos, as well. The type of creative photography that makes a print ad successful."

"I see." She set the portfolio on her desk. "All of that is very commendable, but I want you to know here and now that I have my limits. I want to reach the next generation, but not at the expense of our current customers. I look at the magazine ads. This artsy stuff can be a bit much sometimes. I will not accept any campaign that doesn't mention our product. And I don't want to see black and white photos of anemic-looking couples crawling all over each other. I've heard the old adage that sex sells, and perhaps it does. But I won't resort to that tactic to convince customers to buy our products."

Obviously, despite Rhoda's willingness to argue with Sebastian, her son's opinion held powerful sway. She resolved to remember that. "I hadn't planned on that type of ad for you," Gwendolyn assured Rhoda. "I'm afraid some other manufacturers have cornered the market on those. I understood I would be working with a cow and a cake."

"Oh, and don't forget Bernie. The Saint Bernard."

"A—a Saint Bernard."

"Of course. We always use Bernie in our winter campaigns—unless you have a better idea."

"No, no," Gwendolyn hastened to assure her. Racking her brain, she remembered seeing a Saint Bernard in past ads for DairyBaked Delights. Their popular slogan, "DairyBaked Delights to the rescue!" flashed though her memory.

"We're quite attached to Bernie," Rhoda said. "My father was fond of his Saint Bernard, so he liked to use him in the ads way back when. I've kept up the tradition as a nod to the past."

"I like that."

Rhoda sent her a pleased smile. "If you're as good as I think you are, I'll be giving you more latitude later. That's why I want you to know the rules right off the top. Love of our product is more important than art, I believe."

Gwendolyn's first love was art, but she couldn't express disagreement with her prospective client. She searched for a common denominator. "I think it does help to be familiar with a product you're selling."

"Then I trust this is not the first time you've tried one of our products."

She chuckled. "No. I'm afraid I succumb too often to your baked goods. And I do thank you for making sugarless CreamDreams. They've gotten me through many a chocolate craving."

"Have they now?" Rhoda grimaced. "I'll tell you a secret, but you didn't hear this from me. I don't like the sugarless stuff. But our customers sure seem to."

"I enjoy all your products. That is why I jumped at the chance to photograph an ad for DairyBaked Delights," Gwendolyn said.

"Really?" Rhoda's expression displayed her approval.

"Really." Gwendolyn nodded. "Even though I want this assignment, I wouldn't lie to get it."

Job 32:21–22 popped into her mind. *"I will show partiality to no one, nor will I flatter any man; for if I were skilled in flattery, my Maker would soon take me away."*

For the briefest of moments, she considered sharing the

verse with Mrs. Emerson. Just as quickly, the thought vacated her head. No need to appear any more self-righteous than she already had.

"Good." Rhoda's expression softened from a tough businesswoman to a mother hen. "I didn't think you looked like someone who would resort to deceit."

"Never." Seeing Rhoda's friendly expression, she decided to take a chance. "I'm a Christian."

Rhoda's face lit up. "Even better." She leaned forward and lowered her voice. "We're not supposed to ask, you know." She leaned even closer and lowered her voice another notch. "I do believe you are the perfect photographer to take us into our next phase of development. Don't tell anyone, but we're planning to—"

An interior door to their left creaked open. Startled by the unexpected intrusion, Rhoda and Gwendolyn both nearly jumped out of their chairs as they looked in the direction of the sound.

Rhoda leaned back, swiveled her chair, and smiled too broadly. "There you are, Sebastian." Her voice was louder than necessary.

Gwendolyn shot her gaze to the door through which Sebastian entered the office. She stood in anticipation of a handshake and mustered a smile for her opponent.

## Chapter 2

G wendolyn had to compose herself from taking in a noticeable breath of surprise and pleasure upon spying her adversary. Sebastian Emerson appeared nothing like the bellowing troll she had heard protesting her existence. Despite his reminiscence of Grandpa and his old-fashioned attitude of thrift, Gwendolyn could see by his youthful appearance that Sebastian had not yet celebrated his thirtieth birthday. Sebastian was one of the rare men who was several inches taller than Gwendolyn. A dark suit nipped at the waist accentuated his broad chest and shoulders, suggesting hours spent lifting weights. Deep brown hair was cropped to perfection. She couldn't resist staring up into Sebastian's gray blue eyes.

A spark of interest ignited as he returned her look, only to fade as he apparently remembered he was supposed to be against her. "So you are the photographer." His voice was curt.

*So much for a friendly greeting.*

His mother gave Sebastian a warning look before turning

to Gwendolyn. "This is my son, Sebastian Emerson."

"How do you do, Mr. Emerson." Remembering that most men don't offer their hands in greeting to a woman unless she makes the gesture first, Gwendolyn extended her hand. Sebastian might have been a rival, but she wouldn't stoop to abandoning her manners.

He took her hand. His grip proved to be firm and businesslike, though more warm and pleasant than she expected. "You may call me Sebastian. Mr. Emerson is my father." The smile Sebastian gave her in return was warm enough to make Gwendolyn wonder if Rhoda's son could somehow be molded into a real human. He even went so far as to motion Gwendolyn to one of the seats situated in front of his mother's desk, then sat beside her.

"Gwendolyn," said Mrs. Emerson, who had seated herself in the spacious executive chair behind her desk, "Sebastian is our VP."

"Supposedly," Sebastian muttered.

Gwendolyn knew her expression betrayed her surprise at his comment. She tried to contort it back to normal.

"Unlike yourself, the VP didn't find out about the new ad campaign until this morning," Sebastian said in an aside to Gwendolyn.

"Sebastian doesn't like surprises," Rhoda explained. "But never mind that. The important thing is the photo shoot. Gwendolyn, as we discussed earlier, you'll be working with Pansy during the first shoot. You are familiar with Pansy, I'm sure."

"I assume she's the dairy cow who's been your symbol for a while."

"Exactly. You and Pansy will be selling these." Rhoda handed Gwendolyn two stuffed toys that had been sitting on her desk. One was a white-and-brown cow, and the other was a Saint Bernard with a small plastic barrel that mimicked wood around his neck.

"How cute!"

"We think so." Rhoda smiled. "This little toy is free with three proofs of purchase and $1.99 postage and handling. Not a bad deal, don't you agree?"

"Not a bad deal at all."

"I was told you're good with animals," Rhoda said.

She hesitated. "I haven't had the opportunity to work with a cow," she had to admit, "but I look forward to meeting Pansy."

Gwendolyn cut her glance to Sebastian long enough to ascertain his response to her answer. Instead of the disapproval she dreaded, she caught him in a tender look, studying her as though he were eager to memorize her features. His unspoken message sent embers that made her skin tingle hot before he focused his attention back to the business at hand.

"As I'm sure you know," Rhoda droned, "we're hoping the new campaign will increase our fall sales well into winter."

Gwendolyn nodded. "People love to have lots of baked goods to serve when they entertain."

"Especially over the hectic Thanksgiving and Christmas holidays," Rhoda agreed. "And we do have a superb line of kosher products for Hanukkah as well. I'm sure you realize that many of today's women don't have time to do their own baking."

"And that's where DairyBaked Delights comes to the rescue," Gwendolyn pointed out.

Rhoda chuckled. "I'm glad to see you've just about memorized our ad copy."

"I make it my business to know as much as I can about my clients."

"You're a young woman after my own heart. It sounds as though we're off to a great beginning. And if the first shoot increases our sales," Rhoda added, "we'll be calling upon you for a second shooting. Then you'll be well on your way to a long-term position as our photographer for DairyBaked Delights."

"That would be wonderful." Gwendolyn cut her gaze to Sebastian long enough to see if he would object. Thankfully, he said nothing. She breathed an inward sigh of relief that she hoped didn't show on her face.

Rhoda stood. Sebastian and Gwendolyn followed suit.

Rhoda eyed her from head to toe. "You certainly are statuesque, more like a model than a photographer. It's a wonder you stay behind the camera. You're as pretty as many of the girls in the glamour magazines."

"That hardly matters, Mother," Sebastian reminded her.

"Don't pay any attention to my son," Rhoda told Gwendolyn. "He seems to have some difficulties dealing with humans."

"Don't we all, at one time or another?" Glancing at Sebastian's physique, its fine tone evident even under his suit, Gwendolyn had a sudden thought. "Sebastian, have you ever considered modeling?"

"You have the job, Miss Warner. There's no need to resort to flattery." Though she knew Sebastian wanted her to think he had been insulted by her remark, Gwendolyn noticed his face held a shadow of pleasure.

"I'm sorry."

"Sebastian," Rhoda chastised, "you are the one who ought to apologize for being so ungracious. I taught you better than that."

"I know." He set his handsome face in Gwendolyn's direction. "Sorry. Thanks for the compliment."

"Maybe my compliment was my way of saying that I just want you to be comfortable with the way your company is presented to the public." She hoped her explanation, despite its incoherent logic, absolved her from her unintentional expression of interest in her new boss. "Your mother has already told me that she doesn't want anything too artsy or with blatant sex appeal."

"Right." He nodded.

"I think what you have in mind is just the approach for your product. However," she continued, "you've seen the trend of company leaders going directly to the public." *And none of them are nearly as attractive as you are.*

Her idea took her by surprise. Gwendolyn lost her train of thought. "And I–I—"

"You what?" he asked. "You're suggesting that I should appear in our ads?"

"That's not such a bad idea, Sebastian," Rhoda intervened. "Why don't you consider it?"

"No thanks. Vanity is not one of my weak points." Sebastian surveyed Gwendolyn, his eyes glimmering. "Judging by how you're thin as a reed, you must not ever indulge in baked goods."

"Then you don't know me very well." She placed her hand on her hip. "I have a huge sweet tooth."

"You wouldn't know it to look at you."

She decided not to acknowledge his backhanded compliment. "I can prove it. When we shoot the ad next week, I'll bring the best dessert you ever put in your mouth!"

Sebastian's eyebrows arched. "Really?"

"Yes. And if you don't like it, you can fire me." She extended her freshly manicured hand for a shake to seal the deal. When he grasped her fingers, the touch of his warm flesh sent renewed sparks through to her heart. She hoped the gentle squeeze he gave her hand wasn't a figment of her imagination.

Clutching her portfolio, Gwendolyn headed to the car. In case they were watching, Gwendolyn kept her step light until she slid behind the driver's seat, well out of the range of prying eyes. After placing her portfolio in the passenger seat, she crossed her arms over the unfeeling steering wheel and laid her forehead upon them.

"Now what will I do?" Gwendolyn wailed to the horn. "I have no idea how to cook!"

# Chapter 3

Standing in front of her bathroom mirror on the Saturday night before Monday morning's photo shoot, Gwendolyn looked at her face one last time as she prepared to wash most of its color down the drain. Light foundation, golden brown eye shadow, brown mascara, coral lipstick, and peach-colored blush accentuated her features. After she removed such enhancements, she noticed that she looked younger than her twenty-five years. Did she look like a professional photographer—one who owned her studio—not just a wannabe spending too much of her savings to finance a dream that might prove to be nothing more than pie in the sky?

She sighed. Putting the shoot together—a vision based on her own idea—had proven expensive and time consuming. Thankfully, her assistant, Fernando, was still in college and eager to work cheaply in exchange for experience and a good reference. Fernando had spent the entire week setting up the scene in the small warehouse space she had rented so Pansy wouldn't ruin her studio in the city. Not to mention she couldn't imagine a cow roaming the streets of the nation's capital.

Besides hard work, Fernando offered her some amusement. Taking advantage of his dark wavy hair and olive complexion, he had changed his name to Fernando from what he considered a less than glamorous moniker, Chip. In keeping with the change, he often tried to act as though he had just gotten off the boat—or, rather, the jet—from Milan.

To her relief, the warehouse was already prepared for Pansy's arrival in two days. She pictured the scene. A backdrop depicting snow was in place. Artificial snow was ready to be fanned over the scene to create the effect of a winter storm. The look was so realistic that a pleasant shiver traveled up her spine as she remembered happy times playing in snow. She had envisioned just how she would situate the cow and the model she had hired. She felt nervous about Sebastian's mandate regarding sex appeal. With his concerns in mind, Gwendolyn had spent hours poring over photos of available models. She selected a beauty of understated elegance—a brunette with the right kind of wholesomeness. Surely Sebastian would be pleased.

*Not too pleased, I hope.*

Her cheeks flushed hot. *I'm not jealous. No way. Now where did that thought come from?*

Determined not to dwell on her traitorous heart, she concentrated on how she would impose an image of the product itself onto the scene after the photos were shot.

She sent up a prayer to cover the photo shoot, added her thanks for Fernando, and reminded herself that she'd be giving him a nice Christmas bonus should the DairyBaked Delights account prove profitable.

Freshened in body and spirit, Gwendolyn decided to indulge in a cup of herbal tea before going to bed. Waiting for the water to heat, she sat at the table in the portion of the kitchen that doubled as a dining area in her small apartment. A batch of the latest fashion and beauty magazines heaped on the counter was too tempting to ignore. These popular publications were those in which she dreamed her photos would appear. Instead, she was fighting for a chance to photograph ads for a tiny bakery situated beyond the growing suburbs of the nation's capital city, in the middle of what was still Virginia farmland.

Certainly, the advertising campaign had enough money behind it to offer her a break. Even the first photo shoot guaranteed she would appear often over the next few weeks in the *Washington Post*, the *Richmond Times-Dispatch*, plus smaller local newspapers. Rhoda had even said the ad would be run in color in at least two Sunday editions of both of the larger papers. DairyBaked Delights planned to place a full-page glossy in several regional magazines. Such exposure should have excited Gwendolyn, yet it wasn't enough. She knew her brother wouldn't be impressed unless she surpassed his success by making the big time. That meant going to New York, Paris, and Milan to shoot photos for famous fashion designers and internationally known products.

"Although," she muttered, "Rhoda did mention something about the next stage of development. I wonder. . ."

She shook the thought out of her head. No need to think up grandiose schemes.

Turning her attention back to the magazine, she studied the avant-garde look so many of the two-page glossy ads touted. *I can take photographs that are every bit as eye-catching and creative as these. As a matter of fact, I'm even better than most of these photographers.* She lifted her chin in defiance, though the eyes in the photographs only offered vacant stares in return.

*"Charm is deceptive, and beauty is fleeting; but a woman who fears the Lord is to be praised."* The words of Proverbs 31:30 mocked her.

"Lord, why must You chastise me? You know I love You. Don't I have a right to my own dreams? Is it really wrong to want a little success in this world?"

*But what is success?*

The question disturbed her. What is success, really? Unwilling to search her soul for the answer, Gwendolyn pushed the question out of her mind.

She turned over a page and saw an ad for whipped topping. A luscious-looking slice of pie stared at her from the page.

She gasped. "Oh no! I forgot all about the dessert I promised Sebastian!"

Panic gripped her. Where would she find a recipe? She had no cookbooks and no experience. "Where's Mom when I need her?"

She picked up the phone and called her sister's house, where Mom and Dad were visiting.

"But of course I don't have my cookbooks here with me,"

Mom answered after Gwendolyn told her about the dilemma.

"Mom! I thought surely you'd be making dinners for them. You always tell Sarah how much you want her to learn to cook like you do."

"I know, but it seems ever since they visited New Orleans last summer, Josh has taken a liking to Cajun food. That's just not my thing. Although. . ." Her voice suddenly became too cheerful. "I do enjoy eating it while I'm here. Sarah has mastered seafood gumbo, and it's quite spicy."

Gwendolyn knew her mother's code word—spicy—meant that she'd be hitting the antacid later. "Hmm. Sarah just walked into the room, huh?"

"Yes indeed!" Mom sang.

"Well, you're doing the right thing to be a good mother-in-law to Josh. I'm sure he appreciates it."

"I know he does. And I really do love Sarah." Even though Sarah was in the room, Gwendolyn knew her mother meant the compliment.

Gwendolyn talked to her sister, her brother-in-law, their two kids, and Dad. Making dessert was getting quite expensive. Finally Mom got back on the phone with a new suggestion. "Why don't you call your friends, honey? I'm sure someone must have a good recipe."

Gwendolyn laughed. "My friends? You mean the ones who eat fast food every night? They think cooking means you zap leftovers in the microwave. I don't think so."

"You have a point," Mom conceded. "I have another idea. You're always talking about how great the Internet is. Why don't you try there?"

Gwendolyn snapped her fingers. "The Internet. Hmm. I suppose I could do a search and come up with something."

"I'm sure you could."

As Gwendolyn contemplated the possibilities, the notion that she might find something worthwhile grew. "Great idea, Mom! You're the best. Call me when you get home, okay?"

Moments later, a search yielded results. "Cynthia Lyons' Online Cooking School. Hmm."

She studied the teaser for the school. Pictures of dishes Cynthia taught her students looked good enough to serve at the best gourmet restaurants. "I can't believe this class is free." Gwendolyn looked at a picture of a cookbook. "Maybe I'll buy a copy of her book. In the meantime, I'll see what help I can get by e-mail."

> *Dear Cynthia,*
>
> *Hi! I'm a new student who just enrolled in your school tonight. They said I could e-mail you so here I am!*
>
> *I'm in a pickle. Cute food-related joke, isn't it? I'm in a desperate pinch. Sort of like needing a pinch of salt. Hey, I'm on a roll! (Maybe a cinnamon roll? Ha-ha.) Anyway, I need a recipe quick!! I promised my new boss I'd make him a super dessert. Problem is, I don't have a good recipe! I need to have the dessert by Monday morning. So really, I need to make it Sunday night at the latest. Not much time!*

*Can you give me any suggestions? It needs to be something easy. Cooking is not my forte. I guess if it was, I wouldn't need your school!*

*Thanks for your help.*

*Gotta dash—like a dash of pepper! Ha ha!*

*Yours,*
*Gwendolyn Warner*

Now, if only Cynthia Lyons, whoever she was, would come through!

The next day after church, Gwendolyn eagerly checked her e-mail. A message from Cynthia awaited!

*Dear Gwendolyn,*

*Welcome to the class! I trust you will enjoy learning new ways to cook. I do happen to have a recipe I'll be happy to share with you. It's for key lime pie. Not too exotic, but different enough that your new boss should be favorably impressed. You can use graham cracker crust, but if you really want to wow him, you might try a traditional piecrust. Nothing beats a flaky, homemade piecrust, especially if your boss's mother or grandmother made her own pies.*

"She sure did—and does!" Gwendolyn assured the absent Cynthia. "At least, that's what I'm willing to bet since he's the son of a bakery owner."

She kept reading.

*The recipe I've included is foolproof. I've used it many times myself, and my students have all been pleased with it.*

*Happy cooking!*
*Cynthia*

Gwendolyn printed out the recipes and examined them both. Neither looked too difficult. "Excellent!" She lifted her fist in the air with triumph.

She cleared a section of the kitchen counter and got out her ingredients for the piecrust. How hard could making a piecrust be? She had watched Mom make piecrusts for years. All she did was throw together a little flour, water, and a few other ingredients, chill the dough awhile, and roll it out. Voilà! A beautiful crust. She could certainly do the same. Mom would be so proud!

She noticed that Cynthia's recipe called for vinegar. "Vinegar, huh? Hmm," she wondered. "Does a 't' mean a teaspoon or a tablespoon?" She measured out a teaspoon. "That hardly seems like anything. I'd better try a tablespoon. And I think I'll add a little more for good measure."

The dough rolled up into a nice ball, just as the recipe promised. Gwendolyn placed the bowl in the refrigerator to chill for two hours. She'd take a break and make the pie filling, then roll it out and be all set.

Not until later when she was preparing to complete her cooking task did Gwendolyn realize that she should have made sure she had plenty of eggs on hand. The recipe called for four eggs, but she only had three left.

"That shouldn't matter," she reasoned. "Eggs are so tiny. I'll just use what I have." She looked at the clean counter. "But first, to roll out the pie dough."

She set the oven temperature to 400 degrees to cook the crust. After dividing the dough in half, she attempted to roll it out. Why wouldn't the roller run smoothly over the dough? Why was it sticking to the roller, and to the counter? What a mess! Then she remembered she was supposed to flour the rolling pin and the counter.

Gwendolyn rolled and rolled, but her crust didn't look anything like her mother's. The dough was the ugliest she had ever seen. And the thickness varied from place to place. The buzzer let her know the oven had reached the preset temperature.

"Well. It'll just have to cook until it's right." She placed her ugly piecrust in the oven and hoped for the best. "Besides, no one will care once the filling's in."

Even though she used only three eggs, the pie filling didn't seem any worse for the lack of one little egg.

"This sure is soupy," she noticed after adding the juice. "Oh! It says a half cup, not a cup." She shrugged. "Oh, well. It should congeal just fine anyway. But I wonder why it isn't green like a lime. I've never seen such an anemic color. It looks more like a watered-down lemon than anything else. This won't do at all."

Gwendolyn thought about what to do. "I know." She snapped her fingers and searched her cabinet. "There it is. Green food coloring." She was glad she had helped her niece color Easter eggs the previous year. "I'll use some of that."

She added one drop to the pie mix and stirred, but it didn't turn the nice shade of green she expected. She added another, and another, and several more, stirring after each round. Instead of a beautiful shade of emerald green, the mixture turned a strange shade of aqua. "This is bound to look better once it's done cooking." Cheerfully she placed the pie into the center of the oven and waited.

*Lord, I know this is trivial, but please let this pie turn out okay.*

When the pie came out at the appointed time, Gwendolyn nearly shrieked. The color hadn't improved at all. If anything, cooking brought out the blue even more. Even worse, the crust was black around the edges. Gwendolyn tried to flake off as much of the burnt portion as she could with a butter knife, resulting in minimal, if any, improvement.

She groaned. "What am I going to do?"

Her kitchen clock told her the hour was almost midnight. She had no choice. Her new boss would feast on this very pie the next day.

The next morning, Sebastian stood beside his kitchen sink and drank a tall glass of orange juice blended with a raw egg. "Wonder if Gwendolyn drinks juice for breakfast?" he muttered.

At that moment, he realized he had been thinking of the photographer with chocolate-colored hair and matching eyes ever since he'd met her. "Gwendolyn. Gwendolyn Warner. Why does she haunt me? Why do I wonder about everything about her—even what she eats for breakfast?"

The only answer was Sebastian's basset hound whimpering for his own breakfast.

"Aren't you glad you don't have to worry about such nonsense, Cookie? All you have to think about is sleeping and getting fed every day." Sebastian poured his pet a healthy portion of premium dog food and set the hound's monogrammed bowl on the floor. "Here you go, boy," he said, giving Cookie a quick rub behind the ears.

As the dog chomped his food, Sebastian journeyed into the largest of three bedrooms in the house he occupied. The four-year-old house had been custom-built on a parcel of land that had been part of Grandpa's farm before he started the bakery business. Though modest, when Sebastian approved the plans, he knew the house would be too large for a bachelor. He had not built the home for himself, but for the wife and family he hoped to have one day. Still, Sebastian was in no hurry for One Day to arrive. Though women pursued him, even calling to arrange dates, Sebastian had not found any of them alluring enough to cause him to break his quiet stride of life.

Opening the door to his walk-in closet, Sebastian pondered several suits, shirts, dress pants, and jeans. On the days he had sales calls to make, the decision to dress in a suit was automatic. Sebastian mused that perhaps a suit was no longer required in a world of casual Fridays, but he clung to tradition out of pride, stubbornness, and, though he was loath to admit it, a desire to be different.

Yet today was not a usual business day for the VP. Today he

was scheduled to visit a photo shoot, just to be sure it was going according to plan and, as Mother liked to say, "To remind them that DairyBaked Delights is paying the bill."

Sebastian had been present during other shoots, but those had only involved Reginald and Bernie. The animals wouldn't have cared if Sebastian appeared in a bath towel. But an elaborate set, with a professional model—well, that was something altogether different.

Having finished his breakfast, Cookie joined his master in the bedroom. The dog nuzzled against Sebastian's bare leg.

"You're no help at all." Nevertheless, Sebastian chuckled and gave his buddy a playful pat on the head.

Cookie waddled to his customary position on the oval beige rug beside Sebastian's bed, closing his eyes for an early morning snooze.

"Decisions, decisions." Sebastian pulled a dressy blue shirt off a cedar hanger. Standing in his shirttails, he debated whether to wear a pair of dark blue chinos that had been faithful friends since the day they were purchased. "No one else will be wearing a suit," he told Cookie. "I'll fit right in."

The dog opened one eye. Looking at his master, he wagged his tail in approval.

Sebastian twisted his mouth. "On second thought, I am the one paying the bill." The idea prompted him to don a dark blue suit and matching tie. "There. That's better."

As he perfected a Windsor knot, Sebastian had a horrifying thought. "Cookie, do you realize this is the first time I've ever put on more than one change of clothes for work?"

"Ummm hmmm," Cookie seemed to say.

"What do you think has happened to me, boy?"

He whimpered.

"Yeah, maybe you're right. Although I never thought I'd go for such a tall, thin woman. She looks like a model." He pursed his lips. "The kind of model my sister always admired." Bittersweet images of his older sister came to mind. "Do you think I'm making a big mistake, boy?"

This time, not even Cookie gave him an answer. Sebastian was on his own.

Meanwhile, Gwendolyn waited anxiously for Pansy to arrive. Just that morning, someone named Hal, who said he boarded Pansy and Bernie, called to ask for directions from his farm in Haymarket. So someone else would be bringing DairyBaked Delights' mascots. Had Sebastian forgotten all about the dessert? Strange, she felt sorry that she might not be seeing him after all. If he didn't show, at least after the shoot she could console herself with a big slice of pie. Somehow, the thought didn't comfort her as much as she thought it might.

Two hours later, Sebastian arrived at the warehouse. He was glad he didn't have to venture all the way into Washington. Though the city offered excitement, he had no desire to enter the frenzy full time. Trips to the Corcoran Gallery of Art and plays at the Kennedy Center gave Sebastian the cultural infusions he needed without the everyday hassle of urban living.

Gold hands on the black face of his watch confirmed that Gwendolyn must already be an hour into the photo shoot. Rushing lest he miss the entire session, Sebastian pulled into the first generous parking space he saw and made his way into the dumpy building. He didn't have to note the room number. A catchy tune would have led Sebastian in the direction of Gwendolyn's studio even if he had not visited in the past. He knocked on the door loudly enough to be heard over the music. As he waited for a response, he noticed that the song, a tune he didn't recognize, mentioned Jesus. And not as a swear word. The singer was praising His name!

The volume was turned down so he could no longer hear the words, just a faint tune. He heard footsteps as someone approached the door, and then Gwendolyn answered.

"Mr. Emerson! I was wondering when you would show up."

He looked around, pretending to search for his father. "Dad? Are you here?"

"Sorry." Her face blushed a pretty shade of peach. "Sebastian."

"I would have been here sooner if not for the traffic. I-66 was terrible," he responded, referring to the highway used by commuters heading into Washington from the western suburbs.

"No matter. We haven't started yet. You arrived at just the right moment," she smiled and gushed, leading him into the room where the photo session was to occur.

He looked at his watch. "You haven't started yet?"

"The model is still in hair and makeup."

"Still?" Sebastian glanced once again at his watch.

The melody of her laugh echoed in the studio. "You're spoiled since Pansy doesn't need much preparation to look cute. But hair and makeup for real models takes forever!"

"I see," Sebastian muttered, even though he didn't. As he followed Gwendolyn to the set, he noted her slim figure and gorgeous mane of hair. "I'll bet if you were the model, you wouldn't take more than five minutes," he blurted.

She turned her head just enough so he could see her eyes and answered. "Are you kidding? I'd take all day!"

"I find that hard to believe." Sebastian found himself enjoying the light banter. Already, Gwendolyn had made him feel relaxed, as though he, not she, should have been feeling nervous. She seemed just as at ease as she had the first day they met in his mom's office. Nothing he said or did ever seemed to intimidate her. He found her self-confidence both impressive and charming.

Glancing about the room, he noticed Pansy contentedly chewing her cud. A handsome young man was stroking the side of her neck. A vague feeling of jealousy ripped through Sebastian, taking him by surprise. "Who is that?"

"Oh, I'm sorry," Gwendolyn apologized. "That's Fernando, my assistant."

Fernando sent him a cocky grin and waved.

"I'd be lost without Fernando," Gwendolyn said.

"I'm sure." Sebastian had taken an instant dislike to Fernando. No man had any business being that handsome. He couldn't help wondering if Gwendolyn shared his opinion.

"Do not listen to my beautiful boss lady, Mr. Emerson," Fernando protested in a strange accent that seemed to mock a character in a mafia movie. "She flatters me."

Unwilling to think about Fernando any longer, Sebastian looked for Bernie. As soon as their eyes met, the dog let out several loud barks and rumbled until the cage shook.

"Settle down, boy!" Gwendolyn coaxed.

"Where's Hal?" Sebastian wondered.

"He went out for a latte. He'll be back before we get started."

"He'd better be. Hal's the only one who can keep Pansy under control."

Gwendolyn picked up a petit four and began applying petroleum jelly to the outside with a miniature paintbrush.

"Now what?"

"You've never seen your other photographers at work, have you?" Her voice held an edge that revealed her suspicion.

What could he say? He had always trusted Ebba. "The last photographer we had was in place before I was even born."

"Oh. She just retired, huh?"

"After a long career, yes. And I never once heard her say the first thing about petroleum jelly."

"I'm sure she used it. She just didn't tell you, that's all. It's nothing sinister. Petroleum jelly will make the chocolate coating on your petit fours look even more scrumptious, especially under the right lighting. You'll see."

Sebastian pointed to an oversized fan. "What is that for?"

"For the shots of falling snow, of course." Gwendolyn nodded toward a set depicting a ski slope. "When the time is right, we'll turn the fan on low and use artificial flakes to create a gentle snowfall."

Sebastian pictured the campaign Gwendolyn had explained to his mom. Mom had okayed the idea and then passed on the info to Sebastian without getting his approval first. So what else was new?

Still, he had to admit, he liked the idea. The model would be positioned, half sitting and half lying, as if she had just fallen in the snow. Pansy would be in the background, taking in the whole situation with her big brown cow eyes. Wearing a barrel around his neck replicating the ones on the stuffed dogs, Bernie would look at the model as if he were her best friend. A few petroleum jelly-painted petit fours would be placed in the snow, as if they had fallen from Bernie's barrel. Gwendolyn had suggested this as a way to show the consumer the candy itself.

He pictured the caption, in red script:

*Want to win her over?*
*Let DairyBaked Delights come to the rescue.*
*P.S. Bring the dog.*

"I'm sure I'll be pleased," Sebastian said with a nod.

"Good. I think this ad will get everyone's attention and convince people to buy your goods for holiday entertaining."

Just then, the model appeared. She was wearing ski garb the

color of raspberry jelly. Her face was made up in a flamboyant style. Her lips were the color of raspberries, and her dark hair was streaked with the same color. She did remind him of a bonbon.

"Here she is," Gwendolyn said. "What do you think?"

Fernando didn't hold back his opinion. "She is beautiful, is she not?" He brought his fingertips to his thumb, then touched them to his lips. Making a kissing noise, he drew his hand back toward the model in an exaggerated gesture. *"Bella!"*

Sebastian felt his breakfast threaten to make an encore appearance. Fernando's character seemed to be a guise, not the true persona of a full-blooded Italian male.

Sebastian looked at the model but visualized Gwendolyn instead. *"Bella,"* he whispered.

"Is anything wrong?" Gwendolyn asked.

"No. Nothing." Actually, everything. Sebastian realized he had been staring not at the model or anything else in the room he was supposed to be observing. Ever since he stepped into the room, he could only concentrate on Gwendolyn. He had to leave. He had to, before he made a complete and utter fool of himself.

"Everything looks as though it's going smoothly," he managed. "I see no need to stay and watch the entire shoot. But I shall expect exceptional results." With a curt nod, Sebastian set out to make his exit. In his haste, his knee tripped the latch to Bernie's cage. Enthralled by unexpected freedom, the dog bounded for the set.

"Stop, Bernie!" shouted Gwendolyn. "You'll ruin everything!"

## Chapter 4

The dog wasn't listening. Jumping on the fan's pedestal, he pressed the switch with his massive right paw. A second thump with his left paw sent the fan's blades from a gentle spin to full speed. Mighty gusts of wind filled the room.

Picking up white plastic bits from an open container in its path, the wind swirled them into a frenzy until the inside of the studio resembled a blinding blizzard.

Before the unexpected burst of wind, Fernando had set a few petit fours in the artificial snow that had been placed on the make-believe ski slope. But the platter of petit fours that Fernando held proved to be the dog's goal. Bernie bounded for the treats. His slobbering mouth made contact with the edge of the thick china, knocking it to the floor. Unprepared, Fernando lost his balance and landed on the floor, jelly-covered candies cascading all over his indigo shirt and black pants.

The petit fours that flew from the platter onto the model

landed on her hair. Gravity taking them downward, they left trails of jelly clinging to her smooth locks. Flying artificial snow adhered to the gunk. The final effect gave the impression her hair had been visited by snails that left behind slimy, snowflake-filled trails. Gooey treats spiraled downward and landed on her outfit, leaving greasy brown blotches wherever they hit before making their final free fall to the floor.

Having vanquished his enemies, Bernie bounded for the petit fours and engulfed a mouthful of treats. The pause in the dog's leaping seemed to bring Fernando to his senses, propelling him to shut off the fan. The blizzard ceased.

"You brute!" Fernando screamed as he got up and assessed the spots of jelly and chocolate on his clothing. "Now my beautiful silk shirt and best pants are a disaster!" His dark eyes narrowed as he looked in Gwendolyn's direction. "Someone will have to pay me every last cent it costs to replace this!"

By this time, Gwendolyn had helped the model recover and was ready to put a consoling hand on the assistant's shoulder. "It's all right, Fernando. It's only a shirt."

"Only a shirt! But it is my favorite shirt!"

Sebastian interrupted with a more immediate concern. "Don't let Bernie eat the treats. He could die!"

"He could?" Gwendolyn asked.

"Yes. My dog, Cookie, got into an open box of truffles last Christmas and became violently ill," Sebastian said as he attempted to corner Bernie. "His vet said dogs don't have the enzyme needed to digest chocolate."

"Not to mention, no creature should be eating petroleum

jelly," Gwendolyn added, trying to grab Bernie's collar. "Those are props, Bernie."

"Now, now, Bernie. You don't want to eat that." Sebastian's coaxing failed to convince the animal. The dog's response was to lunge onto Sebastian, the surprise impact knocking him to the floor. Bernie's front paws held him down by his shoulders and his back paws rested on Sebastian's legs.

"Get off my knees! That hurts!"

Wagging his tail, Bernie complied, but not before drooling chocolate, raspberry jelly, bits of chocolate cake and vanilla cake, mauled cherries, coconut, caramel, and petroleum jelly all over Sebastian's suit and hair. Only a quick turn of his head saved Sebastian's face.

"What's going on here?" Hal interrupted.

"Get your dog!" Fernando commanded.

Hal set his latte in an empty corner on the floor and rushed to calm the excited animal before confining him to his cage. Hal's cooing words to assuage the animal seemed to have a soothing effect on the humans as well.

Looking about the trashed studio, Gwendolyn seemed to be making mental calculations as to the amount of damage caused.

"How did he get out of his cage? I had it locked," Hal said as Bernie entered his portable kennel.

"My knee hit the latch," Sebastian admitted. "I'm just glad you got here when you did, Hal."

"So am I," Gwendolyn agreed. "But Hal's arrival was too little, too late, I'm afraid. This place is such a mess, I don't think we'll be able to shoot today."

Her edict resulted in a collective groan.

"When will we be able to reschedule?" Sebastian wanted to know.

"I'm afraid I won't be able to reschedule a shoot now until next week. First, the studio must be cleaned. Then I'm booked with other jobs from tomorrow until next Tuesday."

"I'm sorry," Sebastian said. "Please reschedule whenever you can."

"I'm sorry, too. I know I promised your mom—"

"Never mind. It was mostly my fault. I'll explain everything to her." He looked at the disaster that the studio had become. "Hire a cleaning crew. DairyBaked Delights will cover the expense."

"That is very generous of you, Mr. Emerson," Fernando said.

"Yes, thank you. That will save Fernando and me a lot of valuable time, and allow us to reschedule your shoot sooner," Gwendolyn added.

Fernando cleared his throat. "About my shirt. . ."

Though he felt no special generosity toward the young man, Sebastian knew he had to make amends. He took out his wallet, withdrew five twenty-dollar bills, and handed it to Fernando. "Will that buy you another silk shirt?"

He nodded several times in rapid succession. "Yes! Thank you!"

"Good. I'm glad to have at least one person happy today. I'll see the rest of you later." Humiliated by his error and disgusted by the mess the dog had slobbered on him, Sebastian rushed out the door, determined nothing would stop him this time.

He hadn't even gotten to the elevator when he heard Gwendolyn calling him.

"Sebastian! Wait!"

He pretended not to hear. *Not even Gwendolyn can console me now.*

"Sebastian!"

He was cornered. "What is it?"

Her eyes bespoke her sympathy. "Look, I'm really sorry about today."

"Sorry? Why are you sorry?" he snapped. "You and your staff will be paid for today even though you didn't snap the first picture, and you'll collect your fee for your work next week."

Her mouth opened as if she were about to deliver a rebuttal, but she didn't speak. The hurt look on her face, still smeared endearingly with chocolate, was too much for him to resist.

"Now I'm the one who's sorry. I didn't mean that."

"I know. At least, I think I know." From Sebastian's perspective, her smile lit up the entire building.

"I'm just kicking myself for being such a klutz that I've thrown off the whole day." Sebastian looked at his ruined suit and let out an audible sigh. "I just want to go home and forget this morning ever happened."

Gwendolyn cocked her head toward the model, who had begun wiping off her face. "You could be her." She lifted a strand of her own dark hair, which had become saturated during the effort to calm Bernie. "Or me. Want to help me clean this out of my hair?" To his surprise, rather than being angered as Fernando had been, Gwendolyn giggled like a young girl flush with the excitement of her first slumber party.

"You think this is funny?" he asked.

She stopped laughing long enough to ask, "Don't you?"

Gwendolyn's resilient spirit was difficult to resist. "I suppose we do look pretty amusing. And we probably smell even worse. At least I'm sure I do. Clothes can be replaced, and we humans are washable, aren't we?"

"As far as I know." He grinned in spite of himself.

"Fernando is a player, and he wants to be ready for his next impromptu date," Gwendolyn told him. "He always carries more than one change of clothes. Maybe he has a pair of pants and a shirt you can borrow."

He looked down at his long legs. "I don't know. He's a lot shorter than I am."

"Who cares what the clothes look like? As soon as you get home, you can change and enjoy your day off."

"Enjoy my day off?" he scoffed. "Not when I've got to face Mother and tell her I've run up a huge bill with no pictures to show for it."

"That's all right. You don't have to pay me."

"No. I insist." Sebastian tipped his head to one side and shrugged. "You shouldn't have to pay for a lost day and a cleaning bill when the accident wasn't your fault."

"Maybe you'll feel better after eating my dessert," she suggested.

"Dessert?"

"Don't you remember? I promised to make you dessert."

"Oh, that." Embarrassment covered him as he remembered how rudely he had challenged her. "You didn't really have to do that."

"Didn't I?"

"All right, I suppose I did seem pretty serious about the whole thing last week. If there's enough dessert, maybe we can share it with Fernando and Hal later. A good dessert should put us all in a better mood."

After cleaning the goo from her face and hair and sponging off her soft white sweater and black pants as best as she could, Gwendolyn was ready to serve her dessert. She retrieved the pie and a container of whipped cream from the compact refrigerator and headed toward the table where everyone sat, awaiting a treat.

When she noticed Sebastian, she nearly dropped the pie. Following her suggestion, he had borrowed a shirt and a pair of pants from Fernando. Since the wild floral-patterned shirt was three sizes too small, Sebastian was forced to keep the buttons on the front and cuffs undone. Gwendolyn had to admit her new boss possessed a chest her male friends in the modeling business would envy. She summoned her willpower to keep from staring.

Fernando's blue jeans constricted Sebastian's taut abdomen and full thighs so that he shifted in his seat every few minutes.

Their ill fit wouldn't have been noticeable to the casual observer, except that the jeans were hemmed well above his ankles. If Gwendolyn had seen Sebastian without knowing why he was wearing such a getup, she would have guessed he had been stranded alone on a desert island since he was twelve years old and had been wearing the same outfit since his ship wrecked.

Trying to maintain her composure, Gwendolyn placed the dessert on a table where it wouldn't be visible to the rest of the group. Only the model had excused herself. Gwendolyn wasn't surprised that she passed on dessert.

The burned piecrust hadn't improved in appearance overnight. The color looked bluer than ever. She tried to cover her mistake with whipped topping, but some of the color was still visible from the gaps in the top. Giving up, she brought the dessert to the table.

Sebastian was the first to speak. "Uh, what kind of pie is that?"

"Key lime, of course!" Gwendolyn smiled so broadly she could almost feel the corners of her lips touch the sides of her ears. She looked around the table and noticed that everyone's expressions looked as though they were watching a circus performer rather than anticipating a piece of delicious pie. "Why? Is something the matter?"

Fernando answered. "It is a most. . .interesting. . .shade of. . .teal."

Gwendolyn examined the pie. "Teal?"

Sebastian nodded. "I'd have to say he's right. Sort of a teal green."

"Oh. It must be the food coloring. Yes, I was hoping for a more true green, but it turned out a bit odd. But it will still taste wonderful, I'm sure." She knew she sounded like a television commercial.

"You added food coloring?" Fernando asked.

"Yes. I didn't like the way it looked after I made it. I thought it looked anemic. More like a really, really pale lemon than a nice fresh lime. I was hoping to make it the color of the limes you see in the stores. You know, a nice, pretty shade of green." She shrugged. "Oh, well."

"Oh, well?" Hal grunted. "Sorry, but I think I'll pass. Say, Sebastian, got any more of those petit fours left?"

"I used them all," Gwendolyn snapped.

"Oh." Disappointment colored Hal's tone. "I saw some pumpkin cake in the coffee shop. I think I'll grab me a piece of that before I head on out to the farm."

Fernando's eyes darted from side to side, and he squirmed in his seat.

"You don't have to eat it, Fernando," Gwendolyn said, swallowing to overcome her hurt feelings.

"Are you sure you don't mind? Uh, lime never was my favorite flavor, anyway. I never even liked those lime lollipops they give away at the bank." He grinned. "I always asked for grape. Still do, as a matter of fact."

"Care to go next door with me?" Hal offered.

Fernando gave Gwendolyn a pleading look before he answered. "If it's all right with everyone. . ."

"Cowards!" Sebastian teased.

*Funny. That's what I used to think about you.* To her surprise, Sebastian seemed almost likable.

"But we will be cowards eating pumpkin cake!" Fernando countered as he and Hal headed out the door.

After their exit, Sebastian turned to Gwendolyn, a smile lighting his handsome features. "Looks like we've been deserted, pun intended."

"Cute." Gwendolyn screwed her mouth into a wry grin.

"I thought so."

She looked at the door. "Go ahead." She tried not to choke on her words. "I suppose you want to go with them."

"Not at all."

"Really?"

"Really." The light in his gray blue eyes showed her that he meant it. "I want to try your pie. After all, you promised to make the dessert, the least I can do is to eat it." He winked. "Who knows? Maybe you've invented a new product for DairyBaked Delights!"

Relieved that the troll had permanently retreated to his lair beneath the bridge, Gwendolyn placed her hands on her hips. "You don't mean that."

"Perhaps not about the new product. But I do want to try the dessert."

"Well, I don't want to try it," Gwendolyn admitted.

"Why not?" Sebastian challenged. "What happened to your spirit of adventure?"

"It doesn't extend to food gone wrong."

"Aw, come on. I can look at this pie and tell you put a lot

of work into it. We've got to try it."

"Well, okay." She cut into the pie. The knife slid through the filling without a problem, but the crust was another matter. In her attempts to cut through it, she ended up stabbing it in frustration.

"Whoa!" Sebastian said. "You don't have to kill the pie, do you?"

"No." She stopped stabbing. "But apparently I need to kill the crust."

He chuckled. "Let me help you with that." When he drew closer to her, she caught the aroma of his clean skin. A pleasant woodsy scent of a brand of cologne she couldn't identify emanated from his neck. She wished he could linger, just so she could breathe in his warmth and closeness longer.

"She's putting up quite a fight," he observed.

"Who?" Gwendolyn blurted.

He gave her a strange look. "The piecrust, of course. She's a tough one. Why, who did you think I was talking about?"

"No one," she spouted. "Nothing. I don't know. I'm just not used to anyone calling a piecrust 'she.' "

He chuckled. "I guess not." He placed a slice of pie on her plate. "Well, you gave it the old college try, but I am the conqueror!" He lifted his hands in the air in mock victory.

She laughed in spite of herself and watched him struggle to cut a second piece.

Moments later, he scooped up a dollop of filling. "Ah, there's nothing like toothpaste pie." He placed a spoonful in his mouth. "Mmm, good!"

"Toothpaste pie?"

"Sure is."

She studied it. "You know, come to think of it, the color is a little like the spearmint flavor I use. Well, it won't taste like spearmint. That I can guarantee."

He nodded. "Actually, it tastes great."

As the flavor of lime burst into her mouth, she had to nod in agreement. "You're right. It does taste good. But it looks so awful, and the crust is so tough; I have to say, I failed. I could just die." She looked into Sebastian's steely blue eyes. "And I know what this means. Both my dessert and my photo session flopped. You win," she conceded. "I'm fired."

# Chapter 5

Seeing the photographer's distress, Sebastian realized that in spite of how badly the shoot had gone, and regardless of the fact that the dessert had been a flop, he didn't want to fire her. Feeling ashamed, he recalled how boorish he had been to Gwendolyn when they first met. Although the company was well in the black financially, Sebastian remembered when they weren't, and he still hated to waste money. Mother didn't always exercise the same caution. Sebastian had taken out his anger with his mother on the young woman when she was doing nothing more than appearing for a job interview. She hadn't deserved the treatment he'd given her, and he knew it.

Still, pride made him resist. "Do you think you deserve to be fired?"

Gwendolyn gulped. "Not really." She bowed her head, causing her long lashes to form lush crescents on her pale cheeks. "But I was foolish enough to make a promise I knew I couldn't keep. Now I have to accept the consequences."

He nodded once. How could he fire someone who possessed such humility?

Her coral lips curved into a frown. "Besides, it's not like you'd be losing any good pictures if you let me go now."

Sebastian saw her shoulders sag in defeat. She busied herself by piling the dessert plates she had brought into a neat stack, her chocolate-colored eyes avoiding his.

She was beautiful. That couldn't be denied. But for Sebastian, her appearance had become secondary to the fiber of character she displayed.

"I won't let you go." As soon as the words escaped his lips, Sebastian realized that he sounded more like a suitor than a boss. For once, he hoped they weren't of like minds. Otherwise, she might see he had just admitted he wished he could captivate her forever.

Matthew 12:34 came to mind: *"For out of the overflow of the heart the mouth speaks."* Thinking of this eternal truth, he was all too aware an expression of chagrin passed over his features.

Her gaze met his, her delicate features marked with questions.

Sebastian changed his expression to one that would brook no nonsense. He tried to give his voice an edge of authority. "What I mean to say is, Mother will be upset enough by today's fiasco as it is. How could I tell her I fired her hand-picked photographer on top of everything else?"

Gwendolyn let out a little "oh" that indicated his answer was a disappointment. Sebastian couldn't deny a triumphant feeling that she might return his interest.

Gwendolyn was quick with a comeback. "I'd like to be a fly on the wall when you tell her!"

Her remark stung as surely as if she had slapped him across the cheek, but he couldn't let her know. "So you'd like to see me squirm?" He arched his eyebrow to indicate he was an accomplice to her joke.

"Not really," she admitted. "Although you've certainly seen me embarrassed enough."

"Perhaps." He stirred the dessert with his spoon. "I must confess, this is the best toothpaste pie I've ever eaten."

"My guess is that it's the only toothpaste pie you've ever eaten."

He decided that no reply was necessary. In the company of Gwendolyn Warner, the prospect of toothpaste pie seemed pleasing indeed.

The phone was ringing as Gwendolyn slipped the key into the scratched brass doorknob of her apartment door.

"Coming!" she called to the telephone as though it would respond with more than an urgent summons. After shutting the door and setting down the leftover dessert, she ran the few steps necessary to reach the other side of the living room and picked up the receiver before the answering machine responded.

"You sound winded!" Her mother's familiar voice succeeded in conveying both chastisement and concern.

"Hi, Mom. I just got in from the photo shoot."

"So how did it go?"

Gwendolyn set her keys on the arm of the thirty-year-old couch, a gift from her parents' attic. She plopped on top of a giant sunflower set against a worn background of avocado green. "You don't want to know."

"Oh, don't I?"

"What you really want to know is how the dessert went over."

"You know me so well." Mom chuckled. "Of course I don't even have to ask about the photo shoot. I know it went swimmingly. They always do."

Gwendolyn bit her lower lip and shot a wordless prayer heavenward asking forgiveness for her lie of omission. If she revealed too many disasters, her mother might decide to arrive in Washington the next day and straighten things out in her capable way. "About the dessert. . ."

"What about it?"

"Well, let's just say your title of Best Cook Ever is still safe. Very safe."

Mom's throaty laugh filled the phone line. "Oh, I wouldn't be so sure. With a little practice, you'll soon surpass me."

"Oh, I already have. In the category of toothpaste pie."

"Toothpaste pie? Whatever do you mean?"

Gwendolyn grimaced as she remembered the teal green filling and tough crust. "That's how the pie could best be described."

"But toothpaste?"

"I added food coloring, and. . .let's just say it didn't turn out the nice shade of green I expected."

"And you got this recipe from a woman who runs a bed-and-breakfast? Remind me not to eat there!"

"No, Mom. The recipe was good. Cynthia Lyons' Web site recipe didn't tell me to add food coloring. I did that on my own. And, thinking back, I might have made a mistake or two on the piecrust ingredients. And besides, Cynthia recommended that I use a graham cracker crust. Foolish pride made me try something I didn't know how to make. So I can't lay any of the blame at Cynthia's feet—or on her keyboard." She chuckled at her own humor.

Mom laughed the same way she always did whenever she read the comics in the Sunday paper. Their shared amusement cheered Gwendolyn.

"So are you still going to stay with the class?"

"Sure. I have a lot to learn. Obviously."

When she hung up minutes later, Gwendolyn's initial excitement about the job returned. She thought about the next photo shoot. Her stomach danced the twist. The emotion took her aback. She told herself her reaction was only delight about keeping her job. Other possibilities were too unsettling to contemplate.

The following night, Gwendolyn logged on to the cooking course. Apparently feeling more ambitious than usual, Cynthia had challenged everyone to submit a favorite cake recipe. She offered to hold an online chat for anyone interested in talking about recipes. Gwendolyn sent her grandmother's recipe for sour cream cake, then got the go-ahead from Cynthia to try it.

"Yay!" Gwendolyn typed on the screen. "I hope I can do Nanny proud."

"I'm sure you will," Cynthia answered.

"I don't always succeed in my attempts," Gwendolyn typed.

Someone named Subqueen chimed in. "Well, I can't talk. You should have seen the lemon bars I made the day I met my sister for the first time! Lemon soup bars are what they should've been called—and talk about tart!"

Gwendolyn grinned. Apparently Subqueen was just as bad a cook as she was! Suddenly she didn't feel so alone anymore.

Someone else typed, "I'll bet your lemon bars were better than what I recently ate. I called it 'toothpaste pie.'"

*Toothpaste pie!* Her heart felt as though it had fallen to her feet. She looked at the classmate's screen name: CreamyDream.

*It has to be Sebastian.* She felt tears threaten. *After he tried to make me feel better today, here he is, making fun of my pie, where he thinks I won't see.* She swallowed and stuck her lip out with the false pride of someone who was hurting. *So what? Who cares what he thinks?*

She grabbed a tissue and kept reading.

"In spite of the color, the wonderful woman who made the pie had a great sense of humor," CreamyDream wrote. "It truly was one of the best desserts I ever tasted."

"Because of the woman who made it, huh, CreamyDream?" LzzyGurl typed.

CreamyDream replied with an emoticon smiley face.

Gwendolyn couldn't believe her eyes. "Because of the

wonderful woman who made it?" Sebastian was talking about her? Her tears disappeared just as quickly as they came.

Obviously Sebastian hadn't recognized her screen name. She thanked Cynthia and logged off, whistling a happy little tune.

As soon as he saw IPhotoU log off, a sick realization hit Sebastian in the stomach.

IPhotoU?

Could that be Gwendolyn's screen name? No. No. He hoped not. But somehow, in his heart, he knew IPhotoU was Gwendolyn.

He groaned. How could he have made fun of her pie— however good-naturedly? He must have come across as a crank and, as a result, left hurt feelings in his wake. Sebastian felt devastated. Gwendolyn was the only woman to crack his tough exterior in years. He had been focused on the family business for the past five years. His personal life had been on hold. Finally, a Christian woman he thought he might grow to love—and he had ruined everything.

Over the next couple of days, Gwendolyn found her thoughts returning again and again to her new job. Yet as soon as she thought about how she could make the next photo shoot a success, images of Sebastian popped into her head. They persisted no matter how she pushed them aside.

In the evening, she tried to concentrate on devotions,

focusing on Romans 8:28: "And we know that in all things God works for the good of those who love him, who have been called according to his purpose."

As she contemplated the passage, the words *love* and *purpose* leapt out at her. She set her Bible, still open to the passage, on her lap.

*Lord, why do I feel You are trying to show me something in granting me this job? Are You finally telling me to pursue modeling full time, or do You have something else in mind? Why is it when I think of this job, my mind dwells on Sebastian? You know nothing like this has ever happened to me before. I need Your help, Lord, to sort out my feelings and to see how they fit into Your plan for my life.*

Though the Lord didn't respond with a definitive answer, Gwendolyn noticed her spirit being strengthened. The feeling was like water being added to a half-empty cup. The pouring came from the Lord. The filling increased her confidence that the Lord would soon reveal His will.

# Chapter 6

I can't believe Aunt Jeanette didn't realize I'd have to drive forever to get here," Gwendolyn grumbled as she finally pulled her compact car into the parking lot, miles from her apartment. But she couldn't waste such a marvelous Christmas gift—a year's membership to a new facility with aerobics classes, racquetball and tennis courts, two hot tubs, an Olympic-sized pool, and huge rooms filled with state-of-the-art exercise machines.

She was in a better mood once she'd dumped her coat and gym bag in a locker and headed for the treadmills. She had just entered instructions for a thirty-minute run at five miles per hour, hoping to work her way up to six within a few weeks. Soon she felt the presence of a fellow runner jump on the machine next to hers. Cutting her glance to the right, she nearly tripped when she recognized Sebastian Emerson.

He returned her stare. "Gwendolyn?"

"In the flesh," she puffed, regaining her stride.

"What are you doing here?" Sebastian managed to press

buttons as he spoke.

"I could ask you the same thing. I've been a member for over two months, and I've never seen you here before."

"But we didn't know each other before." His machine increased its speed to 6.3 miles per hour. "I hardly recognized you. Uh, you don't mind if I run beside you, do you?"

"Why would I? You're a member here, too."

They ran alongside each other without speaking until Sebastian finally ventured her name again. "Gwendolyn?"

She snapped her head in his direction. "Yes?"

By this time, he was becoming a bit winded, although not enough to alarm her. "Uh, I have a question. Do you take online cooking classes?"

She nodded.

His lips twisted into a frown. "Cynthia's?"

"Yes."

He groaned. "You were on the chat the other night, weren't you?"

She nodded. "I was surprised to see you on the list. I would have pegged you as someone who knows how to cook all sorts of sweets."

"No. I work in the front office, not in the bakery itself. My grandfather was trained in Germany. He was a baker's apprentice before he came to America as a young man in 1948. I can hardly boil an egg, myself. So I thought I'd learn." He wiped his face off with a small white towel.

Feeling left behind, she set her treadmill a couple of notches higher. "Cynthia's place is a good start. I've learned a lot already."

"So have I. But now I wish I hadn't taken it."

"Why?"

"Because of what I said the other night. Look, if you hate me, I understand. I'm sorry," he said in between huffs of breath. "Especially about what I said about your pie."

She felt her heart soften. How could she not forgive Sebastian, when he was willing to come to her and confess his mistake? She decided to focus on the positive comment he had made about her. "And the wonderful woman who made it?"

His face became redder. Gwendolyn had a feeling the flush wasn't the result of increased exertion. "I'm sorry."

"So you didn't mean what you said?"

"About the pie?"

She heard herself breathing harder. Her throat became sore as air flowed over it through her open mouth. "No. About the wonderful woman."

"Of course I meant it."

*So he meant it!* "Why are you taking classes?" she asked, her huffing matching his.

"No special reason. I live alone, and I get tired of eating out of the microwave, I guess."

She laughed. "Me, too. In that case, why don't we try out some of the recipes together?"

His eyes brightened. "Really? You'd like that?"

"Yes."

"How about Thursday?"

"Sure. You can meet me at my apartment. I'll e-mail CreamyDream my address." She sent him a sly grin.

"Why don't we go out to dinner first, and then come back

and try out our desserts?" he proposed.

"That means I have to get dressed up?"

"Not at all." Sebastian gave her a quick glance. "You're even more beautiful without makeup."

Unwilling to let him see that she was flattered by his remark, Gwendolyn focused on three big screen televisions just in front of them. Each was tuned to a network station. Closed captioning provided dialogue, since the sound was turned off in deference to the rock music blaring from the gym's radio.

"If only that were true," she denied.

He shook his head in rebuttal but changed the subject. "I thought you lived nearer to D.C."

Gwendolyn brightened. "I do. This membership was a Christmas gift from an aunt who has no concept of metro traffic. But it's worth the drive. Lucky you if you live nearby."

"I could almost walk it."

"Then you could probably run it." Gwendolyn was still huffing, but Sebastian was now gliding as though he were on a Sunday promenade.

"So could you. Although you don't need to work yourself to death exercising."

Remembering his earlier remarks about her slight figure, Gwendolyn bristled. "I like to keep in shape, that's all."

"Then you must be in shape enough to join me in a game of tennis."

Wary of another challenge after the pie fiasco, Gwendolyn searched for an excuse. "Isn't it a bit cold?"

"Not on the indoor courts."

"I didn't bring my racquet."

"They have loaners at the front desk." A triumphant grin indicated he enjoyed his checkmate. "And don't tell me you have to get home. It's still early."

Sebastian had anticipated her trump card and played it before she could. "All right. You win."

"Not yet. But I will."

"So you're not afraid you might lose the match to a girl?"

"Should I be?"

"Maybe. Although I might let you win. Wouldn't want to do permanent damage to your male ego." Grabbing the white hand towel she had thrown over the treadmill's display, Gwendolyn patted the sweat from her face as the treadmill slowed for a one-minute cooldown. "I'll get a racquet and meet you on the court."

"Ad one!" Sebastian called before he delivered a robust serve. He had won five games to her four. The game in progress had ended up in a deuce, so they were playing for two advantage points to determine the winner. If he earned the last point, Sebastian would win the set.

Gwendolyn had positioned herself well, just in front of the baseline in the backcourt. Despite her teasing, she discovered early in the set that she needed to fight for every point. Sebastian had proven his talent for placing the ball where Gwendolyn would have to expend the most effort to return it.

This time was no exception; the ball barely cleared the net, well into the service area.

She dashed for it. Her forehand stroke sent the ball higher than her intent. Taking advantage of her mistake, Sebastian charged the net and leapt high in the air, returning the ball with a forceful overhand smash, a power stroke too difficult to return.

"Good game." She extended a congratulatory hand.

Sebastian grinned. "Thanks for letting me win." His hand made contact with hers, causing that spark again.

With regret, she broke the grasp. "You're welcome. Although I could have played a better game with my own racquet," she protested teasingly.

"Excuses, excuses." He shook his head in mock sympathy. "You'll have to bring your racquet next time."

*Next time. Why did that sound so good?*

A few moments later, she and Sebastian approached the desk so she could exchange the borrowed racquet for her membership card. Gwendolyn was taken aback by a query from the woman at the desk. "You're Gwendolyn Warner? The model?"

She nodded.

"I saw your ads for Lustre Lipstick." She studied Gwendolyn but protested as she returned her card. "You don't look like Gwendolyn Warner."

"No one does." Turning on her heel, Gwendolyn exited, an obviously amused Sebastian following beside her.

"Good retort. I think she was stunned."

"I stole that line from Cary Grant." She stopped in front of her car.

Sebastian's eyebrows shot up. "But I don't get it. I thought you were a photographer."

"I am. But I did some modeling awhile back." She kept her voice curt to discourage inquiry. Her modeling days were over. She hurried over to her car.

"This is your car?" His voice betrayed his surprise.

Gwendolyn opened the door of the ancient Ford Aspire. "I *aspire* to something better, but this is all I can *afford,*" she quipped.

A chuckle was her reward. "Don't tell me you plan to give Cary Grant credit for that line as well."

"No. I made it up all by myself. Although I won't promise someone else hasn't thought of it, too."

"You mean, such brilliance might be duplicated?" As she laughed, he changed the subject. "So when will you be back?"

"Tomorrow or the next day."

"That soon?" He appraised her figure in a way that reminded her of a personal trainer. "You really don't need all this exercise."

"I want to stay healthy."

"Yes, but I don't think you will add a day to your life. The Lord is in control."

"I agree."

His mouth dropped open in apparent shock. "You do?"

"Yes." She placed her hands on her hips. "Just because I used to be a model doesn't mean I don't read the Bible."

"Then I owe you an apology. I jumped to the wrong conclusion." He thought for a moment. "So tell me, how can a

Christian woman pursue a career devoted to vanity?"

His unforeseen question left her with no quick response. Instead, she felt an unwelcome surge of anger. "It was nice playing tennis with you, Sebastian. See you another time." Without looking back, she jumped behind the wheel of the car. Ignoring his protests and apologies, she sped out of the lot.

Sebastian's question about reconciling her Christianity with her profession was provocative. Too provocative.

She wasn't sure she wanted the answer.

# Chapter 7

The next Thursday, Sebastian knocked on Gwendolyn's apartment door. Even though she had left the gym in a huff, she hadn't called to cancel their plans to have dinner together.

"Coming!"

*Good. So she hasn't conveniently forgotten.* His heart thumped at the melodious sound of her voice, muffled though it was through the door. An instant later, Gwendolyn appeared before him. Her hair was styled in loose curls that framed her creamy complexion and dark eyes. She had chosen a soft coral sweater and black dress pants with low heels. As always, she looked beautiful.

"Come on in." She stepped to the side and eyed the dessert. "Can I take that?"

"Sure." He hesitated. "About the other night—"

"I'm sorry," they said in unison. At the realization, they chuckled.

"Look," Gwendolyn said, "I shouldn't have peeled out of

the parking lot like that. I was being childish. You posed a perfectly reasonable question, one that I don't have an answer for. I was too embarrassed to face the facts, so I ran away. Can you forgive me?"

"I'm here, aren't I?" he responded only half-jokingly. "No one has all the answers. Least of all me. If I came across as challenging you, I'm sorry. As Mother told you, I have trouble relating to humans sometimes."

The cordial look on her face was his reward.

Gwendolyn lifted the transparent green plastic container to eye level and examined the contents. "What is this?"

"Noodle pudding."

"Oh, yes. I remember that recipe. I didn't have the nerve to try it."

"I tasted it," he admitted, following her into the small kitchen just off the side of the common area. "I think it's pretty good."

Gwendolyn set his container on the kitchen counter, then pointed to a closed cake container. "I made Nanny's sour cream cake."

"Mmm. Now that sounds good. I don't remember her posting that, though."

"She didn't. It's from my own grandmother. I've called her Nanny ever since I was two years old."

"Oh, a family heirloom."

"The recipe is, anyway. I'm not so sure I'd want to eat a family heirloom," she joked. "I think it turned out okay. It looks good, anyway." Gwendolyn lifted the cover to reveal a perfectly formed Bundt cake.

"Looks good. No frosting, huh?"

"Doesn't need any. Besides, that's what makes it so portable. Not a lot of sticky icing to contend with."

"True." He rubbed his chin. "Looks like something DairyBaked Delights could package."

Gwendolyn let out a musical laugh. "I could just see Nanny now, if she thought her cake might go national—"

"Maybe even international."

Only an instant flew by before she gasped. "So that's what your mom was about to tell me? You plan to go international?"

"That's a long way off. We've just come out of a corporate reorganization and are just recovering from that. Plus, we haven't even broken into the Midwest market in the U.S. yet. So don't say anything."

"Your secret is safe with me." Gwendolyn cut off a slice of cake and placed it on a blue and white dish. "Here," she said, handing him the dessert. "Life is short. Eat dessert first."

"But won't we spoil dinner?" Despite his protest, he took the dessert and sat down at the small kitchen table.

"Maybe. But I can't wait to try the noodle pudding."

"And we can have more dessert after we get back from dinner, huh?" he ventured.

"Of course!" She took the seat beside his.

He grinned. Gwendolyn's love for life was making her more and more attractive to him. He took a bite of cake. "Say, this is good!"

"Thanks. And so is your noodle pudding. So, have I made

up for the toothpaste pie?"

"And then some! Oh, I almost forgot," Sebastian said. "Bernie got into an altercation with one of Hal's cats and got a scratch on his face. The vet said he'll need at least a week, maybe a little longer, to heal well enough to appear in a photo."

"Another week? But—"

"I know. We'll miss Thanksgiving."

"I don't suppose we could shoot it without him."

"Not a chance."

"So what will we do?"

He shrugged. "We'll just catch the latest trend. We'll run an old Thanksgiving ad and call it a classic."

"I'm sure people will enjoy that." Gwendolyn seemed to be trying to hide her disappointment.

"But I don't like that idea as well as running something fresh." Sebastian let out a resigned sigh. "Maybe everything's turned out for the best. Since the new photos will be geared to spring, we won't have to worry about plastic snow."

"After what happened last time, I'm not sure I ever want to work with plastic snow again, anyway."

"Maybe the beach."

"Whatever you say. You're the boss."

Sebastian cringed at the designation. Could it be possible that she couldn't see his real feelings for her?

Gwendolyn expected him to escort her to his car but, instead, he offered his arm so they could walk to the restaurant. She remembered the only steak restaurant within walking distance. "You must be taking me to the John Paul Jones."

He nodded. "Ever tried it?"

"Are you kidding?"

"Why would I be kidding?"

She avoided his gaze. "The truth is, I can't afford it."

"Perhaps DairyBaked Delights will change that."

Gwendolyn smiled to herself. *At least he's finally decided he likes me—as a photographer, anyway.*

They chatted as they waited for dinner to be served. Gwendolyn was pleased to discover it was easy to talk to Sebastian. Even more importantly, they agreed on the things that mattered in life.

She felt her heart softening toward him, glad he was proving to be somewhat human after all. Quite a far cry from the first day they met, when Gwendolyn was certain she could never like such a stuffed shirt.

The steak placed before Gwendolyn was so large, a portion of the fatted tip hung over the edge of the plate. Thankful for the concept of doggie bags, Gwendolyn was just about to reach for the steak sauce when Sebastian's hand touched hers.

"Care to say a blessing?"

"A blessing?" Gwendolyn was accustomed to muttering a few words of thanks for meals consumed in private, but never in public. She perused the room and noticed every table was full.

"We don't have to, if you're embarrassed."

A sense of shame engulfed her. "I guess I shouldn't be."

Sebastian flashed her a smile and took her hands in his. Their comforting warmth left her feeling secure. The prayer he spoke was barely above a whisper. "Our Father, we thank You for Your bountiful provision and the time we have this night to share in it. In Christ's name we pray, amen."

He gave her hands a squeeze before releasing them. Feeling self-conscious all the same, Gwendolyn darted her glance over the room. None of the other patrons had noticed their gesture. To her surprise, her relief was mingled with disappointment. Perhaps their willingness to pray before a meal could have inspired others. Biting into the savory meat, she resolved not to be shy about saying blessings in public in the future.

"Enjoying your steak?" Sebastian seemed pleased.

"Mmm!" was all Gwendolyn could muster with her mouth full. Nodding, she dug into the baked potato slathered in butter and sour cream.

"I must confess, I'm surprised to see you eating so well." He took a sip of coffee.

She swallowed, an unpleasant thought occurring to her. "Please don't tell me this is a test."

"Of course not. What would make you think that?"

"You know perfectly well." Putting down her fork, Gwendolyn realized the voice that exited her lips was more snippy than she had intended, yet she couldn't stop herself from continuing. "Sebastian, you have no idea what my life has really been like. You seem to think I'm too thin."

"Says who?"

"You did. The day I first met you in your mom's office, and you asked me if I ever touched a piece of chocolate."

"Oh." He stared at his empty plate.

"You just don't understand."

Mimicking her, he put down his own fork and leaned forward. "Then why don't you make me understand?" His voice held no dare.

"I'll try." She sighed. "All through school, I was teased and taunted for being a bean pole. Until ninth grade, I was taller than anybody else in class, including the boys. After they started catching up to me in height, I hoped and prayed the teasing would stop. But it didn't, because then they decided I was too skinny." Remembering those lonely times, she clutched her stomach. "I would go home every night and drink milk shakes until I was about sick, hoping to gain weight. But no amount of high-fat foods, or anything else, helped. I was known as 'the bean pole' until graduation day."

"Your classmates don't get extra credit for originality."

"They didn't have to. I got the point."

"I'm sure you did." Sebastian's mouth softened, and he shook his head slightly in a gesture of sympathy. "You're right. I had no idea. That must have been terrible for you."

"It was." She sighed.

"But you judge others. You just had to hire a model yourself."

"True. But I always try to judge favorably. And when I look for friendship, I don't go by looks."

"Maybe God was trying to teach you something through your high school experiences," he pointed out.

She nodded. "I learned a lot."

"Good. So you're not still doing crazy things like drinking yourself silly with milk shakes, are you?"

Gwendolyn shook her head. "No." She smiled in spite of herself and swept both arms over her body. "Can't you tell?"

"No. You're perfect. Perfect just the way you are."

"I wouldn't have known it. . ." The faraway look on Sebastian's face caused Gwendolyn to lay down her imaginary sword. "What's the matter, Sebastian? What are you thinking about?"

He shook his head as if returning from Oz. "Nothing."

"I know that's not so. I told you about my miserable school experience. The least you can do is tell me about yours."

"I wasn't the one who was miserable."

"Then you were the bully." Having seen the competitive and disagreeable side of Sebastian, this wasn't a stretch for Gwendolyn to imagine.

"Actually, I wasn't." He half-smiled. "I was thinking about Candy."

"Candy? Oh, you mean your petit fours."

"No. My sister, Candy."

"Sister?" Gwendolyn didn't bother to conceal her surprise. "I had no idea you had a sister."

Sebastian extracted a photo from his wallet. Faded with time, it was the portrait of a sprightly blond teenager. Gwendolyn speculated that Rhoda must have looked much like Candy when she was that age.

"So beautiful," Gwendolyn said with unabashed admiration.

"And so thin. At least in this picture." He studied it. "Too thin. And do you want to know why?" His eyes narrowed as his voice took on a hard edge. The misty eyes were gone. "Because of people like you. Skinny people. People who never knew what it was like to be fat."

"But, Sebastia—"

"Can you imagine what it must be like for a girl to be overweight, especially when her parents own a bakery?"

Gwendolyn stiffened as she thought back to her own experiences. "Yes, I can."

"I doubt it. Because even though people teased you, at least you're built like a model. Just think about what it's like for a plump girl to see people like you everywhere she turns. Women she's supposed to emulate, to admire, to adore. And she can't be like them. Because she isn't made that way."

"Look, I never said everyone should be like me."

"You don't have to. Just your photographs are enough." He let out a sigh. "I'm not saying you're to blame. You're in an industry that demands thinness."

Reaching for his hand, she managed to touch it before he pulled it away, clasping both hands around his cup of coffee.

She retreated and stirred her own coffee. "Obviously you're upset. And understandably so." Gwendolyn caught his gaze. "Tell me about her."

"Candy was one of those girls who was chubby as a child and even more plump as a young teenager. People would say, 'You have such a pretty face.' "

"How thoughtless."

He nodded. "Maybe they wouldn't have been so insensitive had they known how much worse their taunts made her feel." Sebastian folded his arms across his chest. "Anyway, she wanted to be popular, and finally, with Mom's help, she dieted until she was almost as thin as you. Unfortunately, it worked. She became popular."

"Why is that so unfortunate?"

"Because if her weight loss hadn't changed things, maybe she wouldn't have been so determined to keep the weight off. At first, the popularity and praise seemed great. She seemed more secure than ever. But eventually she became addicted to the praise and began to agonize over every fluctuation in weight. She worked harder than ever to stay reed thin. She kept on losing more and more weight. Before our eyes, she went from looking healthy to a waif. It was awful."

"It must have been," Gwendolyn agreed. "But it seems her weight loss was motivated by kids at school, not the media."

"Think again. I noticed Candy's open admiration for models in magazines and thin actresses in movies and on television."

Gwendolyn held her breath, bracing herself for whatever news he had to share.

"Over a period of two years, Candy finally lost so much weight that she had to be hospitalized. Thankfully, she recovered."

"I'm so glad to hear that."

He nodded. "She's fine now, but she doesn't want to have anything to do with the bakery."

He leaned closer. "I convinced Mom and Dad not to use

human models in DairyBaked Delights' ads for many years. I don't want my family to do anything to contribute to any other young girl's loss of self-esteem—or health."

Gwendolyn felt her own eyes mist. "So that's why you were so opposed to me using a model."

"Yes. And now that I think about it, I'm still opposed to it." Without warning, Sebastian threw down his napkin. "Gwendolyn, this evening's over. I'm taking you home."

# Chapter 8

Over the next few days, as much as she wanted to talk to Sebastian, Gwendolyn sensed that he needed to work out his issues for himself. She made no contact with him but concentrated on her work. Photographing reed-thin models, she couldn't help wondering if Sebastian was right about unrealistic media images.

The knowledge that Sebastian was angry with her was even worse. Almost a week had passed with no contact from him. His silence made her wonder if she was supposed to show up for the scheduled photo shoot for DairyBaked Delights. But each day that she didn't hear otherwise was another day she could hope the assignment was still hers.

Even if Sebastian never could be.

During evening devotions, she sought answers through prayer. She hoped the Lord would grant her peace or lead her to the right verse of scripture. But she found none. Perhaps her mind, or heart, was not yet open to His leading.

The day before the second photo shoot for DairyBaked Delights, Gwendolyn was thumbing through the day's mail when she spotted an envelope bearing the return address of Kline and Birmingham Studios, Inc., in New York City.

Hands trembling, Gwendolyn opened the envelope.

*Dear Miss Warner:*

*After reviewing your portfolio, we believe your photographs and previous work experience show you have the potential to become a name in the photography profession.*

*I would like to meet with you at your earliest convenience so that we may discuss how your association with our studio may be of mutual benefit. Please contact me at your earliest convenience to schedule an interview.*

*Sincerely,*
*Irma Horton*
*Kline and Birmingham Fashion Photographers*

Surprised, Gwendolyn slowly sat on the couch. She read and reread the letter, unable—or perhaps simply unwilling—to believe it. After Gwendolyn had memorized every word, she was still not ready to let go of the letter. She began to stare at the paper, a quality rag bond a gentle yellow, its red letterhead suggesting youthful vigor and energy, much as she pictured a big, vibrant New York studio.

This was the letter she'd been wanting for years.

But instead of elation, Gwendolyn felt unable to move.

Weeks ago, she would have taken the news as a sure sign that God was answering her prayers and telling her He wanted her to be a commercial photographer. Now, she wasn't so certain.

She remembered a verse she once memorized for Sunday school, Deuteronomy 13:4: *"It is the Lord your God you must follow, and him you must revere. Keep his commands and obey him; serve him and hold fast to him."*

She knew what she had to do. And tomorrow she would set her plan in motion.

Gwendolyn donned a pair of black wool trousers, an emerald green angora sweater, and a strand of pearls with matching earrings and bracelet. As she touched lipstick in Coolly Coral to her lower lip, the doorbell rang. "Coming!" She glanced one last time in her dresser mirror. Satisfied with her reflection, she darted to the door to discover her visitor was Sebastian.

"Why do you look so surprised? You did look through the peephole this time, didn't you?"

She gritted her teeth in embarrassment. "I guess not."

"You really must change your habits." His voice was teasing, but soon became serious. "And I should change mine. I want to apologize to you for my behavior the other night. My sister's reaction to media images happened years ago. I shouldn't hold you personally responsible for something you had nothing to do with."

"No, I understand. What your family went through was traumatic, and I am part of a profession that perpetuates those images. I'm so sorry your sister was hurt. But I'm glad you told me about her. From now on, I'm going to be very careful about what assignments I accept, and what creative direction I take with those I do accept."

"I can't ask for any more than that." He smiled. "I come bearing gifts."

"I wondered why you were hiding your hands behind your back."

"I have a surprise." He presented Gwendolyn with a narrow white box about three feet in length. Gwendolyn guessed the box concealed a bouquet of flowers. "So, am I invited in?"

Playing along, she put the box up to her ear. "Well, since I don't hear a ticking sound. . ." Flashing him a smile, Gwendolyn stepped aside for him to enter.

"You thought I was still angry."

"Not only angry, but determined to fire me," she observed as she shut the door.

His lips pursed. "I'm sorry about that. Because I definitely want you to stay on as my company's photographer—if you'll still have us."

"Yes!"

"In that case, these are yours." He handed her the box.

"You mean, you were going to take this back if I said no?"

He grinned. "Well, Mom likes gifts, too."

"Oh, you!" she teased.

Opening the box, Gwendolyn inhaled with delight when she discovered a dozen long-stemmed red roses. "These are beautiful!" Selecting one that was on the verge of blooming,

Gwendolyn stroked a silken petal with her fingertip.

With her unspoken permission, he followed her into the kitchen so she could put the flowers in a vase. "I admit, after our conversation the other night I was ready to see Mom and demand we buy out your contract. But thankfully, I decided to wait until I cooled off. Then after a lot of soul-searching, I came to my senses. And I'm thankful you were gracious enough to accept my apology." She felt his gaze upon her as he watched her arrange the flowers. "You're dressed mighty well for so early in the morning. I hope this doesn't mean you have a shoot scheduled with Sara Lee."

"Hardly," she answered. "As a matter of fact, I was on my way to see your mother."

His eyebrows furrowed. "You were?"

She nodded. "I was going to tell her that I didn't want to use a human model in the ads if you were opposed to one."

"Really? You were really going to tell her that?" His mouth dropped open as though he didn't believe it were possible. "What I think matters to you that much?"

"It always has." Gwendolyn tried not to cringe when she recalled Sebastian's opposition to her the first day they met. She leaned against the counter and folded her arms. "But more important to me is what the Lord thinks. And I have to tell you, I've been struggling with this career."

"Really? But you seem so committed."

"I am. At least, I thought I was." *Until I met you.*

"If it's such a struggle," he asked, "then why do you pursue it?"

"I sort of fell into it, and at the time it seemed as though it was the right thing to do. You see, my brother is a professional photographer."

"He is?"

"I was his assistant before I broke out on my own. I didn't make a big deal about being related to him for obvious reasons."

"So creative talent runs in your family."

"I like to think so." She nodded. "But your comments about models hit home with me in more ways than one. Remember, I used to be a model myself. Nothing big, mind you."

He looked her over from head to toe, but his admiring glance made her feel loved. "So I haven't seen you in any of the big magazines? I'm sure if I had, I'd remember."

She chuckled. "Thanks, but I think it was God's plan for me not to be a huge success. While he was learning his craft, my brother used me as his subject many times. Of course, he wanted exposure for his pictures, so my photos eventually wound up with local people who thought I'd make a good model. Some of them had the power to follow through on their instincts. I've done lots of runway shows for retailers around here."

"I can't imagine you looking snooty and prancing around."

"Oh, yeah?" Lifting her nose and straightening her lips, Gwendolyn narrowed her eyes just so. She could see from the expression on Sebastian's face that she had succeeded. Slouching ever so slightly as she inserted a hand in each front trouser pocket, Gwendolyn strode around the small living room.

"Bravo!" Sebastian clapped. "But didn't you list a lot of bridal shows? I think I'd be put off if I were your groom." His mouth twisted into a wry grin.

Gwendolyn affected a fake Eastern European accent. "What do you mean by that? Do you not consider it an honor for me to step on you with my spike heel?" Though her shoes boasted modest stacked heels, Gwendolyn twisted a heel into the carpet.

Sebastian crossed his arms over his face in mock surrender. "Scary!"

Giggling, Gwendolyn placed her hands on her hips. "I'll show you something a lot less scary. Here's my 'happy bride' look." She affected a pleasant expression that fell just short of giddy. Pretending to wear a full-length skirt, she cavorted around the room, her manner and style giving her the effect of one floating upon a cloud.

"I have to give you credit. Modeling seems to require a degree of acting. I can't believe you never made the big time."

She paused, thinking back on her career. "I could have made a decent living. I think that's one reason why my brother, Bruce, was so mad at me for abandoning modeling for photography. I went from being his asset to becoming a rival. He thought I was wasting money on getting a photography degree when I could have dropped out of high school to be a model."

"He didn't really advocate that, did he?"

"No," she admitted. "College was another matter. Tuition, you know."

"I know. But schooling is never a waste, at least in my book." He chuckled at his pun.

"Cute," she said with a grin.

"So you want to be a famous fashion photographer?"

"I once thought I did. I even thought that since I hadn't made any real effort to be a model at first, perhaps that was God's plan for my life. But now I'm not so sure."

"I remember when the dessert flopped. You didn't try to worm your way out of our agreement. You were ready to accept the consequences." He looked into her eyes. "Maybe you were having doubts?"

She shook her head. "Not then. I wanted that job desperately. Quitting was the last thing I wanted to do. But if you had held me to our agreement, I would have left that day. Keeping my word is more important to me than any job."

" 'Charm is deceptive, and beauty is fleeting; but a woman who fears the Lord is to be praised,' " he said.

"Oh, the Proverbs 31 woman." Gwendolyn waved her hand dismissively. "If you expect me to live up to her, I'm afraid you're in for a rude awakening." She chuckled. "Although I'm glad to see you're reading your Bible."

"Yes, more so than usual," he admitted.

"Me, too." Her voice took on a faraway quality. "Searching for answers."

"Did you find yours?"

"I think so."

"Good. I think I found mine, too." Stepping toward her, he took her hands in his. "Gwendolyn, I've come to realize that just because Candy couldn't face her problems in a healthy way doesn't mean everyone else is like her."

"I know. But I've been contemplating what you said, and I

feel the same way you do. I wouldn't want what I do for a living to contribute to anyone else's problems."

"That's just it. I see now that people make decisions about their lives every day. Maybe seeing someone thin will inspire them. Or make them depressed." When he let out a sigh, she knew he was thinking about his sister.

"What you told me about your sister made me think a lot. As I told you before, I really don't want to be responsible for something like that."

"I know you don't." Sebastian paused as though he were contemplating what to say next. He looked her in the eyes. "You live a healthy lifestyle, right?"

"I try."

"You don't crash diet or go on binges or do other unhealthy things to stay thin, do you? Or drink milk shakes just to put on a pound or two?"

She shook her head.

He chuckled. "As long as you're being responsible about the way you eat and exercise, you can't be expected to shoulder the blame for people's reactions to your image, whether you're in front of or behind the camera. Just as I have no control over whether someone has an allergic reaction to chocolate." He gave her hands a light squeeze. "Honor God by doing your best and then leave the outcome in His hands."

"What about using beauty to sell products? That seemed to be a concern of yours."

"Who was I kidding? People want to see beautiful models." Sebastian caught her gaze and held it. "And if the truth be known, I want to see a beautiful model—and photographer—every day. Her name is Gwendolyn Warner."

Gwendolyn became conscious of her heartbeat. She didn't want to spoil the moment, but she had to allay her fears. "Sebastian, I have to know. Do you really want to see Gwendolyn the famous photographer, or Gwendolyn the local portrait photographer?"

He didn't hesitate to answer. "I've spent a lot of time thinking about that very question since I last saw you. Do you want the truth?"

Feeling scared, she whispered, "Yes."

"I'd like to see Gwendolyn as a happy and fulfilled woman, regardless of the career she chooses."

She breathed a sigh. Sebastian's words had set her free. Free to be the woman she wanted to be.

"Sebastian, there's something I have to tell you." Stepping back, she let go of his hands.

"Oh?"

"I've been asked to interview with a studio in New York City. I think the meeting is just a formality. I expect them to offer me a contract."

He hesitated for only a split second. "Then go. Make your dreams come true."

"Do you really mean that?"

"Yes, I do." He clasped her hands once more. "But will you come back to me?"

"That's just it, Sebastian. I no longer want to go. I don't want to leave."

"Really?" His gaze grew soft. "Because of me?"

Did she dare admit the truth? She looked into his eyes and decided that she could take the risk. "Yes. Because of you."

"In that case, will you be more than my photographer? More than my friend?"

"Yes! If that's what you want."

"That's what I wanted from the moment I saw you." Wrapping his arms around her waist and shoulders, Sebastian pulled her closer to him.

Feeling the warmth of his lips as they drew closer, Gwendolyn lost herself in his kisses—the first of many to come.

# SOUR CREAM POUND CAKE

1 cup butter
$\frac{1}{2}$ cup lard or vegetable oil
6 eggs
3 cups sugar
3 teaspoons vanilla extract
3 cups plain flour
$\frac{1}{2}$ teaspoon salt
$\frac{1}{2}$ teaspoon baking powder
1 cup sour cream
2 teaspoons lemon juice

Cream butter and oil.
Add sugar and sour cream to mixture and beat until well mixed.
Add eggs one at a time, beating well after each egg.
Sift flour, salt, and baking powder in large bowl and add to mixture.
Add vanilla and lemon juice, mixing well.

Pour into greased, floured Bundt pan. Be sure to use a traditional Bundt pan, because the recipe doesn't work as well with tube or loaf pans. Put in cold oven, baking at 300 degrees for 1 hour and 30 minutes, or until top is golden brown. Times may vary with ovens.

## TAMELA HANCOCK MURRAY

Tamela Hancock Murray lives in Northern Virginia with her wonderful husband and two beautiful daughters. In true family tradition, they enjoy sweet treats more than they should. Tamela's great-grandfather, a wiry Englishman, drank his tea with seven teaspoons of sugar. Her paternal grandfather made pies for almost every occasion in his hometown. Tamela's daddy, Herman Hancock, to whom her story is dedicated, has always done his part to keep Hershey's Chocolate in business.

# A Letter to Our Readers

Dear Readers:

In order that we might better contribute to your reading enjoyment, we would appreciate your taking a few minutes to respond to the following questions. When completed, please return to the following: Fiction Editor, Barbour Publishing, Inc., P.O. Box 719, Uhrichsville, OH 44683.

1.  Did you enjoy reading *Sweet Treats*?
    ❑ Very much—I would like to see more books like this.
    ❑ Moderately—I would have enjoyed it more if _____

    _____

    _____

2.  What influenced your decision to purchase this book?
    (Check those that apply.)
    ❑ Cover          ❑ Back cover copy      ❑ Title      ❑ Price
    ❑ Friends        ❑ Publicity            ❑ Other

3.  Which story was your favorite?
    ❑ *Cupcakes for Two*        ❑ *Bittersweet Memories & Peppermint Dreams*
    ❑ *Blueberry Surprise*      ❑ *Cream of the Crop*

4.  Please check your age range:
    ❑ Under 18        ❑ 18–24        ❑ 25–34
    ❑ 35–45           ❑ 46–55        ❑ Over 55

5.  How many hours per week do you read? _____

Name _____

Occupation _____

Address _____

City _____ State _____ Zip _____

E-mail _____

# If you enjoyed

## *Sweet Treats*

### then read:

# HIDDEN MOTIVES

*Four Romances Emerge from Mysterious Shadows*

*Watcher in the Woods* by Carol Cox
*Then Came Darkness* by Gail Gaymer Martin
*At the End of the Bayou* by DiAnn Mills
*Buried in the Past* by Jill Stengl

# HEARTSONG ❤ PRESENTS
# Love Stories
# Are Rated G!

That's for godly, gratifying, and of course, great! If you love a thrilling love story but don't appreciate the sordidness of some popular paperback romances, **Heartsong Presents** is for you. In fact, **Heartsong Presents** is the premiere inspirational romance book club featuring love stories where Christian faith is the primary ingredient in a marriage relationship.

Sign up today to receive your first set of four, never-before-published Christian romances. Send no money now; you will receive a bill with the first shipment. You may cancel at any time without obligation, and if you aren't completely satisfied with any selection, you may return the books for an immediate refund!

Imagine. . .four new romances every four weeks—two historical, two contemporary—with men and women like you who long to meet the one God has chosen as the love of their lives. . .all for the low price of $10.99 postpaid.

To join, simply complete the coupon below and mail to the address provided. **Heartsong Presents** romances are rated G for another reason: They'll arrive Godspeed!

## YES! Sign me up for Hearts❤ng!

**NEW MEMBERSHIPS WILL BE SHIPPED IMMEDIATELY!**
**Send no money now.** We'll bill you only $10.99 postpaid with your first shipment of four books. Or for faster action, call toll free 1-800-847-8270.

NAME _____

ADDRESS_____

CITY _____ STATE_____ ZIP_____

**MAIL TO: HEARTSONG PRESENTS, P.O. Box 721, Uhrichsville, Ohio 44683**
**or visit www.heartsongpresents.com**